Copyriƒ

The right of Peter Jay Blac   s
been asserted in accorda   t

1900.

1 2 3 4 5 6 7 8 9 10

OAKBRIDGE
K040424
ISBN 9781739549633 (paperback)
ISBN 9781739549640 (eBook)
A CIP catalogue record for this book is available from the British Library

Black, Peter Jay
Murder on Ivywick Island / Peter Jay Black

London

RUTH MORGAN INVESTIGATES...

MURDER
on Ivywick Island

PETER JAY BLACK

1

Greg Shaw screamed. Not in a deep, manly shout for attention, nor a heroic call for help, but a high-pitched squeal reminiscent of a six-year-old running from an imaginary monster.

Ruth slammed both feet onto the motorhome's brake pedal, and it took one and a half football fields in length for the behemoth to come to a juddering stop.

To be fair, not the worst braking distance she'd experienced in her tin palace.

Trevor, back in Vanmoor Village, must have upgraded the discs or whatever. Bless him.

Ruth cocked an eyebrow at her grandson as the gangly teenager's bottom jaw worked, but no words came out.

"Yes. Thank you, Gregory." She'd reacted to the almighty bang, so the scream was completely unnecessary, let alone the panicked hysteria.

This was one of those times Ruth wondered if a hapless maternity ward nurse with poor eyesight had switched her grandson for another baby. There was no way she was ever this dramatic in her youth. Sara, Greg's mother, could be intense, but still not to the extent he currently exhibited.

Greg wrung his hands, and his cheeks drained of colour. "We're going to prison," he croaked.

Maybe he gets it from his father's side of the family, Ruth mused. *That certainly would explain it.*

She set the parking brake and switched off the engine. When it had come to a rattling stop, Ruth unfastened her seat belt and said in a calm voice, "Shall we go see what's happened?" She climbed from the driver's side, eager to figure out what calamity had befallen them this time, so they could get moving again.

Ruth exited the motorhome and trooped back along the road, searching for the exact location of the dreaded impact. The mere fact she'd not seen what object they'd hit, and therefore not had the time to swerve, filled her with suspicion.

Greg trotted after her, muttering something about Ruth's terrible driving.

She took offence. Her driving style wasn't bad, more like unique. Where normal people would gauge a road too narrow for their vehicle, or a bridge too low, she'd always be up for the challenge. Gave life an extra level of excitement.

A stone wall bordered the forest to their left.

Greg squeaked and motioned to a crumbled section.

On the other side, between the trunks of two oaks, lay a man in his fifties, with a weathered face, a grizzled beard, and thinning red hair jutted from the sides of his head.

He wore a tatty parker jacket, torn at the elbows; a woollen hat with more holes than a slice of Swiss cheese; and a pair of Doc Martens boots that looked as though they'd seen at least two world wars.

He stared unblinking at the sky.

"I said your driving would kill someone one day." Greg looked at Ruth, wide eyed. "I just assumed it would be me."

She sighed. "The day's still young." Ruth leaned over the wall for a better look. "At least he's breathing. That's a good sign."

Sure enough, the man's chest rose and fell, and then he groaned.

"I'll call an ambulance," Greg said.

"No," the man croaked. "I'll be all right." He hacked and winced. "Oh dear." His eyes spun into the back of his skull.

Ruth scanned him from top to toe. He had no visible bruises or scrapes, and no part of him oozed any type of liquid. *Interesting.* She frowned and looked him over again, then the ground nearby.

Greg slipped a phone from his pocket, but Ruth grabbed his wrist.

"What are you doing?" He tried to pull free. "This man could die."

"Not in the next minute he won't." Ruth let go of her grandson. "Stay right here. Don't move." She raced back to her beloved motorhome and circled to the front. The impact had dented the bumper and grille. "Can I not go five minutes without something dinging my house?" Ruth knelt and inspected the damage.

By the look of it, a skilled tradesperson could hammer everything back into shape. Perhaps she could find one of those handy types at their destination. Ruth glanced down the road. Which was only another mile or so. "Typical."

She ran a hand over the now concave bumper and then rubbed her fingers together. Particles of sand. Ordinary beach sand by the feel. Her eyes narrowed.

Ruth straightened and stood at one end the bumper and

grille, noting the level of the impact relative to the ground, with no damage above waist height.

"As I suspected." Fists balled, she stormed back to the crumbled wall.

The man now writhed about with his eyes squeezed shut, face twisted in agony. He moaned. "It's broken. All broken. Hurts so much. The pain. What have you done to me?"

Trembling, Greg raised his phone again, but Ruth snatched it out of his hand as she passed him.

"Hey."

Ruth stepped over the remains of the wall, then over the man too, and made her way deeper into the forest.

"Where are you going?" Greg called. "Grandma?"

She glanced back as the man opened one eye and watched her.

A little way in, Ruth looked about. "Where is it, then?"

"Where's what?" Greg said.

"I'm fading." The man slumped. "Slipping away. There's a tunnel. Bright light."

Ruth held up a hand. "Don't die just yet. I'll be right with you. Give me a minute." She took several paces farther into the forest and stepped behind one of the oaks. "Ah-ha. Here we go." She snatched up a rope.

"Don't touch that," the man croaked. "That's my personal property." He clutched his chest and screwed up his face. "It hurts. Hurts so bad. Bleeding on the inside. Spleen."

"What's that for?" Greg asked as Ruth returned with the end of the rope.

She handed it to him. "Pull."

Greg stared at her.

"Do it, please, Gregory. And hurry." Ruth looked at the time on the phone. "We haven't got all day."

Greg yanked on the rope, hand over hand, coiling it at his feet, while something dragged across the ground. Attached to the other end was a sandbag. He pulled it toward him a bit further, and then stopped. "What's that for?"

"Excellent question." Ruth put her hands on her hips and glared at the man.

Greg looked between them with a furrowed brow.

"It's a poor attempt at a scam," Ruth said when the man didn't answer. "A weak plan, and an even weaker execution."

The man stopped writhing and blinked at her.

Ruth gestured to the sandbag. "You threw that in front of my cherished motorhome as we went by. Once it hit the bumper, you dragged it back with the rope. You then lay down and started those amateur dramatics that would quite literally fool no one." Despite the situation, she smirked. "You'll win no theatrical prizes with that performance."

The man sat up, and grumbled, "Everyone's a critic."

Greg's face fell. "You tried to con us?"

"That's why he insisted there was no need to call for an ambulance," Ruth said. "Perhaps he was about to suggest we could buy his silence and fund his long road to recovery." She inclined her head. "Or maybe he planned to feign a serious spine injury and claim against our insurance." Ruth sighed. "Which is it? I'm fascinated to know."

The man shrugged.

Greg scowled at him. "Seriously? You gave me a heart attack. How could you?"

"Where is it?" Ruth eyed the man's trousers and jacket.

"Where's what?" he said in what he clearly thought was an innocent tone, even under the circumstances.

"Oh, for goodness' sake." Ruth stepped past him again and searched behind the other tree. "Ah, here we go." She kicked a pile of twigs aside and snatched up a rucksack.

"Hey, that's mine," he said. "Put that back. Private property."

Ruth found a wallet in the front pocket and opened it. However, it was empty: no bank cards or a driver's licence. "What's your name?"

"I'm not telling you."

Ruth returned the wallet to the bag and slung it at him. "Call the police, Greg."

"Wait." The man glared at her. "Josh."

"Josh what?"

"Green."

"Is that your real name?" Greg asked.

"Yes."

"Well, Josh Green, I can safely say I hope to never see you again," Ruth said.

Greg snarled at him. "You should be ashamed of yourself."

If she weren't in a hurry, Ruth would have dragged Josh to the nearest police station. Instead, she stepped over the wall and took Greg's arm. "Let's go. We'll be late."

As they headed back to the motorhome, Ruth called over her shoulder, "When we reach Tayinloan, I'm informing the police of what you've done, Josh Green. You'd better be far away from here when they come looking." She climbed back into the motorhome and strapped herself into the driver's seat.

Greg sat in the passenger side and frowned at her. "How could you let him get away with it? At least have him pay for the damage."

"I don't have time to sit around for the police to take

statements." Ruth started the engine. "And I can safely assume Josh doesn't have the money to pay for repairs."

Never mind all the hassle of calling the insurance company and then filling out a billion forms.

Besides, it was already late morning, and if they delayed any further, her sister, Margaret, would never let Ruth hear the end of it.

She checked mirrors for any more local thespians ready to leap out, and then pulled away.

A mile farther down the road, a sign came into view:

Fàilte gu
Welcome to
TAIGH AN LÒIN
TAYINLOAN

Greg's face screwed up and his lips moved as he tried to make sense of the words.

Ruth looked at him askance. "What's the matter? Your Scottish Gaelic not up to snuff?"

"It's a little rusty," he muttered.

Ruth chuckled. "Don't worry. Everyone here speaks English, for the most part." She let out a sigh of relief, as they'd now made it to their destination on the west coast of Scotland.

Tayinloan sat some one hundred and twenty miles from Glasgow, and the only way they could to get to it with Ruth's American-sized motorhome was to first drive sixty miles north over the border, and then double back a further sixty miles south along the Kintyre peninsula.

She followed the road, with fields and woodlands on either side, until they found a narrow lane on the right, flanked by grazing land as far as the eye could see, and the odd farmhouse here and there, looking all picturesque and whimsical.

After hard right, past more stone houses and sheep herds, Ruth pulled into a car park.

In the top corner, next to a couple of wooden sailboats on wooden chocks, someone had sectioned off a large area with bright orange traffic cones.

"And here we are." Ruth pulled the Motorhome close.

Greg jumped from the passenger seat, headed down the steps and outside. He moved several of the cones, and Ruth pulled into the space.

As the engine came to a rattling stop, Ruth stared across the ocean to Cara Island, and the Isle of Gigha dominating the horizon. A car ferry chugged its way toward them, but Ruth and Greg's destination lay beyond those, an island so remote only the oldest locals knew of its existence.

Ruth's stomach tightened in anticipation, and she looked back at her grandson standing inside by the motorhome door.

"I've got the suitcases ready. And—" Greg nodded at an oak box—sixteen inches wide and tall, twenty-two long— with a brass handle, air vents down each side, and metal clasps holding it together. "His Highness is in there." He said this last part through tight lips.

Ruth climbed from the driver's seat. She slipped on her black woollen coat, pink scarf, matching pink hat and gloves, and then grabbed the box, plus her handbag, and followed Greg out.

At the door, Ruth paused and looked back. "Behave yourself while I'm gone," she said to the motorhome. "I know what you're like. No drinking or wild parties. And no, I repeat *no* inviting double-decker buses over to spend the night. You know what happened last time. Understood?"

"You're weird," came Greg's voice from outside.

Ruth grinned, and locked the door.

Greg gripped a suitcase in each hand and waddled across the car park.

Ruth called after him, "Where are you going?"

"The ferry."

"We're not going on the ferry," she said with a sparkle in her eye.

Greg turned back, his brow furrowed. "Then how are we getting there?"

Ruth pointed to the horizon as an inflatable dinghy with an outboard motor bounced across the water toward them.

Greg took one look at it and dropped the suitcases. "No way." He shook his head. "I'm not going on that thing. No chance."

"How are you getting there, then? Swimming?" She eyed the rough sea. "Good luck." She headed to the shoreline with her oak box and handbag.

Up close, the inflatable dinghy turned out to be robust and of a more moderate size than it first appeared. Although an open deck design, the rigid inflatable boat was twenty feet long, with a double pilot's chair, and a bench seat wide enough for three at the back. Its solid underhull slid up the beach and came to a stop.

As Ruth and Greg made their way along a path with their belongings, an elderly gentleman in a heavy parka threw a ladder over the side of the boat and climbed down.

Ruth's eyebrows lifted in surprise. "Captain Barney?"

A crooked smile swept across his weather-beaten features. "Ruth Morgan. It's been a while." He had a Glaswegian drawl, softened by the English accents of his employers, but with the dialect of local island-living thrown into the Frankenstein mix.

Astonished, Ruth set the oak box down and hugged him. "Thirty-eight years." Although saying that out loud was both incredible and frightening.

Captain Barney's bushy eyebrows lifted. "Ye were a wee lass when ye were banished from the island."

Ruth chuckled. "Hardly wee. I was twenty-seven."

Captain Barney hadn't aged a day. In fact, Ruth now wondered if he'd been born looking the way he did.

She motioned to Greg. "This is my grandson."

He set the suitcases down, waved awkwardly at Captain Barney, and kept eyeing the boat, turning greener by the second. "How far is it?"

"Six nautical miles, give or take." Captain Barney grabbed one of the suitcases.

"Why were you banished?" Greg asked in a low voice.

"I'll tell you later." As Greg and Barney loaded the boat, Ruth climbed on board.

Captain Barney pointed. "Sit up front wi' me."

Greg helped him push off, and a minute later they raced across the ocean.

Even though the day was overcast and cold, Ruth pulled a pair of oversized sunglasses from her bag and slipped them on, shielding her eyes from the wind and spray.

It didn't seem to bother Captain Barney at all. His eyes remained open and unblinking.

Ruth's grandson had done the opposite: he squeezed his eyes closed, pressed his lips together, and sat rigid on the rear bench, taking deep breaths.

"Is he a'right?" Captain Barney asked.

"Travel sick," Ruth said.

"A few hundred more trips, boy will get used to it." Captain Barney adjusted the throttle. "Ye still polis?"

"Polis? Oh, a police officer?" Ruth shook her head. "Left the force a long time ago. I'm a food consultant now."

Captain Barney's brow furrowed.

This was a common reaction.

Ruth cleared her throat. "I advise hotels and restaurants on their recipes and menus."

"Is that how come Margaret and Charles want ye here?" Captain Barney asked. "Or a personal visit?"

Truth was, Ruth didn't know. Margaret wouldn't tell her what was so urgent, only that she had to come to Ivywick Island right away.

Ruth had been keen to return to the island since her banishment all those years ago, and what with Charles' father dying recently, no doubt leaving the entire estate to him, it was her first opportunity.

The last time she had set foot on the island shores was almost four decades prior with her late husband, John, and that visit had almost ended both their lives.

Despite all that, Ruth wanted to know what had her sister so rattled, and why Margaret had insisted she get there as quickly as possible.

Why couldn't she explain what the problem is over the phone? Why did I have to physically come here?

Ruth looked back at Greg and mouthed, "Are you okay?"

He gave a rigid nod, and then threw up over the side.

C aptain Barney pointed past the bow of the boat as a landmass came into view. "Ivywick in all her glory."

The island sat in an isolated part of the ocean: a five-hundred-acre teardrop-shaped lump of rock jutting from the sea, lined with cliffs and beaches.

Hung over the side of the boat, Greg moaned as Captain Barney swung the vessel to the left and aimed for the narrowest point of the island.

"Do you still live there?" Ruth asked.

"Aye," Captain Barney said. "Wee cottage at the north."

Ruth pictured the stone and slate building next to the lighthouse at the top of the highest cliff. "And you have those sheep too?"

"Not identical ones," Captain Barney said with a twinkle in his eye. "Thirty ewes and one lucky tup."

"Tup?" Ruth asked.

"Male sheep." His brow furrowed. "Lighthouse stopped workin' twenty years ago."

"Oh, really?" Ruth said. "Why?"

He shrugged. "Coudnae tell ye." Captain Barney slowed

the boat, deftly navigated a cluster of treacherous rocks, and glided alongside a pontoon. He then set the throttle to neutral and nodded at Greg. "Tie us off, lad."

Clearly grateful to have reached dry land, Greg stumbled onto the pontoon and, under Captain Barney's tutelage, secured the ropes around bollards at both fore and aft.

Then Greg returned for the suitcases, helped Ruth out of the boat with her oak box, and a minute later, they headed to shore.

The pontoon ended in a concrete ramp leading up to a cliff railway—a single carriage elevator on a steep track, carved into the rock face.

Greg and Captain Barney stepped inside with just enough room for the luggage.

Ruth tensed as she handed the oak box over to Greg and remained where she was.

Captain Barney eyed her. "I remember. Yer claustrophobic."

"Cleithrophobic," Greg said.

Captain Barney cocked a bushy eyebrow. "What's that?"

"Fear of being trapped," Ruth said through a clenched jaw.

"We can leave the door open, if that suits ye?"

Ruth shook her head as she pictured them reaching almost the top of the cliff only to then tumble out. "Go on without me. I'll meet you up there."

"Ye sure?"

She nodded.

"Fair enough." Captain Barney slid the door closed and hit a giant green button on the wall. A second later, the elevator carriage ascended the track.

Ruth watched them go for a minute, and then with a heavy heart, she headed up a steep flight of steps.

Halfway to the top, she gripped the railing and bent double, breathing hard. "If I wanted this much exercise, I'd join a gym." She shuddered at the thought.

After a minute of gathering herself, Ruth straightened and continued the climb.

She'd forgotten about these stairs.

As she ascended each painful step, Ruth vowed to have a strong word with Margaret, and ask her and Charles to fit a giant escalator instead.

However, Ruth didn't want to push her luck. She was keen to improve her relationship with her sister, and this was her best chance yet.

Some family alone time.

Clearly Margaret wanted Ruth to visit for some desperate reason, and Ruth had no idea what that could be, but she wanted to keep levelheaded and calm during their stay. No matter what her sister threw at her.

They'd spent most of their lives at loggerheads, their personalities often clashing, and enough was enough. Time was finite. Ruth and Margaret needed to find common ground and make amends for past mistakes. Starting with the Tammy Radcliffe incident.

Finally, Ruth reached the top of the cliff steps, where the boys waited.

Captain Barney welcomed her with a crooked smile. "Ye enjoy that?" He set the oak box at her feet.

Panting, lungs on fire, legs burning, Ruth leaned against a post. "Not even a little bit."

She considered making a harness out of rope and having them drag her up the side of the cliff next time.

Once she'd caught her breath, Ruth picked up the oak box and followed Captain Barney through an archway.

Ahead sat a mansion house, four storeys tall, with towers

and battlements; a converted and expanded ruined castle complemented with red brick infilling the original grey stonework—a thoughtful melding of the modern with the ancient.

Greg's mouth dropped open. "You weren't kidding about this place, Grandma." He waved a finger at the sections of ruined castle. "This has to be, what?" He looked at Captain Barney. "Fifteenth century?"

"Don't ask me, lad."

At the top of the nearest gable end of the newest addition was a circular window, stained glass with a starburst pattern. Above that, mounted right at the peak, sat a giant weather vane, comprising letters for each compass direction, and topped with the silhouette of an owl.

Ruth, Greg, and Captain Barney followed a cobblestone path alongside a manicured lawn, flanked with topiary and shrub borders.

A man wearing a flatcap, jeans, weatherproof mac, and wellies worked on a hedge maze with shears.

"A'right, Alec?" Captain Barney called.

Alec looked over at them, tipped his cap, and kept working.

A sign nearby read:

Welcome to
Amgine Hall

When Ruth, Greg, and Captain Barney reached the giant oak double front door, the right half swung open, and a butler in his late sixties greeted them.

He wore a fine black suit, white shirt, red tie, with is grey hair combed back. "Can I help you?" he asked in a hoarse voice.

"Hi, Carter." Ruth grinned.

He didn't return it, and studied her for a moment. "Mrs Morgan?" His tone was unsure, though he must have known they were coming.

"The one and only."

Carter didn't bother to reach for their cases, and he stepped aside.

"I'll be goin'." Captain Barney winked.

"Thank you so much," Ruth said. "It was really great seeing you again."

"Don't be a stranger." He nodded at Greg and headed back down the path.

Ruth stepped across the threshold into an opulent entrance hall with a marble floor and a set of stairs arching to the next level. Portraits lined the walls, men and women with stern expressions. "Exactly how I remember it."

Greg whistled. "Nice place."

Margaret, a couple of years older than Ruth, strode toward them. She wore a dark blue designer dress, matching shoes, and a silk scarf. Margaret had wavy grey hair cut into a neat bob, an alabaster complexion, and her facial features were sharper than an axe. She kissed Ruth on each cheek, and then stepped back to appraise her sister over the tops of her glasses. "Are you shorter?"

"Shorter than what?"

"The last time I saw you."

Ruth considered this question. "I don't think so."

Margaret waved a hand. "Well, you look shorter."

"Maybe you put your contact lenses in backward," Ruth suggested.

"Don't be ridiculous." Margaret sniffed. "You know I can't wear contacts. They scratch my eyes."

Ruth muttered, "That would be a shame."

"Pardon?"

Ruth forced a smile. "I've missed you too, sis."

"And who is this strapping young man?" Margaret said with a twinkle in her eye. "By Jove, could it be Sir Gregory?"

Greg snickered. "Hi, Aunty Margaret."

"*Great aunty,*" Ruth said.

"Just aunty is fine." Margaret pecked him on each cheek. "Although, it has to be said, and widely acknowledged, that I am indeed rather great." Her attention moved to the oak box Ruth held. "How's Merlin?"

"He's fine." Ruth stiffened at the *yap, yap, yap* of a chocolate and white Chihuahua as he hurtled toward her, claws clattering at a billion miles an hour.

She swore under her breath, cursing herself for having forgotten to tape extra-large sandwich bags over each shoe.

Sure enough, Billy Connelly—named after Margaret's favourite Scottish comedian—jumped at Ruth a few times and then cocked a leg, but she'd anticipated his move, pulled her right foot clear of the stream, and Billy peed on the marble floor instead.

Ruth sneered down at the mutt. "Too fast for you this time, buddy boy."

Margaret scooped him up. Like Ruth and Merlin, she travelled nowhere without Billy, and had brought him to Morgan Manor many times in the past. He'd peed on everything there too. "Drinks before lunch?"

Ruth pulled her new phone from her pocket. She'd stopped off in a town on the way and bought a smartphone as a replacement for her old one. Ruth studied the time: 11:20 a.m. Not bad, considering their tortuous journey from Vanmoor.

Margaret nodded at the suitcases and oak box. "You can leave those here." Her expression darkened. "Charles' valet quit on us, but I'm sure Carter can take them to your rooms."

"Ooh, a valet." Ruth's eyebrows waggled. "Fancy." She looked over her shoulder, but Carter had vanished.

"Your husband, John, had a valet when you first met, did he not?" Margaret said. "And a butler, as I recall. Plus, a footman, a housekeeper, several maids, a cook, a handyman, two gardeners, and a gamekeeper. Unless I'm missing someone?" She inclined her head. "Remind me, Ruth, when you married, didn't you chase them all off?"

"We kept a gardener and a cleaner," Ruth said in a defensive tone. Besides, a cleaner made sense, and green-fingered Ruth was not. But having people to cook for her and her family always seemed frivolous, given Ruth's love for the culinary arts.

John had resisted getting rid of the house staff at first, but he eventually came round to the idea that Morgan Manor didn't need so many people to take care of it nor them.

Margaret cleared her throat. "And you've now left poor Sara in that great big home to fend for herself while you gallivant around the country like a common traveller."

Ruth let out a slow breath, keeping her nerves and temper in check. This would be a long, *long* week. "I'm fine taking this to my room." She lifted the oak box. "I need to let Merlin out myself, otherwise he gets antsy."

"To be fair," Greg said, "that's his default mood."

"Have it your way." Margaret sniffed. "Third and fourth guest suites on the left." She adjusted her grip on Billy and pointed to the top of the stairs. "But come straight back. We have much to discuss, and little time remaining, no thanks to you."

Ruth clicked her heels together and saluted.

"Ever the clown," Margaret said. "And at your advanced age."

"I'm two years younger than you."

Margaret strode off. "Allegedly."

Ruth poked her tongue out at her sister's retreating back, then headed to the stairs, muttering a few choice words under her breath for good measure.

So far, her plan of reconciliation was not going well, but Ruth was determined to not drop it easily.

Greg followed with the suitcases. "I'd forgotten how funny Aunty Margaret is."

"Yeah. Hilarious."

At the top of the stairs sat a plinth with a statue of a horse, and further along the landing was an archway. Ruth strode into a corridor, counted doors, then opened the third one and stepped into her bedroom.

Well, in fact it was a suite of rooms, with a vestibule complete with storage space for coats, hats, and boots, and a baroque mirror—judging by the date: eighteenth century— opposite an oil painting of a woman wearing a white dress and standing at the base of a flight of stairs.

The woman had to be one of Charles' ancestors.

Beyond the vestibule was a sitting room with two comfy sofas facing one another, a glass designer coffee table between, and a balcony with a spectacular view of the ocean.

Next was a spacious bedroom with a king-size bed; a walk-in closet; and a bathroom with a copper rolltop bath, and a shower large enough to hose down an elephant.

Ruth had to admit that, despite her deep love for the motorhome, it still was nice to indulge in a soupçon of luxury from time to time. Not to mention sleep in a big bed.

She set the oak box on the sitting room floor.

Greg placed her suitcase in the closet and went to leave.

"Wait." Ruth hurried over to her grandson and gripped his shoulders. "Remember, our primary objective during our stay here is we must, I repeat, *must*, at all costs, uncover the secret to Margaret's steak and ale pie."

Greg rolled his eyes. "Not this again."

Ruth fixed him with a hard look. "I'm deadly serious. I have been trying to get it out of her for forty-five years." She gritted her teeth. "It drives me insane. Margaret won't share. Sisters are supposed to share. She's got some mystical ingredient I can't work out." Ruth released Greg and stepped back. "We'll torture her if we must. Nothing a couple of hours of waterboarding won't sort out. We can take it in turns. She'll buckle eventually."

Greg sighed.

"Too much? Fine." Ruth rubbed her hands together. "Thumbscrews it is. Anyway, promise you'll help me."

"Whatever."

"Thank you."

Greg waved a hand and left.

"Okay, my darling." Ruth unfastened the metal clasps on the oak box and hinged the front aside. "Sorry I've had you cooped up all this time."

Merlin, an eight-year-old black Burmese cat, lay curled up on his velvet cushion. He opened his eyes, let out a raspy meow, stretched, and then slinked from the box.

As he examined his new surroundings, Ruth filled his bowls with fresh water and a sachet of cat food, and slid the litter tray from the base of the box.

Merlin hopped up onto a sofa. Ruth massaged his ears, and he purred. She then opened the French doors to the balcony a crack to give him some air, then went to freshen up, telling herself she would not let Margaret get under her skin.

Ha. Fat chance.

Thirty minutes later, Ruth strode into Amgine Hall's main sitting room. It had a parquet floor, a Persian rug, wood-panelled walls, and several high-backed chairs around a stone fireplace.

Greg was already seated, sipping a lemonade.

Margaret plucked the stopper from a crystal decanter, poured her younger sister a large measure of brandy.

"A bit early for drinking, isn't it?" Ruth glanced at a carriage clock on the mantelpiece: it was a little before midday.

"Trust me," Margaret said, "once you hear what I have to tell you, you may request a second, and then a third."

"Ominous." Ruth examined the photos on either side of the clock. The first was of Charles, in his twenties, standing with his parents. All three Andrews family members had serious expressions. Charles' mother, Jean, wore a silk dress, and her neck, wrists, fingers, and ears dripped with diamonds.

Ruth's gaze moved over the other portraits. In fact, Jean displayed her wealth in each photograph. As did an older lady, who Ruth assumed was Charles' grandmother.

Margaret held out the glass of brandy.

Ruth took it and dropped into a chair. "Wait a minute, where's Charles?"

Margaret's expression glazed over as she poured herself a drink. "Who?"

"Your husband." Ruth frowned. "Surely you remember

you have a husband, Margaret? After all, you've been married forty-seven years." She'd never seen her sister so distracted and distant. Usually, Margaret's senses were as sharp as her tongue.

Margaret snapped out of her trance and sat opposite. "He's in the east guesthouse."

Ruth's eyebrows lifted.

"Working," Margaret added as she picked up Billy and placed him on her lap. "Charles is trying to raise funds. It's a desperate time."

"For what?" Greg plucked a slice of lime from his glass and looked about for somewhere to offload it.

Ruth pointed to a coaster on a nearby side table.

"Which brings us neatly to why I asked you here," Margaret said to her.

Ruth braced herself. "What's so urgent and secretive that you couldn't tell me over the phone?" Although, she had to admit her sister had piqued her curiosity.

Margaret took a sip of brandy. "As you're aware, Henry, Charles' father, passed away recently."

It came as no real surprise, considering the guy had celebrated his ninety-second birthday not too long ago, and had been a chain-smoker, sucking down several cigars a day. Even so, he'd outlived his wife by twenty-five years, and she'd been a salad-munching tennis fanatic.

"Henry left Amgine Hall and the entire Ivywick Island estate to Charles?" Ruth asked.

Margaret grimaced and took another sip of brandy, as if fortifying herself.

Greg now coaxed a slice of lemon from his glass and set it on the nearby coaster with the lime.

Margaret let out a slow breath. Whatever bothered her,

it clearly pained her to talk about. "Charles has a half-brother. Noah." She shuddered. "A ghastly man."

Ruth's mouth dropped open. "You never told me Charles has a brother." Mind you, Margaret rarely shared personal details with anyone, even Ruth.

"We'd all but forgotten about him," Margaret said. "Noah moved to Australia before Charles and I married. Rarely hear from him." Her eyes darkened. "Thank goodness."

Ruth shuffled in her seat as she realised the implication of another close relative in the Andrews family. "I'm guessing Henry's bequeathed a large sum of money to Noah in his will? That's what has you so agitated?"

"Nothing so simple." Margaret looked toward the door. "We have no doubt Henry has left the estate in its entirety to Charles. No doubt at all."

Ruth finished her brandy and set it on a side table. "What's the problem, then?" Although she had another guess lined up.

Margaret tensed. "Henry's will is missing."

"Missing?" Greg blinked.

"We searched his private study, plus several other rooms, but all to no avail." Margaret adjusted Billy on her lap. "Without that will, we have no way to prove Henry left the estate in its entirety to Charles."

"Meaning this Noah guy will get fifty percent," Greg said. "Half-brother, half of everything."

Margaret grimaced. "Precisely."

"You expected Henry to have left hints as to the will's whereabouts?" Ruth asked. "But he didn't?"

"None whatsoever," Margaret said. "It's very unlike him. We anticipated uncovering the first clue in what would have no doubt been an elaborate game, but have thus far found no sign of it, nor of the will itself."

Ruth stared at her sister, not quite understanding the issue. "The solicitors must have a copy."

Margaret's expression became dejected. "Miller and Rowe burned down the day of Henry's passing."

"Where were their offices?" Ruth asked.

"Local. Tayinloan. Everything was destroyed. Complete negligence. Of course, we could sue them, but that doesn't get—"

"You out of your immediate pickle," Ruth finished, understanding the issue.

"A rather clumsy way of putting it," Margaret said. "But yes. A pickle indeed." She studied her sister. "Well? What say you? Games and mysteries are your thing. We must find the start of Henry's trail and follow it to the will's hiding place."

Ruth pondered the dire situation. Without a copy of Henry's will in hand, the solicitors would have no choice but to split the estate between the sons.

Margaret sat back. "We expected Henry would leave some type of riddle to its whereabouts, as per his modus operandi—the man couldn't make anything simple, and was so very fond of games—but, as I say, we've found nothing thus far. We're at a total loss."

"What if you never find it?" Greg asked. "Can't you and Uncle Charles buy Noah's share? Pay him for his half of the island?"

"We've put a great deal of our own finances into this estate already," Margaret said. "Paid for renovations to the cottages, maintained the grounds, even financed the staff's wages. Henry's remaining money went into his own medical care. His bank account is all but empty. Charles and I have very little left. Our pensions would cover the running costs, but that's all."

Charles was a retired bank manager, and Margaret the ex-CEO of a car company, so they no doubt had sizeable pensions between them, but the island would be expensive to run with its five hundred acres and full complement of staff.

Ruth sighed. "And what does Noah have planned?"

Margaret's jaw muscles flexed. "He's a successful businessman." She sniffed. "Well, according to him anyway." Margaret's gaze moved to the door and back again. "He has the capital to buy our share. Has told us as much. Noah wants to turn the island into a hotel and spa for rich music- and movie-mogul types." She shuddered. "Ghastly."

Ruth snorted and then straightened her face. "Oh, you're serious? He really wants to do that?"

"Deadly serious," Margaret said. "Noah is on his way here, solicitors in tow. He's made his intentions very clear, and we don't have a legal leg to stand on. Without Henry's will, Noah takes Charles' legacy."

"Can't you refuse to sell?" Greg asked.

Margaret absently stroked Billy. "In a dispute such as this, the law forces us to put the island on the market, and it will go to the highest bidder, which will be—"

"Noah," Greg finished.

"We can't let that happen." Margaret met Ruth's gaze. "You must help us. We need to find Henry's will. That's why I asked you here." She scooped up Billy and stood. "We all know how you put mystery solving before all else. So here's a problem. Solve it."

Ruth did her best to ignore the slight against her character, and got to her feet too. Although she did not know where to start hunting.

Margaret motioned to the door. "Lunch first."

"Hold on," Ruth said. Now was her chance. "When I find Henry's will, which I hope to do, I would like two things from you in exchange."

Margaret levelled her gaze. "Which are?"

"First." Ruth raised an index finger. "I'd like us to have a better relationship. Goodness knows we've spent decades at each other's throats. I've had enough. We need to work on it. So I'll forget all the nasty things you've said to me in the past, and I want you to forgive my indiscretions too."

"All of them?" Margaret's eyebrows shot up. "Including the broken vase? What about what happened the day Dad had his wisdom teeth removed? His smashed window? The way I took the blame?" Margaret stared at her. "Oh, and the fish tank fiasco? You expect me to forgive you for that nightmare too?"

"Yes," Ruth said through tight lips. "Everything."

Margaret blew out a puff of air. "There's a lot, Ruth."

"We'll start with the Tammy Radcliffe incident and work our way out from there," Ruth said. "A mammoth sisterly therapy session where we fix everything, apologise, and move on once and for all. What do you say?" Ruth held her breath.

Margaret shook her head. "We can certainly try, I suppose. It's a tall order."

Ruth stood her ground. "I'd like your best effort."

Clearly seeing how much it meant to her, and no doubt feeling the same, although buried way deep down inside. Margaret gave a small nod, "I'll check on Cook," spun on her heel, and swept from the room.

Ruth called after her, "You haven't asked me what the second thing is."

3

R uth and Greg sat opposite each other at a long table in what was modestly known as the *grand dining hall*. Once part of the original castle, its builders had paneled the walls to head height, and added a vaulted ceiling held aloft by thick oak beams.

Various armour and medieval weaponry adorned the stonework above the panels. Ruth eyed a nasty mace with rusty spikes, trying not to picture the gruesome outcome of its intended use.

Greg pointed to a golden suit of armour covered in thousands of foliate scrolls, warriors, and Roman women. "Parade armour of Henry II of France. Some of those images are from mythology: Apollo and Daphne."

"I'll take your word for it," Ruth said.

Her grandson's fascination with history stretched back to when he was finally old enough to lift a book. Greg was currently on a gap year, tagging along with his dear old grandmother as she travelled the country for her food consultancy business.

However, Greg was ultimately bound for Oxford Univer-

sity later in the year, where he'd study history and
archaeology.

His eyes sparkled as he took in all the antique objects,
and then he peered at the silver place settings. Greg picked
up a goblet and examined it. "I feel like I'm in King Arthur's
court."

"Queen Arthur," Ruth said.

Margaret swept into the room. "Sorry about that."

"Speaking of which." Ruth forced a smile at her sister.
"Everything all right?"

"There was a problem with the Aga stove," Margaret
said. Billy raced after her, and his nails clacked as he went.
"Poor Cook almost had a heart attack from the stress." She
scooped up the micropooch and set him in his own custom
high chair. "Fortunately, Ray is a whiz with a screwdriver."
Margaret sat at the head of the table and laid a napkin
across her lap.

"How long before Noah arrives?" Ruth asked.

"He'll reach Tayinloan at four tomorrow afternoon. He'll
be with us by half past four." Margaret's jaw tightened. "We
simply must locate the will by then, or we'll lose everything.
They've drawn up all the paperwork."

"Here they are. My favourite people." A giant bear of a
man, six foot five and broad shouldered, strode into the
room. He had flaming red hair flecked with grey, and a
handlebar moustache, trimmed and combed to perfection.
He also wore an immaculate suit and bow tie.

"Charles." Ruth leapt to her feet, hurried over to him,
and they embraced. "I'm sorry for your loss."

"Thank you." He released her, his expression solemn.
"That means a lot. The place isn't the same without the old
guy around."

Greg stepped forward with his hand outstretched. "Hello, Uncle Charles."

Charles pulled him into a rib-shattering hug. "Nice to see you again, young man." He let go of the lad and gave him the once-over. "You're catching up to me. At least another six inches taller than the last time we saw you." A flicker of a frown crossed his features. "How long ago was that?"

"A little over a year since you stayed with us," Ruth said.

"Good gracious. Is it really? Astonishing."

"Any luck?" Margaret asked him.

"I explored one last avenue," Charles said as the three of them sat. "Slim chance, but I'm waiting to hear." He shook his head. "If only we still had my mother's jewellery collection."

Ruth recalled the photographs in the sitting room. "Where is it?"

"Long gone, I'm afraid." Charles adjusted his bow tie. "I believe my grief-stricken father sold it all shortly after my mother's death."

Ruth tried to imagine where Henry may have stashed his copy of the will, but with a house as large as this one, it could take them a lifetime to locate it.

They only had a day, and she couldn't envision her sister and brother-in-law living anywhere else.

Now with the promise of building a better relationship with Margaret, one Ruth had always wanted her whole adult life, she was eager to prove her worth.

Ruth pictured holding Henry's will high above her head in triumph, while Margaret and Charles smiled, clapped, and congratulated her.

Butterflies ravaged Ruth's stomach at the prospect.

"I trust you're hungry?" Margaret asked Greg. When he nodded, she said, "Excellent."

A housemaid and manservant glided into the room and set down ornate platters, bowls, and tureens bursting with foodstuffs.

There was a bewildering assortment of sandwiches cut into neat triangles—everything from salmon to cheese and pickle. Plus, sausage rolls, mini pies, handmade crisps, mixed salad . . .

Ruth gaped at it all. "Are you expecting an army?"

"I wasn't sure what you'd like," Margaret said to Greg, and she poured herself a glass of water. "So I asked Cook to err on the side of caution. We have a big day ahead of us." She looked at Ruth askance. "Well, what's left of it."

"Don't worry, Aunty Margaret." Greg tucked a napkin into his collar and cracked his knuckles. "I'll take care of this for you." Then he helped himself to at least three of everything.

Ruth selected a cucumber sandwich and studied Charles as he poured himself a coffee from a cafetière.

Under the bright lights of the dining hall, he seemed pale, with bags under each eye, as though he hadn't slept for days.

Ruth supposed that, given the threat of losing his ancestral home, he hadn't.

Charles chuckled at Greg's ability to vacuum food from plates. "That's the spirit, young man. Still a couple years' worth of growing left in you yet." His phone vibrated. Charles studied the display, and his shoulders slumped.

"Any luck?" Margaret asked as she cut a steak sandwich into small pieces and then placed them on the tray in front of Billy.

He tucked in with as much gusto as Greg.

"I'm afraid not." Charles slipped the phone into his pocket. "All financial avenues exhausted. We're on our own."

Margaret's gaze hovered on him for a few seconds, and then moved to Ruth. "Then it's on you to find the will."

She swallowed. "No pressure."

"Come on, Ruth." Margaret used a pair of tongs to pluck a mini pastie from a nearby serving plate. "You're the best person for the job."

Ruth took that as a rare compliment, but it didn't ease her burden. After all, she still had no idea where to start.

"Heaven knows you like puzzles." Margaret's gaze fixed on her. "Solve this one and—" She tensed for a second, and then, as though it took an immense amount of effort, she muttered, "We'll work on us."

Ruth lit up. "You promise?"

"You have my word," Margaret said through a tight jaw. "Anyway, an unhealthy enjoyment of conundrums is something you have in common with our dearly departed Henry."

Charles gave a sage bob of his head. "Very true. You could say my father was rather obsessed with them."

Margaret sliced off a minuscule sliver of pastry and folded it on itself. "And it's why I specifically asked *you* to come, Ruth. No one better suited for the task ahead of us." She slipped the pastry into her mouth and chewed.

With her sister in a grateful mood, Ruth chose that moment to press her luck. "About my second request."

Margaret swallowed. "We'll work on our relationship, but beyond that, some things are too high of a price to pay."

Ruth levelled her gaze. "It's time you gave it up."

"Over my dead corpse."

"That's the spirit."

"Give what up?" Greg asked. "Oh. Are you talking about the steak and ale pie recipe again?"

Margaret's eyes narrowed. "Trying to recruit the boy to do your dirty work, Ruth?"

Ruth cleared her throat and focused on Charles. "Before we start, I'd like to look at the cave. Maybe it's linked to the hidden will in some way."

"That won't be possible. Father sealed it off after the . . . incident." Charles sipped his coffee. "He strictly forbade anyone to go in. No one's set foot in there for almost four decades."

"What cave?" Greg asked with a mouthful of mini sausages. "Has it got something to do with why you were banished from the island?"

"It has," Margaret said before Ruth could answer.

Greg glanced between the three of them. "What happened?"

"Thirty-eight years ago, your grandfather and I explored a cave on the beach," Ruth said as memories rushed forward. "John saw a light coming from beyond a crack in the back wall."

Margaret shook her head. "He was hallucinating."

Ruth bit her lip.

"That's not all John claimed to have seen," Charles said in response to Greg's inquisitive expression. "He thought he spotted someone on the other side. Only a shadow, but a person moving about a hidden room."

Margaret tutted. "This island always attracts superstitious nonsense and wild stories."

However, Ruth pictured John with his face pressed against the rock, peering through the crack. He'd waved her over to come see, when part of the ceiling had collapsed. They'd been lucky to escape with their lives. "Henry found out we'd been in there," Ruth said to Greg. "Despite it being off-limits. He went ballistic."

"And banished you?"

Ruth nodded. "I really wanted to check it out now. Henry might have hidden the riddle in there." She murmured, "He was clearly protecting something that day."

"I very much doubt it," Charles said. "It's always remained forbidden to go down there. My father was unyielding in that regard." He held up a hand before Ruth could respond. "Not because he was hiding something, but because it's dangerous. John almost lost his life."

Abandoning her plate, Ruth sat back and folded her arms.

"There's a metal barrier sealing off the entrance." Charles noticed Ruth's despondency. "Fine. If we locate my father's missing will before Noah arrives, you have my word that I'll spend as long as it takes to track down that key."

Ruth's attention moved to a medieval axe on the wall.

"Don't even think about it," Margaret warned.

Once lunch was over, Ruth suggested they get cracking, starting with rooms in the house Henry had frequented the most. She waited with Greg in the entrance hall before Margaret returned with a key.

"This way."

They followed her down a narrow corridor next to the stairs. Margaret stopped at a set of doors carved with ornate flowers and unlocked them.

Greg looked about. "Where did Billy go?"

"Having an afternoon nap in his room." Margaret pocketed the key.

Greg gaped at her. "He's got his own room?"

"Naturally." She pushed open the doors and stepped on through.

The space beyond stood fifty feet on each side and stretched upward for a further two floors, topped with an arched ceiling. Balconies with metal balustrades ran round each level, and a spiral staircase connected them. A parquet floor formed the outline of a labyrinth in the middle of the room.

At the far end sat a giant stone fireplace, with a pair of high-backed chairs facing it, covered in blankets. A portrait of Henry Andrews hung above the mantel, and to the left sat a large blackboard on a wheeled stand. Shelves lined almost every inch of the rest of the vast room, crammed full of books and boxes.

Greg's eyes popped from their sockets. "Are all these games?"

"Puzzles, to be more precise." Margaret sat at one of several card tables and gazed round at it all. "Henry's life-long obsession."

Ruth stepped to a nearby bookshelf and read some spines: *Advanced Game Theory*, *One Thousand and One Riddles for All Ages*, *Mixed Puzzles Volumes 1–20*, plus countless books packed full of word searches and sudoku.

During her previous visits to the island, and even though she was aware of Henry's fondness for games and puzzles—it was legendary, after all—Ruth had not stepped foot inside this room.

She turned on the spot, trying to take it in, and then faced her sister as sudden realisation swept through her. "You think Henry hid the will in here?" It would take them months to check every book and box.

"Not likely," Margaret said. "But, knowing Henry, we can

assume the trail starts here, if we can only find the first clue."

Greg examined a Rubik's Cube. "Why didn't he just tell Uncle Charles where he hid the copy of the will? Why play games?"

"Because that's how my father treated life." Charles strode into the study with a three-foot-long roll of paper tucked under his arm. "He made everything into a puzzle."

A twinge of excitement coursed through Ruth at the prospect of unravelling one of Henry's challenges.

Charles set the roll of paper on a nearby table. "As a child, tasks set by my father dominated every Christmas and birthday." He balled his fists. "Never content to simply hand over presents, he'd hide them somewhere on the island, and then invent elaborate riddles for me to follow."

This got Ruth's undivided attention.

A frown creased Charles' brow. "I never discovered my thirteenth birthday present. I'd asked for a new bike." He unrolled the paper and placed chess pieces at each corner to hold it flat. "My father would leave the first clue in the same place for me, so I'd have a chance of uncovering the rest."

"But you've searched thoroughly for it?" Ruth asked.

"That's what's so odd. It's missing. I resorted to this as a possible way to locate the will directly." Charles motioned to the table. "Come see."

Ruth hugged herself as she joined him. "Why's it so cold in here?"

"My father switched off the heating in this room, and . . ." Charles gestured to a window. It was open an inch, with a heavy bolt securing it in place. "He insisted on constant airflow. Didn't want humidity ruining his collection." Charles then swept a hand over the blueprint. It was of the house, complete with several outbuildings. "As you're aware, my ancestors bought this island, complete with its ruined castle, and renovated. They kept the original castle intact, and each generation thereafter added to it with modern building techniques." He tapped the blueprint. "I obtained this from the local planning office, in the hopes of finding the will's hidden location."

Ruth nodded. "Logical." It certainly made for an impressive building. "What are all these?" She indicated several blacked-out areas.

Charles' eyebrows knitted. "I don't know how my father managed it, or who he bribed, but these are redacted areas. Parts of the house he did not want to divulge publicly."

"You've checked them out?" Greg asked as he peered at the blueprint too.

"Each and every one." Charles indicated a black mark in the corner. "The pantry. Nothing there." His finger moved to another splodge. "The boot room. Also, nothing there." Charles huffed out a breath.

Ruth wondered if this could be part of Henry's game. All distractions from finding the hiding place. She scanned the drawing, eager to begin the hunt. *But where to start?*

Margaret pointed to a blacked-out section of the next floor. "The will is probably in that locked wardrobe."

"I told you, Margaret," Charles said. "My father's wardrobe is an antique. I'm not breaking it open unless we must. Let's look for the key too, if we must, but assume for now the will is not in there."

Ruth pursed her lips and studied her brother-in-law. "If Henry wrote his will with you as the sole beneficiary, and he knew of Noah's attempt to lay claim to half the estate, why make it a game unless he wanted to make sure you were the only one to find it?"

"Precisely."

Ruth stared into space. "Henry could not have known someone would burn down the solicitors', unless—"

"I don't believe he left a will with them," Charles said. "They have no recollection of him doing so. That's something Margaret and I disagree on."

"Charles thinks the copy here is the only one," she said.

"Right," Ruth said. "That would make sense."

"Bit of a coincidence the solicitors' burned down on the same day Uncle Henry died, though," Greg said.

Ruth inclined her head at Charles. "You've already checked out the blank areas on the blueprint, so where do we look?"

"My father had a long, drawn-out decline in health. He had plenty of time to set up one of his elaborate games as a final hoorah." Charles brushed his handlebar moustache with his fingers. "And despite the infuriating riddles throughout my life, he wasn't a spiteful man. He loved me. Margaret too. And therefore, I know my father would have left the first piece of the puzzle for us to find. In plain sight. It's just not where I expected it to be. Something's gone wrong." He tapped the blueprint. "My father was a civil engineer. These redacted areas could mean something or nothing."

"Henry wasn't aware of something," Margaret whispered. "A secret Charles kept from him."

Ruth's stomach tensed. "Which is?"

"I didn't solve any of his puzzles myself," Charles said. "I always had help. Even from a young age."

Greg smiled. "Your mum?"

Charles nodded. "On my thirteenth birthday, she was away on a business trip. It was the only time I didn't solve my father's riddles and get to my present in time. He threw away the clues before she returned."

Ruth sauntered down one side of the room, scanning the shelves. "But Henry still thought you solved all the others?"

"After Jean's death, I tried helping," Margaret said. "It turns out puzzles and riddles aren't my thing either." She cleared her throat. "So, we paid the staff to assist us twice a year. We solved them as a team. Henry and I dropped bonuses in each of their pay packets as a thank you. Became quite the tradition."

"You bought their silence." Ruth clucked her tongue. "Now, Margaret, that's not very honest."

"We did what we had to. You of all people should know that."

"But even if we could find the start of this," Charles said, "we're not comfortable asking them to help us. We want to keep it in the family this time. Too much is at stake."

Given the importance of what they sought, that was a good idea.

Ruth stopped at the fireplace and stared up at Henry's portrait.

A hint of a smirk played on his lips, as if he'd known the trouble he would cause. She wasn't sure this wasn't part of his plan all along.

"Where would he usually leave the first clue?" Ruth turned back to the room, and she stiffened.

Greg's face fell. "Grandma? What's wrong?"

Ruth pointed a shaking finger to the floor by the nearest bookshelf. It was a section obscured from the rest of the room by the high-backed armchair and its draped blankets.

Lying supine, his grey eyes staring at the ceiling, lifeless, was the body of Carter, the butler.

4

In the study, Margaret, Charles, and Greg hurried over to Ruth. She held up a hand to stop them, but it was too late.

Charles stared down at the body. "Dear me. Carter?"

Margaret gasped and clapped a hand over her mouth.

"He was here this whole time?" Greg turned away and looked as though he was about to be sick.

Poor lad. He'd had a rough day.

Ruth ushered all three of them to the door. "Call the police."

"W-What on earth happened?" Margaret said as they stepped into the hallway. Her hands trembled, and she looked paler than usual, which was saying something.

Ruth glanced back in the direction of Carter's body at the far end of the study. "How long will the police take to get here?"

"It depends on whether Captain Barney needs to collect them. An hour." Charles put an arm around his wife. "Maybe a little quicker than that." He shook his head. "Carter. This can't be happening. I don't believe it. He's been with us for years. My father adored him. Don't recall a time without the fellow."

Ruth peered down the hallway. All seemed quiet. "Tell the police you'll not let anyone else into the study until they arrive. Keep the rest of the staff away."

Charles went to leave with Margaret and Greg, but he turned back when Ruth didn't follow. "Are you not coming?"

Greg murmured, "Oh no."

"Ruth, really," Margaret said. "Your morbid curiosity will get the better of you one day."

Greg coughed.

Ruth shot him a look.

It was true. Overwhelming nosiness did glue Ruth's feet to the floor, but not for macabre reasons. "I want to check a few things out."

Greg moaned.

"You go with them," Ruth said to him. "I won't be long."

He hesitated, and then sighed. "I'll stay with you."

"Gregory." Margaret glared at him. "I don't think you should—"

"I want to help Grandma." Greg hung his head. "I'm kind of getting used to it now."

"Help with what?" Margaret's face dropped. "And what do you mean you're getting used to it?" She shot daggers at Ruth, and then her eyes widened in realisation. "You're not for one moment suggesting this was anything other than a tragic accident?"

Charles gaped at Ruth too. "You can't be serious."

She held up her hands. Although something in her gut told her it wasn't an accident, and she wanted a good look to prove her instincts correct, she opted to go with a white lie to keep the peace. "I'm not suggesting anything."

"Oh, thank goodness." Margaret clutched her chest. "You

had me there for a moment. Can you imagine? Murder? Here?"

Ruth avoided her sister's gaze and addressed Charles. "Don't tell the police what I'm doing. I'll be careful not to touch anything. I'm only having a look." She knew from experience that the quicker you reached a crime scene while it was still hot, the chances of figuring out what happened increased exponentially.

Ruth did her best not to let on that she thought something nefarious had happened to Carter. That would send Margaret into a tailspin.

Charles stared into the study for a few seconds and then nodded. "Very well."

"Oh, one other thing," Ruth said. "Do you know why Carter would have been in there?"

Charles pursed his lips. "Now you come to mention it, no. As far as I knew, not another soul, apart from us, has stepped foot inside my father's study since his passing."

"The door was locked when we got here," Greg said.

Margaret pulled the key from her pocket. "I fetched this from the boot room."

"When was the last time you opened the study door?" Ruth asked as she took it from her.

Margaret frowned. "A few days ago, wasn't it, Charles? When we tried once more in vain to look for your father's will or the first riddle?"

He nodded.

Ruth examined the lock, but there were no signs of forced entry. She straightened. "Does anyone else have access to this key?"

"Theoretically, the entire staff," Charles said. "My father used to keep it on his person at all times, and there are no other copies, but when he died, we hung it up in the boot room with the others." His brow furrowed into a deep line. "I have no idea why Carter would go in the study without asking first. It's totally out of character."

"When did you last see him alive?" Ruth asked as her brain switched into detective mode. "And what would he usually be doing right about now?"

"This morning, when you arrived at the house. Sometime after eleven, as I recall." Margaret checked her watch. "And I think Carter should've been in the cellar now, putting away the wine delivery from yesterday."

"Which means . . ." Ruth gazed back into the study. "Carter was somewhere he wasn't supposed to be."

"What are you suggesting?" Margaret said. "That he was up to no good?"

"He's served the Andrews family for over half a century," Charles said. "Sure, Carter can be a bit gruff with people on occasion, but he's a perfectionist. Runs a tight ship. There's no one more trustworthy and loyal." Charles' eyes glazed over. "A tragic loss. He'll be sorely missed."

Ruth softened her expression as a wave of sympathy washed through her. After all, they'd lost someone close to them. "I'll take a quick look and let you know what I find. Perhaps we can figure out what he was doing."

Maybe it was an accident, and Ruth was being paranoid for no good reason. Even though the strong sinking feeling deep in the pit of her stomach told her she wasn't.

Charles hesitated again, stared at Margaret, and then sighed. "Please be careful, Ruth. We don't want you getting into trouble with the police."

Ruth ushered Greg inside the study and went to close the door but stopped. "Stick together." She looked between Margaret and Charles. "Don't leave each other's side." She then closed the door before Margaret could ask what she meant by that.

Greg faced Ruth. "You think it's a murder, right?" His shoulders hitched in response to her nod, and he whispered, "Why do you believe that?"

"For one simple reason," Ruth said. "If Carter took the key from the boot room, and it really is the only one, then how did he return it *after* he died?"

Greg blinked. "A copy?"

"The door was locked, remember? Perhaps Carter locked it once inside this room, but if he doesn't have a spare key on him, we'll know for sure." Ruth rested a hand on her grandson's shoulder. "Are you positive you want to help?"

"Don't ask me to touch the body."

"We won't be doing much touching of anything," Ruth reminded him. "Only what's absolutely necessary. As for you, observe only." She took a deep breath and steeled herself. "Stay right here until I call for you."

Ruth then moved slowly around the perimeter of the study. She scanned every item, searching for anything unusual or out of place, but given the sheer number of objects, plus her unfamiliarity with them, it was no small task.

On her second circuit, Ruth stopped at Carter's body and knelt beside him.

The poor man lay on his back, twisted to one side, with his left arm bent beneath him, his legs pulled up, one over the other, and his neck misshapen in such a way his right ear touched his shoulder.

Ruth winced.

He wore a dark suit, polished shoes—one of which now half hung from his right foot—and a leather loop on his belt.

Ruth grabbed a poker from the fireplace, ensured it was clean by wiping it on her skirt, then tapped each of Carter's pockets. "No key." She returned the poker to the fireplace.

Strewn about Carter were a few dozen wooden pieces: some rectangular, others square, none of them more than a few centimetres long, by one wide.

Ruth's attention drifted to the balconies above.

Greg followed her gaze. "You think someone pushed him?"

Ruth looked back at Carter. Judging by the way he'd hit the floor, with his body lying in that fashion, the likely answer to Greg's question was a resounding *yes*.

She pictured a tussle between Carter and his assailant on the balcony, and the subsequent fall. As far as Ruth could tell, Carter had broken his neck, so it had been quick.

At least she hoped so.

Ruth pointed to the balcony directly above. "Can you get up there, please?"

Greg motioned to the spiral staircase. "This way?"

"Yes, but be careful." Ruth stepped back. "Make sure not to touch the handrail. Can you do that?"

"I think so." Greg headed up the stairs, then along the balcony until he reached the end. "What am I searching for?"

"Anything out of place." Ruth took several more steps back so she could get a clear look. "What about those shelves behind you?"

Greg faced them. "Board games. They're all mystery and puzzle based. Surprise, surprise. A few escape rooms. Hey, this one seems fun." He leaned in. "A popup mystery role-playing game. It's got a spooky, haunted-house-type theme. I love haunted house stuff."

"Greg? Focus. Nothing seems disturbed?"

"Not that I can see." His gaze moved to Carter, and he swallowed.

"Try the next floor up." Ruth pointed to the other balcony above Greg's head.

As he made his way to the spiral staircase, Ruth circled the body, hunting for clues, any minute details she may have overlooked, but apart from the wooden blocks, nothing stood out.

"Grandma, there's something here."

Ruth hurried to the other side of the room. "What have you found?"

Greg now stood on the second balcony. "A set of steps."

Ruth pressed her back against the wall. Sure enough, a set of folding steps faced the bookshelf.

Greg peered at the uppermost shelf. "There's a gap. Carter took something." He ascended the steps and stretched up on tiptoes. "These are all wooden puzzle boxes."

"The kind you hide trinkets inside?" Ruth asked.

"Yeah. I think so."

Ruth's gaze dropped back to the blocks scattered across the floor. "Then we know what Carter had in his hand when he fell. These are parts of a puzzle box."

Greg stepped back onto the balcony and stared down at her. "It still could've been an accident, right?"

Ruth cocked an eyebrow at him. "Last time we thought something was . . ."

"It turned out not to be. Yeah, I know." Greg sighed and motioned with his hands. "You could be right. Carter was at the top of these portable steps. He stretched up for the puzzle box, like this, and then fell backward, over the railing. The railing is at least a foot away from the shelves, so I think if he'd slipped off the steps accidentally, he would've hit them, and not gone over?"

Ruth pictured the fall to the hard floor, and cringed. She couldn't help but think there may be a connection between the missing will and Carter's demise. The timing seemed too close to be a coincidence. "What were you up to?" she murmured. Ruth shook herself. "Come down, Greg." She then knelt and peered under the chairs, but there was nothing there either, only more wooden parts of the puzzle box. It had either been empty at the time of Carter's fall, or someone had taken whatever was inside once it had smashed open, then they'd locked the study door on their way out.

Ruth's brow furrowed. "Why lock the door, though? To buy time for your escape? To make sure no one discovered Carter's body right away?"

Ruth was determined not to jump to conclusions without sufficient evidence, but given the odd circumstances, that was proving difficult.

As she strode across the study, her attention moved to the window that was open by an inch or so. Since the bolt secured it in place, she assumed it an unlikely escape route for the killer.

She joined Greg at the base of the spiral stairs.

"We're done?" he asked.

Ruth opened the door and gestured him through. "We are." She scanned the study one last time and vowed to get to the bottom of what had happened to Carter.

Back in the entrance hall, Charles strode toward them. "What did you discover?"

Ruth tried to act casual. Now was not the time to explain her gut—and now evidence—pointed to this being a case of murder. "Carter was checking out the puzzle boxes when he fell."

Charles stared at her. "You suspect it has something to do with my father's will?"

"I'm not sure." Although Ruth failed to understand why Carter or anyone else wanted to go after Henry's will, money was more than enough incentive for murder, so there was a possible motive. But a will alone would not result in a windfall for anyone other than Charles. Not unless Carter knew something about its contents that Charles did not.

Ruth clenched and unclenched her fists. Now she needed to figure out who'd had the means and opportunity to murder the butler.

However, if Margaret got wind of her theory, she'd fly into a rage and level unfounded accusations at the staff, which would do none of them any good. So, Ruth must tread carefully, and not arouse suspicions. She had to at least pretend as though Carter's death had been an accident.

Speaking of which, Ruth's sister marched across the hall, clutching Billy under one arm. "Well?"

"Carter was looking for the will," Charles said.

Ruth's stomach tightened.

"Preposterous," Margaret snapped. "He would never steal from us. You know that, Charles. What a ridiculous notion. Henry's will has no value to anyone other than us." Margaret glared at Ruth. "I assume this is one of your wild theories?"

"I only think it's strange Carter should be in there," Ruth said in a defensive tone, flashing back to when they were kids. "I don't know what he was doing." She gave Greg a look, signalling for him to keep his mouth shut about her murder theory.

Right now, they needed to remain calm and level headed.

"Carter has been with us for decades," Margaret persisted. "Always above reproach. The mere idea of anything less is utterly ridiculous."

"Could he have been trying to find the will for you?" Greg asked.

Ruth blinked at him.

It was a possibility she hadn't yet considered. Perhaps, Carter had hoped for a finder's fee.

"As far as I know, Carter didn't know we were hunting for it," Charles said. "Margaret and I kept that to ourselves."

Well, that puts paid to that idea.

"We didn't want to worry the staff," Margaret said.

Greg shrugged. "Carter might have overheard you discussing it. People can do strange things for money."

Ruth faced him, unable to help herself. "Like that time last year when your mum dressed you up as a bunny rabbit for that children's Easter party, and then you danced around singing a sweet ditty about hiding eggs." Ruth inclined her head. "How much did that gig pay you? Must have been a lot."

Greg's cheeks flushed. "I have no idea what you're talking about."

"Can we not joke at a time like this?" Margaret said. "Need I remind you, Ruth, someone close to us has died. As always, you're focussed on the mystery, and never the damage it's caused."

Ruth composed herself and addressed her brother-in-law. "Are the police on their way?"

Charles studied his watch. "They should be here within the hour."

"The news devastated the entire staff." Margaret set her

crazy Chihuahua on the floor. "Captain Barney has gone to ferry the police across. Meanwhile, I've asked the others to remain in their rooms or the kitchen until further notice."

"What did you tell them?" Greg asked.

Margaret lifted her chin. "That there's been a tragic accident." She shot daggers at Ruth. "What else would I say?"

Billy sniffed at the brass legs of a potted plant stand, and Ruth kept a wary eye on the pooch, ready to yank her feet clear if he decided now was a good time to claim her shoes as his own, via a stream of urine.

"Ruth, if you think there's even the slightest chance Carter was searching for my father's will," Charles said, "then we have to know how far he got." At Margaret's scowl, he added, "It may explain why the riddle is missing. Perhaps Carter removed it for some reason."

Given the locked study door, Ruth could almost bet her life someone else was involved, but she remained tight-lipped on the subject.

"You should speak to the staff," Charles said to her. "One of them may have seen Carter acting suspiciously."

"Charles," Margaret snapped. "That's a job for the police, if they decide it's at all necessary."

Ruth had to agree with her on that point.

Anyway, forensic science had advanced on the order of many magnitudes over the decades, meaning there could be a raft of clues she'd not found in the study; a stray fibre, a strand of hair, a spot of saliva or blood . . .

Charles took Margaret's hand. "What about the staff?"

"You're not suggesting they had something to do with this?"

"It's a terrible situation," Ruth said. One of several she'd recently found herself in. All of which she'd decided not to share with Margaret. Ruth didn't feel strong enough to stand up to her sister's disapproval, especially under the current circumstances. "I don't think there's any harm in asking the staff a few questions. In case they can shed light on why Carter was in the study. It would help the police."

"Ask away," Charles said before Margaret could respond.

She shot him a look, and he squeezed her hand. "Fine." Margaret let out a breath. "If they are willing to talk to Ruth, then so be it."

Charles winked and let go.

"Is there somewhere private we can chat with them?" Ruth looked about with a twinge of unease knotting her stomach. "A location nearer to the servants' quarters, but not too close? Away from the study."

"I have the perfect place." Charles motioned for them to follow him, and he strode across the hallway.

Margaret tottered after him, with Billy hard on her heels.

5

Ruth and Greg followed Charles and Margaret through the house and into a conservatory constructed of stone and glass. Off to one side sat a low circular wall covered in a sheet of glass.

Greg glanced into it. "A well?"

"The original one," Charles said. "When my father added this to the house, he refused to build over it, despite the well drying up decades before I was born."

Around the rest of the room sat various exotic plants in ornate pots, along with padded wicker chairs.

Ruth waved Greg to one of them, and then addressed her sister. "Please fetch two or three staff members."

A phone rang deep within the house.

"Hold that thought." Margaret scooped Billy up. "I'll be back in a minute."

Seizing her chance to speak to Charles alone, Ruth closed the doors, composed herself, and faced him. "If your father left a series of clues and puzzles to follow, but the first one isn't where you'd hoped, then how on earth can I stand a chance at finding the trail?"

Perhaps that's what Carter had found, and now the killer had taken over the hunt. Ruth cursed herself for not searching Carter's pockets more thoroughly. However, that risked leaving behind her own DNA or trace evidence.

Charles dropped into a chair with a deflated expression. "You're our last hope, Ruth. It was my suggestion to ask for your help. Without you, we lose this estate."

"You uncovered nothing among Henry's belongings?" Ruth pressed. "Even something seemingly unrelated?"

"When working on these silly riddles, my father made a point of destroying his notes," Charles murmured. "In case I tried to cheat."

Ruth paced back and forth, hands clasped behind her back. "Where exactly did Henry usually leave the first clue?"

"My father would always place it in a box on his desk. He'd insist I read the riddle in front of him, out loud." Charles looked away. "I guess he wanted to gauge my reaction, which was always confusion followed by a blank stare at the nearest wall."

"Desk?" Ruth's brow furrowed. "There wasn't a desk in the study."

"In his office." Charles waved a hand. "But you needn't bother about it because it was the first place Margaret and I looked."

Ruth stopped pacing and steeled herself. "You didn't tell me Henry had an office."

"I didn't get the chance," Charles said apologetically. "I was about to show you when . . ." He swallowed. "Anyway, it matters little. As I say, we searched Father's office several times since his passing."

"Where is it?" Greg asked.

"Off the study."

"There weren't any other doors," Greg said.

"It's there. Only hidden."

Ruth pinched the bridge of her nose, trying not to lose her cool. "Charles." She forced a smile. "Dearest Charles. You need to tell me things like that right away. Don't hold back pertinent information."

Charles' expression dropped. "I've not been thinking straight. Stressful time. My deepest apologies."

The door opened, and Margaret stepped through.

Ruth kept her focus on her brother-in-law. "Can I see your father's office, please?" They needed to focus on searching the study now and question the staff after.

"That'll have to wait," Margaret said. "Captain Barney called. He's on his way back with the police. They will be here in twenty minutes."

Ruth's face fell. "That soon?" She motioned for Charles to stand. "Show me the office before they seal off the study."

The four of them rushed from the conservatory.

In the hallway, Ruth hesitated and swore under her breath.

Margaret turned back.

"One minute." Ruth raced upstairs and checked on Merlin, who had curled up on her bed and was now fast asleep, and then she grabbed a pair of gloves from her coat pocket. Ruth hurried back downstairs, where she met Greg, Margaret, and Charles outside the study door.

With only fifteen minutes remaining until the police arrived, Ruth's anxiety gnawed at her insides. She addressed Greg first. "Keep an eye out and let me know the second they're here."

She could not afford to get caught in the study. That would result in a lot of questions and the potential for a criminal record at best, prison time at worst. Especially if

Carter's death turned out to be more than an accident, as she suspected.

However, if they didn't search Henry's office now, they may not get a second chance for a while, and with Charles' half-brother set to arrive in—Ruth glanced at the grandfather clock in the hallway—a little over twenty-four hours, time was of the essence.

She took a calming breath, trying to remain clear headed and relaxed, and faced Margaret. "If we don't get out of the study before the police arrive, would you mind keeping them talking until we do? Preferably in the sitting room. Somewhere they can't see us leaving."

"What would you like me to talk about?" Margaret asked in a breezy tone. "Something more important than a murder." She tapped her chin. "Hmm . . . How about the weather? The state of the United Kingdom's foreign policy?"

"Your sarcasm has really gone up a notch since we last saw you," Ruth said. "Congratulations."

Margaret clicked her fingers. "I know. Let's discuss the French Revolution and its culmination in Napoleon Bonaparte's ascent to emperor."

"Cats have thirty-two muscles in each ear," Greg said. He noticed Ruth's raised eyebrows. "Mum. She's always banging on about useless cat facts. Drives me insane." He screwed up his face. "Some of it goes in, unfortunately."

Ruth pinched his cheek. "Your grandfather would have been so proud of you both."

"And *you* should have no trouble entertaining the police." Margaret sniffed. "After all, you're the chatterbox of the family."

Ruth blinked at her. She estimated Margaret had used at least double her word count in their lifetimes, and that was with only a two-year head start. "Right." She shook herself and returned to the task at hand. Ruth nodded at Charles. "Please take me to your father's office." She handed him the key to the study door, and everyone went their separate ways.

Ruth followed Charles into the study, and once inside, she hurried past him.

"Where are you going?" Charles called after her as Ruth made a beeline for the other end of the study.

"Checking something," she said. "Wait there. I'll be right back." Ruth jogged over to Carter's body, knelt, and pulled on her gloves. She then felt inside his pockets, both in Carter's trousers and jacket. The fireplace poker would've only rattled keys or hit hard plastic, but now she checked for papers. "Nothing." Ruth clambered back to her feet. "He doesn't have anything."

Of course not. That would have been too easy.

Halfway down the left-hand wall of the study, Charles stopped in front of a set of shelves crammed full of jigsaw puzzles. "No one knows about this secret room, other than myself, Margaret, and my father." He reached under the fifth shelf from the bottom, toward the corner, and pressed a hidden lever.

There came a solid clunk from beyond.

"What about carter?" Ruth asked.

"I didn't think so, but now I'm not so sure." Charles then swung the bookshelf from the wall, and revealed the entrance to a compact room, ten feet on each side.

More shelves lined the interior, filled with antique books and an impressive collection of executive toys. There was everything from Newton's Cradle, Foucault's pendulum, and a kinetic model of the solar system, to magnetic sculptures, a miniature pool table, and a silver spinning top.

"My father designed and made most of these." Charles

indicated a mechanical Ferris wheel and a metal spire construction with a similar design to the Eiffel Tower.

Henry had painted three intricate solar system icons on the hub of the Ferris wheel. However, unlike his model, these only had a sun and a few planets each, orbiting at various angles.

A selection of hand-carved wooden puzzles adorned an oak desk that dominated the back wall, along with a Tiffany lamp and an assortment of gold fountain pens and inkpots.

Ruth examined a complicated mechanism that filled an entire shelf. It had a series of ramps, pulleys, and gears. "What's this?"

"A Rube Goldberg machine." Charles plucked a metal ball bearing from a pot, set it on a platform at one end of the device, and flipped a switch.

The ball whizzed down a chute, along a narrow ledge, and then dropped into a bucket. The added weight pulled down on a string, which in turn lifted a miniature hammer that then knocked a marble from its perch. And on the machine went: the marble followed a winding path, faster and faster, hit a series of dominoes on levers, which released a spring and hit another marble, sending that one down a steep ramp. The mechanical dance finished in a pirate's Jolly Roger flag being raised at the end.

Ruth shook her head. "Impressive. Do it again."

Charles chuckled. "Takes too long to reset. We're in a hurry, remember?"

Ruth straightened. "Of course."

Charles pointed at a wooden box in the middle of the desk. "This is what we came to see."

The box had an intricate labyrinth pattern carved into the lid.

Ruth tugged at her gloves and opened it, but the box was empty.

"My father would leave the first riddle in there. Every time without fail. Until now, that is." Charles returned to the door, peered out for a moment, and then faced Ruth again. "Margaret and I have checked this room a hundred times." He pointed to the books. "Rifled through every page." Then he motioned to ten ornate boxes in a glass cabinet. "Went through those too. Nothing. The riddle is gone."

Ruth lifted the ornate box from the desk and peered underneath. There were no markings or any obvious secret compartments. "Given his length of employment at the house . . ." Ruth ran her fingers over the lid and sides of the box, hunting for any hidden switches. "Carter could have told someone else about this hidden room."

Charles' expression turned stoic. "I suppose it's possible, although extremely unlikely. Carter is— *was* loyal, and a valued member of this household."

Ruth thought it through. They a had modest sized complement of staff. "Could that have changed when your father died?"

"I don't think so."

"And you're convinced beyond any doubt that Henry would have left the riddle in here before he passed away? And nowhere else?"

"I'm positive," Charles said with a look of conviction.

Ruth believed him. She set the box down. "In that case, we can assume that either he never got round to finishing the riddle, and therefore didn't leave it here, or that someone has taken it." She inclined her head and studied Charles' reaction. "You knew your dad best, so which do you think is most likely?"

Charles folded his arms. "I believe my father would have

prepared the riddle some time ago. Years previously. This was a long time in the planning and execution. Other birthday and Christmas riddles would have come and gone in the meantime, but my firm belief is he would have placed the final one in that box." Charles straightened his bowtie. "My father was fully aware of his own mortality. However, I simply can't go along with the accusation that Carter stole the riddle, so I am at a loss as to what's happened. It makes little sense in my mind."

Ruth could understand his reticence to admit a long-serving member of their household could deceive them, but she remained neutral in her opinion. There simply wasn't enough evidence to formulate a decision on the matter either way.

Whether or not Charles liked it, there was still a high probability that Carter had betrayed him.

Ruth paced the office. "No matter how remote the possibility, perhaps Carter not only knew Henry hid the riddle in this very room, but he also followed the trail your father left. After all, Carter died while retrieving a puzzle box. What else could he have been doing?" Ruth left out the fact she now firmly believed Carter had not been alone when he died.

Charles went to answer, but then gave a small shrug.

Ruth scanned the rest of the shelves. They were running out of time. On the middle row of the last bookshelf, between a crossword compendium and a boxed set of twelve-sided dice, sat a picture of Henry and Jean, with her usual adornment of jewels.

Greg appeared at the open door. He panted and bent double. "They're here. The police. Quick."

As Ruth raced from the office, she removed her gloves and stuffed them into her pockets.

Charles pushed the shelves closed, and then the three of them jogged across the study. They'd just stepped into the corridor and closed the door behind them when Margaret rounded the corner.

She escorted three people. The first was a tall man in his forties. "This is Detective Murray."

He had thinning hair, week-old stubble, and wore a dark grey suit and a long woollen coat.

"A swift response to our call." Charles extended a hand.

Detective Murray shook it. "We take any unexpected deaths seriously, sir." He had a soft Scottish accent, as though he'd lived in England for some time, or maybe America. The detective motioned to an older white-haired woman who accompanied him. "This is Doctor Cleaves."

She carried a leather bag, wore a black suit under a heavy tweed jacket, and Ruth gauged the doctor to be a similar age to her, although tanned, which was odd, given their current northerly location. Ruth put it down to either regular trips abroad or an addiction to sunbeds.

Charles shook Doctor Cleaves' hand too and then motioned to Ruth. "My sister-in-law, Ruth Morgan." He motioned in Greg's direction. "And her grandson, my nephew, Greg Shaw. They're staying with us for a few days."

Detective Murray looked between them, his eyes narrowed, sizing them up, and then he refocussed on Charles. "Where's the deceased?"

"Allow me to show the detective," Ruth said before Charles had time to respond. "I know how traumatic this has been for you. I'd be happy to help."

He gave a solemn nod. "You are the one who found him, after all, so it makes sense." Charles stepped aside.

"Excuse me." The third person, a woman in her twenties with dark hair, wearing a heavy coat, scarf, and hat, stepped from behind the detective. Unlike him, her Scottish accent was stronger, but she pronounced every word with clinical precision. She held up a hand. "Could I use your bathroom?"

Ruth contained a smile. During her time on the force, she'd made that excuse plenty of times to surreptitiously check out the rest of the house.

"I'll show you the way." Margaret gave Ruth a hard look, as if warning her not to do or say anything stupid, and then led the officer back down the hallway.

Ruth opened the door to the study. Detective Murray and the doctor slipped inside. She signalled for Greg to stay close by, and then went in after them. Ruth remained by the door while Detective Murray conducted his preliminary scan of the room.

He let out a low whistle. "Impressive."

Not quite the first observation Ruth had expected from a trained officer.

6

Detective Murray sauntered over to the table with the blueprint, stared down at it for a few seconds, then continued along the room until he found Carter's body behind the chair. "Here we go." He tutted, shook his head, and then his gaze moved up to the balconies. The detective waved his companion over. "You're clear, Doctor."

Ruth frowned. Detective Murray had spent almost no time inspecting the scene around the body.

As Doctor Cleaves examined the deceased, the detective moved slowly around the room again, hands clasped behind his back, as if on a leisurely stroll around a mildly interesting art gallery.

"You discovered the body?" He didn't look at Ruth.

"I did. Right before Charles called you."

"Why were you in here?" Detective Murray looked down at the blueprint again, and his brow furrowed.

Ruth pondered her answer for a second but decided on the truth. Not all of it, though. "Charles' father died, and I've come to see the family. It's a tough time for them."

The detective lifted the corner of the blueprint.

"Shouldn't you be wearing gloves?" Ruth asked.

He stepped away from the table and continued around the room. "You missed the funeral." Detective Murray ran his finger along the shelves as he scanned the titles of the puzzles. "Why did it take you so long to get here?"

Ruth stared at him. "How did you know that?"

"Henry Andrews was part of the community. We all went to the funeral." Detective Murray looked over at her, eyebrows raised, waiting for an answer to his question.

"Unfortunately, I got waylaid," Ruth said. "An accident with my motorhome."

"Ah right. The *thing* in the ferry car park." He said this in the same way many people mentioned Ruth's motorhome: through a clenched jaw, accompanied by a scowl of disapproval.

She gave him a coy look in return. "Hard to miss." Ruth could understand a giant land yacht wasn't to everyone's taste, but it made her happy.

Detective Murray continued his laidback sweep of the room. "Go on."

"Well, that's it really. I arrived late this morning with my grandson." Ruth wasn't about to admit Henry hadn't been Ruth's biggest fan, so not only would it not have been proper to attend his funeral, but she wouldn't have felt right going it anyway. Well, not unless Margaret had wanted Ruth there, and she'd never mentioned that to her.

"What is your line of work?" Detective Murray asked as he examined the spiral staircase.

"I'm a food consultant." To Ruth's surprise, this didn't result in the usual smart remark or million questions. However, what confused her more was the fact he hadn't yet asked any questions about Carter.

Does he think I killed him? If so, then why?

She looked over at the doctor, who did wear gloves as she examined the body and made notes on a clipboard.

Now it was Ruth's turn to ask the questions. "Is this your first visit to Ivywick Island?"

"It is," Detective Murray said. "In fact, we remarked on the way over here that the only other time either of us have heard of anything unusual happening here was"—he motioned between himself and the doctor—"the redheaded boy."

Ruth perched on the edge of a table and folded her arms. "What was that about?"

"Way before our time," the doctor said.

Detective Murray ran a finger along the staircase's handrail. "Forty years ago. The only file still open."

That was a couple of years before Ruth and John had been banished from the island. She gave the detective an inquisitive look.

He half shrugged. "Fishermen spotted a redheaded boy on the beach. The lad waded into the water, dove beneath the surface, and they lost sight of him. By the time Sergeant Bell took statements and then came out here to investigate, there was no sign of the boy."

"He drowned?" Ruth asked, knowing full well what the answer had to be.

"No one knows," Doctor Cleaves said. "The body never washed up."

"The Andrews family and their staff knew of no one fitting the description. No children that age, and none on the mainland either. Never learned the boy's identity or received details of any more sightings. He simply vanished." Detective Murray ascended the spiral staircase.

Ruth pursed her lips and murmured, "No one can vanish."

If he had drowned, the strong tides surrounding Ivywick would have washed a body ashore within hours.

Detective Murray headed on up the staircase, all the way to the uppermost balcony. Once there, his eyes darted from the handrail to the floor, until he reached the set of portable steps at the end.

He then faced the shelves and peered up at the empty space. "Looks like the deceased removed something."

"A puzzle box," Ruth said. "It's down here. Broken apart." She pointed to the wooden pieces scattered about Carter's body.

Of course, he should have already spotted them.

After a cursory glance at the steps, the railing, and the shelves, Detective Murray then made his way back down.

Ruth's narrowed gaze followed him.

It wasn't usual for an investigating officer to allow a possible suspect to remain at a potential crime scene while they investigated.

As Detective Murray stepped from the spiral staircase, he addressed Ruth. "Any idea what he was doing? Why the butler removed the item?"

Ruth shook her head. "We've been trying to puzzle that out for ourselves." She smiled. "Pun intended."

Detective Murray shot her a sour look. "I don't think this is the right time for jokes, madam." He scanned the floor at the base of the staircase and then locked eyes with her again. "Anything else you can add?"

Ruth pressed her lips together and shook her head.

Besides, all she had to go on right now was wild speculation, and she didn't feel the need to spend the next hour or two explaining about a missing will and riddle.

Detective Murray studied Ruth, as if trying to perceive

any uneasiness in her demeanour. All these questions, and he hadn't noted down any answers.

"Are you not going to look for fingerprint evidence?" She asked. "Fibres?"

He strode over to the doctor.

"The injuries look consistent with the fall." She pointed to the relevant parts of the body. "Broken neck. Suspected fractured skull. We'll know more if an autopsy is required."

"And that's the million-pound question." Detective Murphy looked to Ruth and back again. "Fell or pushed?"

"There's no other visible bruising or scratch marks," Doctor Cleaves said.

Detective Murray's gaze moved back up to the handrail above. "No sign of a struggle there either. Looks to be an accident. Toppled backward off the ladder as he took an item from the shelf. Agreed?"

"That would be consistent with what I'm seeing here," Doctor Cleaves said. "He landed mostly headfirst."

The study door opened, and the young female officer entered.

"What did you discover?" Detective Murray asked.

She slipped a notepad from her pocket and read from it. "I spoke to one member of the household staff. The others are in their rooms."

"Out of earshot of the owners?" Detective Murphy asked as he sauntered over to her.

"Yes, sir. Her name is Betty Miller. She's the head housekeeper."

Ruth could understand why they'd want to talk to staff away from Margaret and Charles, so they could speak freely, but couldn't figure out why the detective openly discussed this in front of her.

"I know the Miller family," he said. "Live in Muasdale.

My son went to the same school as her granddaughter. What does she have to say about the victim?"

"She informed me the deceased was a, quote, '*lovely man.*'" The officer continued to read from her notes. "Worked on Ivywick Island since he was a teenager. Well respected. Never argued with anyone. She knows of no one who'd wish him ill, and hasn't seen anything suspicious." The officer closed the notepad and returned it to her pocket. "She's understandably shocked by what's happened."

Detective Murphy took a deep breath, and then looked back at Doctor Cleaves. "Are you satisfied?"

She stood. "I am."

"In that case, we'll question the owners, and then call it a day." His half smile at Ruth didn't reach his eyes. "Thank you for your time, madam."

She gaped at him. "What about the body?"

"Body? Oh, yes." He looked over at Doctor Cleaves.

"I'll contact the funeral director," she said. "It might be some time before they can get here, so we'll need to store him somewhere cold."

Ruth gawped at her.

"Agreed, Doctor." Detective Murray smirked. "Can't very well leave him here, can we?" He cleared his throat. "I'll ask the owners if they have somewhere suitable outside." He strode across the study and opened the door. "After you, madam."

Ruth hesitated, and then realising he meant her, she hurried on through. "Oh." She turned back. "What about the fire? It was local, so did you investigate?"

"Fire?"

"The solicitors' burned down, no?"

"Oh, that fire." Detective Murray nodded.

Ruth stepped to him and lowered her voice. "Did you catch the person responsible?"

He stared at her for a few seconds. "Sure."

This answer caught Ruth off guard. "You did? Who was it?"

Detective Murray's eyes narrowed. "What business is it of yours?" When Ruth didn't respond, he let out a breath. "It was a couple of kids. They set fire to a skip full of cardboard out back. The skip caught the roof alight and razed the whole building." He went to leave.

Ruth stepped in front of him, blocking his path. "They admitted it?" she asked. "Those kids?"

"Not at first." He seemed irritated with her. "But we got it out of them eventually. Excuse me." Detective Murray strode past.

In the hallway, Ruth plonked herself down on a padded bench seat next to Greg.

Doctor Cleaves and the female officer wrapped Carter in one of Margaret's guest bedsheets and took him out to the coal shed.

After a few boilerplate questions from Detective Murphy, who then explained their findings to Margaret and Charles, ruling Carter's death an accident, he and the other two left.

The front door closed, and Charles sighed. "Poor Carter." He turned to Ruth. "So, nothing more than a tragic accident."

Ruth nodded, and then shook her head. "Someone murdered him for sure."

Margaret threw her hands up. "Come on, Ruth. Detective Murray just told us that—"

Ruth waved a finger at the front door. "He doesn't know what he's talking about."

"And we're to trust that you do?" Margaret asked. "After being out of the police force for over thirty years, you suddenly know more?"

"I—"

Margaret shot daggers at her. "You always think you know best, don't you? Just like the time with Dad's car."

Ruth groaned. And here it was—as regular as clockwork.

When Ruth was seven years old, and Margaret nine, they'd accompanied their father on a visit to the dentist. They had then persuaded him they could stay in the car, remaining sensible and adultlike, rather than having to wait in the boring reception area while he had a root canal.

However, after twenty minutes of constant nagging and whining about being bored in the car, despite the radio, Ruth convinced Margaret they should pop across the road to the corner shop, grab several bags of sweets, and race back.

Dad would never know.

Margaret, with some reluctance, agreed. They then raided their father's stash of car park change, and off they went.

However, when the pair of them returned to the vehicle, they realised their huge mistake: they had locked the keys inside.

Not wanting to bother their father with the expense of calling a locksmith, or feel his wrath at full tilt when he came out of his mini surgery, no doubt with a sore mouth and a mood to match, Ruth decided it would be a fantastic idea to smash a side window.

Her thinking was they could then blame it on a fictitious gang of passing yobs, and Dad's insurance would cover the cost.

No harm, no foul.

In a moment of reckless bravery, and before Margaret

could stop her, Ruth hurled a brick through the side window just as a police car pulled up.

Ruth didn't stop running until she got all the way home.

When he discovered what had happened, their dad flipped out. Being the oldest, and supposedly responsible for Ruth's actions as well as her own, Margaret's punishment was far worse: grounded for a month and double chores. *Ouch.*

All Ruth got was her TV privileges revoked for a week.

She offered to share some of Margaret's chores, but her sister refused.

Margaret had never forgiven her for that day either, and she had brought it up in almost every argument since.

Ruth couldn't understand why. After all, as an adult, she'd more than made up for her crime by joining the police force, not to mention being a law-abiding citizen ever since. As far as Ruth was concerned, she'd repaid her debt to society, but Margaret had her own set of laws and punishments.

All this meant that Margaret rarely trusted Ruth, certainly not her instincts or judgement. Margaret knew Ruth had some skills when it came to investigating, that she was the best bet to sniff out the will's whereabouts, but Margaret still questioned Ruth's actions and motives at every turn.

Ten minutes later, in the sitting room, with all this in mind, Ruth cupped her hands around a mug of tea and braced herself, while Margaret paced in front of her, growing angrier with every step.

"How can you think for one second that someone

murdered Carter?" she snapped. "Detective Murray ruled it an accident."

Ruth remained calm. *Deep breath in, deep breath out.* "Have you seen Detective Murray before?"

Charles sat on the sofa opposite. "At the funeral."

"Before that?" Ruth asked.

"Well, of course we haven't." Margaret scowled at Ruth. "Unlike you, we don't have frequent run-ins with the law. What's your point?"

"That he might be new to the job and made a mistake," Ruth said. She hated to say it out loud, but like any other service or industry, you had employees with varying levels of competency. The police force was no different.

"Grandma, do you think you could be a little paranoid this time?" Greg asked in what he clearly thought was a soft tone. "After that business in Vanmoor?"

Margaret stopped pacing and put her hands on her hips. "What business? The village where you broke down? What happened?"

Ruth glared at Greg and waved Margaret's question away. "I'm telling you." She thrust a finger at the door. "Carter died in suspicious circumstances. I'd stake my reputation on it."

"You're a food consultant," Margaret said. "How would it affect your reputation?"

"Well, there's one way to find out if you're right," Charles said. "We'll call the police again and demand they send a different detective. We'll get a second opinion." He went to stand, but Ruth waved him down.

"I don't want them to know it's a murder," she said. "Not yet."

Margaret dropped to the sofa next to Charles, straightened her skirt, and said, "Why ever not? If there's a killer among us, don't you think we need to act?"

"Calling the police and telling them someone murdered Carter would cause a huge investigation," Ruth said. "They'd lock down the island. Treat the whole place like a crime scene. Interview everyone. That could take days. Possibly longer. In the meantime, we'd have no way to look for Henry's will."

"If they lock down the island," Greg said, "that Noah guy won't be able to come here."

"No, Ruth's right." Charles straightened his bowtie. "If we demand another detective, that could take some time to arrange. Noah arrives tomorrow."

Ruth took a gulp of her tea and set it to one side. "Someone murdered Carter, and I want to understand who and why. It has to be linked to the will."

Margaret sat back and crossed her arms. "I mean, Ruth, who? Who'd do such a thing?" Her attitude had softened.

"Until I speak to all the staff, how can I answer that?"

Even then, Ruth would have to do her best to see through lies, which would be difficult, given how someone had already gotten away with murder.

"I think Grandma is right," Greg said. "It's too much of a coincidence. Someone's after the same thing we are."

Margaret gave him an incredulous look.

Ruth thought back to the broken puzzle box pieces—nothing inside. *Was there a note when Carter found it? Was the riddle in there, and now the killer has it? How close are they to finding the will?*

Ruth moved her attention to Charles. "I'm sorry, we have to work with the assumption that Carter and at least one other person knew about the riddle prior to this morning and have been actively searching for the will."

Margaret scowled at her sister. "If you truly believe all these conspiracy theories, then why on earth didn't you tell Detective Murray?"

Ruth glanced at the doors at either end of the room and lowered her voice to a whisper. "Because the killer now assumes we all think Carter's death was an accident. And that's exactly how we'll continue to act. The murderer will not be so wary if they're under the impression we've taken the events at face value, and the police have left the island." Ruth took a breath. "If the killer is not careful in how they proceed, we stand a chance at catching up to them."

Margaret's eyes widened. "Catch up to a murderer?" she said in a shrill voice. "Oh, yes, brilliant, Ruth." She waved a fist. "Have you lost your mind?"

7

After a couple of minutes of silence, the only sound coming from the incessant tick of a carriage clock on the mantelpiece, Charles stood, and walked to the drinks cabinet.

He poured himself a whiskey, and then sat in an armchair away from his wife.

She glowered at him. "Don't tell me you agree with Ruth? You really think there's a killer among the staff? They're determined to find Henry's will? And not only that, but we have to—how did you put it, Ruth?"

"Catch up to them," Greg said.

"Not helpful," Ruth murmured.

"Yes. Thank you." Margaret refocused on Charles. "Catch up to a murderer."

Charles sipped his drink. "Makes sense they're after the will."

Margaret's eyebrows shot up. "For what purpose? It's valueless to anyone other than us."

"How do we know they haven't gotten it already?" Greg asked.

"Because they haven't approached Charles and Margaret for money." When this resulted in three confused stares, Ruth continued. "It seems to me the only reason they'd be after the will is to then hold it to ransom." She looked between her sister and brother-in-law. "The murderer gets to the will first, and they threaten to destroy it unless you pay." Ruth sat back. "Apart from Carter, do you have a full complement of staff here?"

"Yes." Charles took another sip of whiskey.

"I checked they're remaining in their quarters or the kitchen, and told them to await further instruction," Margaret said.

Ruth pursed her lips as she thought the situation through. "If the killer is among them, they'll be stuck with the others."

"But if they sneak off and find the will or the next part of the riddle," Charles said, "they'll then be in a hurry to leave the island."

"Yeah," Greg said. "No way they'd stick around."

"They can't leave," Margaret said. "Barney has the only boat."

"My bet is they'll have arranged for another one to collect them when the time is right, or have some other way to escape," Ruth said. "And I don't think they'd risk hiding the will on the island for fear of someone else stumbling across it." She shook her head. "No. Their best bet is to run, and once they're in a safe place, make their demands."

Margaret steepled her fingers. "What are you planning? To question the staff one by one?"

"That's exactly what I'm going to do." Ruth didn't expect the killer to confess, but she needed to understand the staff's movements over the past day or so. "I want to figure out what conversations they've overheard."

With a house as large as theirs to maintain, and so many staff moving about the place, it would be easy for any one of them to eavesdrop.

"That's how Carter knew about the will?" Greg asked. "He overheard Uncle Charles and Aunty Margaret talking about it?"

"At least Carter must have known," Ruth said with a small shrug. "But perhaps they all know."

"Ridiculous," Margaret said, although she didn't seem so sure about that, and she threw an uneasy glance in Charles' direction.

"If we're pretending Carter's death was an accident," Greg said, "how can you interview the staff?"

"I'll say we want to understand what Carter was doing in the study, as it's supposed to be off-limits." The killer may see through the subterfuge, but it was the only idea Ruth had at that moment. She stood. "Before I talk to them, though, can someone take me to Carter's room?" She needed to see if he'd left any clues behind.

"Carter doesn't have a room," Margaret said. "He has a cottage." She let out a slow breath and got to her feet. "I suppose I can show you."

Greg went to stand too, but Ruth rested a hand on his shoulder. "Wait here with your uncle." She faced Charles. "I assume you've checked behind every painting in the house?"

Charles raised his glass. "First thing we did." He gulped the remainder of his whiskey. "Alas, no hidden safes."

"In that case," Ruth said, "could you and Greg go to the study, remove the rest of the puzzle boxes, and open them?"

Greg's face fell. "There has to be a hundred or more."

"One hundred and eight by my count," Ruth said. "We don't know whether Carter found the right one. We'll need to check them all." She motioned, and followed her sister from the sitting room with a twinge in her gut that guaranteed there were some large pieces of the puzzle missing. Both literally and figuratively.

Down a short hallway, Margaret opened a door to a boot room. She handed Ruth a woollen coat and a scarf, and then put hers on too. Margaret snatched a set of keys from among others on a row of hooks. She then faced Ruth, clutched the keys to her chest, and her eyes glazed with tears. "This is horrible. Simply horrible."

Surprised by this sudden show of emotion, Ruth cupped her sister's cheeks in her hands. "I'm sorry this has happened to you, Margo. I really am. But you have my solemn promise I'll find out who did this to Carter and bring them to justice."

Not to mention find the will.

Margaret sniffed. "I know." She cleared her throat, lifted her chin, and they walked from the boot room and closed the door. "Oh, Ruth," she said over her shoulder as she marched along the corridor. "Dare to call me Margo again, and there'll be two murders in one day."

Ruth chuckled.

At the end they headed through a door and stepped into a walled garden with rows of raised beds.

As the cold air hit her, Ruth applied some lip balm. Little about the house and grounds had changed in the decades since her last visit. They followed the path past statues of angels and Greek gods, plus an ornamental koi pond.

"You fell into that." Margaret waggled a finger at it. "Do you remember?"

Ruth glared at the stupid pond. "No."

"Of course you do," Margaret said. "It was awfully funny.

You'd had one too many glasses of champagne and decided to balance along the edge like a tightrope walker. It was at that moment we all realised a future in the circus was not in the cards for you."

Ruth pictured herself stumbling sideways and then the shock of the freezing water driving the air from her lungs. "I have no idea what you're talking about."

"Yes you do." Margaret smirked. "You kicked Henry's prized Doitsu in the side of the head. He was livid."

Ruth followed Margaret through an archway, and after a few more minutes of walking across several more walled gardens, with the main house receding into the distance, they finally came to a cottage.

The compact building had a thatched roof, leaded windows, stone walls, and was enclosed by a white picket fence.

Margaret opened the front gate, and they strode up the path, past low hedgerows and a manicured lawn.

The front door stood under an open-sided porch, flanked by hanging baskets filled with flowers. Ruth touched one of them to check whether they were silk. They were, which made sense considering it was winter.

Margaret opened the door, and they stepped into a lounge with oak beams only an inch or two above their heads, a comfy sofa covered in blankets and cushions, and a high-backed Oxford chair next to an open fireplace.

On the mantelpiece were various photos of Carter and views of Ivywick Island.

Despite the cozy feel created by the décor, soft furnishings, and low ceilings, Ruth shuddered.

"It feels wrong being in here."

"Why?" Margaret said. "Carter was in our house all the

time. For many years. This is our property too. He lived here rent-free."

"You really do have a soft heart beneath that iron exterior." Ruth walked over to a bureau, swung down the front and peeked inside.

Apart from a few pens and a diary with nothing but shopping lists, it was empty. She checked the drawers next, but all they had were a couple of blank notepads and a stack of bank statements.

"Does Carter have any next of kin?" Ruth moved to a set of shelves and scanned the titles—mainly nonfiction books on World War II. She riffled through some pages.

"His sister passed away last year," Margaret said. "Carter never married nor had any children."

Once done with the bookshelf, Ruth walked into a compact kitchen with a breakfast table, oven, and a sink. She checked inside the cupboards and then stepped into a utility room with a washer–dryer. Everything was clean and tidy.

She glanced into a downstairs cloakroom, then headed on up to the next floor.

On the landing were two doors. The first led to a bathroom, and the second to the only bedroom.

Ruth walked slowly around the bedroom, scanning the double bed, the bedside table, and a wardrobe. She checked inside the latter, and slipped her hand into jacket and trouser pockets.

Margaret stood by the door. "Anything?"

Ruth huffed out a breath and shook her head.

"If he had it, Carter must have destroyed the first riddle," Margaret said. "Threw it away."

"Did he have a phone?" Ruth walked round the bedroom for a second time. "Perhaps he took a picture."

Margaret shrugged. "Not that I've ever seen. Who would he call? He lived alone, and he could reach us by walking to the main house."

Judging by his minimalist lifestyle, and the fact Carter hadn't had a mobile phone on him upon his death, Ruth didn't hold much hope of finding copies of the riddle.

She opened the drawer in the bedside table. "Here we go." Ruth lifted out a smartphone.

Margaret's eyebrows raised. "Dark horse. I never knew."

Ruth powered it on, and notifications of several emails flashed up. Unfortunately, they didn't elaborate on who the sender may be nor their contents. To make matters worse, Carter had locked his phone. It required a passcode.

She returned the phone to the drawer, and then sauntered to the rear window. Ruth stared at the horizon. The lighthouse was visible in the distance, along with the house next to it that Captain Barney occupied.

Ruth's gaze dropped to the cottage's back garden.

Like the front, it too had neat hedgerows and a picket fence surrounding it, along with flower borders, a single metal chair and table, and a small wooden shed.

"Better check that out." Ruth gestured to it.

As they made their way back downstairs, Margaret said, "You realise even if we find Henry's riddle, not only will we have to solve it, but that's merely the start of his shenanigans." She looked at her watch. "Noah arrives in a little over twenty-four hours. Some of Henry's riddles took us a week or more to solve, and I expect this one to be far more complex and irritating."

Not allowing her sister's negativity to affect her, Ruth strode through the front door, rounded the cottage, and headed down the back path to the shed. There was no lock on the door. She supposed the crime rate on Ivywick Island was zero, therefore it didn't need one. However, after Carter's death, they all might want to rethink that.

Ruth opened the shed door, found a light switch inside, and flicked it on. "Now this is more like it."

A bench sat in front of a window with heavy curtains drawn across. On the bench were all manner of tools and parts—gears, levers, open boxes with nuts and bolts, screwdrivers and ratchet sets hanging from hooks, oilcans on shelves, more boxes of parts labelled and stacked head high. Organised chaos.

Ruth snatched up a strange tool with a five-pointed metal star at one end. "What is all this?"

"Carter's one and only vice," Margaret said. "His model Spitfire." She looked around the shed. "I can't see it, though."

Ruth set the unknown tool down and grabbed a radio control unit from a nearby shelf. "This?" She toggled the power switch on. A green LED sprang to life, and a meter displayed the power as being up in the healthy range. "Fully charged." Which indicated Carter may have used it recently, but unfortunately, it wouldn't lead them to the Spitfire's current location. "Where did he fly?"

"The heathland next to the old lighthouse," a deep voice said.

Margaret wheeled. "Charles." She clutched her chest. "Don't sneak up on us like that. What are you doing here?"

"I can't stay cooped up in the house," he grumbled. "Needed some air. Thought I'd come and see how you're doing." Charles gave his sister-in-law an apologetic look. "Greg is dealing with the puzzle boxes."

Margaret rested a hand on his shoulder. "I'll help him. You stay with Ruth." She pecked Charles on the cheek and left.

Ruth held up the radio controller. "Carter's model Spitfire? The heathland?"

"I can take you there." Charles stepped from the shed.

After setting the controller down, Ruth followed him to the back gate and on through.

Finding the model Spitfire might be a long shot, but if it was so important to Carter, then she wanted to understand why it was missing. When it came to murder and mystery, there was no such thing as a coincidence.

As the two of them followed a path through woodland, she said, "You came flying with Carter?"

"A few times," Charles said. "When the weather and my schedule permitted." His expression glazed over. "He had quite the knack for it." Charles shook himself. "Offered to let me fly the darned thing, but I was always content to watch."

The forest ended, and heathland stretched in front of them, all the way to the cliff's edge. To the left stood the lighthouse and Captain Barney's accompanying cottage.

Charles pointed to a narrow strip on the ground, free of heather, four feet wide, and extending a hundred feet in a straight line.

"The Spitfire took off from here?" Ruth asked. "Where did he fly it?"

"In circles," Charles said. "A radio model is limited by its range and one's eyesight."

"And you said Carter was a good model flyer, right?" Ruth asked. "Skilled?"

"Yes. Superb."

He must have flown it recently. Why?

Ruth pictured the Spitfire taking off from the makeshift runway, and then Ruth turned on the spot as the model plane flew in a circle, swooped over the forest behind them, and then came back around again until it reached . . . She stopped and pointed. "Bingo."

8

C harles squinted up at the lighthouse in the distance. "What's it doing all the way up there?"

On the gallery—the circular walkway that ran round the uppermost part of the lighthouse—behind the iron railing, lay the crumpled remains of something painted in green, brown and shades of grey.

They made their way across the heathland toward it.

"Any ideas, Ruth?" Charles said. "It can't have been an accident, could it? Carter was a skilled flyer."

"Not an accident." It had been a deliberate act, and Ruth had a good idea why Carter had done it, although she couldn't be sure what his ultimate goal had been. "My bet is we'll find Henry's riddle hidden in that model."

Charles' eyebrows arched.

The only other way the Spitfire could have crashed up there was if Carter had become distracted while flying. However, Ruth doubted that was what had happened because the lighthouse was such a small target, given the vast landscape of the island. *You'd have to be unlucky to hit it.*

No, her assumption was he'd done it on purpose, and when that sank in with Charles, he'd feel betrayed.

"Perhaps the killer knew about my father's riddle and Carter wanted to stop them from getting it," Charles said. "So he took a picture, or memorised it, and then, rather than destroy the original, he flew it up to the lighthouse where we'd find it later."

Ruth wasn't convinced by this explanation. She could get on board with the idea Carter hadn't wanted to destroy the original or have it fall into the wrong hands, but she was certain he hadn't intended for anyone else to find it, including Charles.

At her dubious expression, he said, "Still doesn't explain why Carter didn't just come to me, does it?"

"No," Ruth said in a low voice. "It does not."

Charles sighed. "Why not tell me someone was after the will and planning to extort ransom money? We could have found it together. He didn't have to die."

"I don't know the answers." Ruth empathised with his feeling of betrayal. "With so little information to go on, we could only guess as to what Carter was doing. I'm sorry."

"Maybe the killer threatened our lives if Carter told me about what was going on," Charles suggested.

"Among the staff, is there anyone capable of doing that?" Ruth asked.

Charles stared at the ground as they walked. "I don't know any of them well enough to make a judgement. I suppose they could say and do anything behind our backs. This whole situation has me questioning everything I thought I knew about people."

"Whatever the case," Ruth said as they joined a gravel path that led to the lighthouse, "I think we've found Henry's riddle. Which is a relief. Let's take that as a small victory."

Plus, it meant they not only stood a chance of finding the will before the murderer, but also of exposing them in the process.

After all, the killer would have to shadow them, keep a close eye on what they were doing, ready to strike at the right moment, which meant they could slip up.

Charles peered up at the gallery again, and the remains of the Spitfire as he and Ruth approached. "Why on earth did Carter go to all this trouble?"

"I guess he wanted to put the note somewhere obscure," Ruth said. "But not destroy it. Burying it could be risky."

Hiding the note this way meant anyone searching Carter's house would come up empty, as they had. At this point, all theories were simply that—nothing more than uninformed guesses.

"Maybe it's a backup plan in case something happened to him," Ruth said.

Charles grunted in either agreement or doubt, but Ruth chose not to pursue any more of her extraneous theories until they had hard facts to consider.

They strode past Captain Barney's house—a modest stone cottage with a slate roof.

However, Ruth's gaze moved to the clifftop at the end of the path.

"Still thinking about the cave?" Charles asked. "You want to catch the phantom?"

Ruth glanced at him. "Phantom?"

"It's what the staff call it." Charles rubbed his forehead. "Bunkum, if you ask me. A phantom? Apparently, the same one John swore blind he spotted in the cave on the day of the accident. When the staff heard about that, the conspiracy theories flowed, and haven't stopped." He shook his head. "Four decades of it."

Ruth widened her eyes. "The house staff believe it too?"

"Every time something goes missing, the phantom did it. When an object breaks—it's the phantom's doing. A door unlocked? Guess what? The phantom did that too." Charles laughed. "Ever since the news of John's sighting got around, the phantom became the staff's go-to thing to blame."

Ruth wanted to solve the decades' old mystery of the cave, only to be denied by a simple locked gate. She tried to hide her disappointment and focus on the job at hand.

The clifftop was only twenty feet away. Beyond that was nothing but ocean and horizon, while to the left a faint slither of dark green and brown represented the mainland.

Charles opened the lighthouse door and waved Ruth inside.

The ground level interior stood almost empty, with a few crates and wooden boxes scattered about. Ruth peered into the first. "What's this?" A thick grey plastic filled the inside.

Charles came for a look. "No idea. Perhaps a busted old inflatable boat?"

Ruth's gaze moved to a machine on the floor with an air cylinder attached, and then she lifted the lid on another crate. Sure enough, a compact motor sat inside. "Captain Barney's?"

"More than likely." Charles brushed two fingers over his moustache. "His fascination with boats is boundless. In Captain Barney's home, pictures of boats fill every available wall."

Ruth faced the room.

A rusty wrought iron staircase ascended to the next level.

She hurried over, checked the stability, then headed on up, with Charles close behind.

Broken planks and debris filled almost the entire floor

above, and each subsequent level had disintegrated and fallen away, only leaving the final one intact far above their heads.

This uppermost section held the lantern, made heavy by its iron mechanism and surrounding panes of thick lensed glass. Steel I-beams braced against the walls reinforced the whole contraption.

The remainder of the staircase twisted on up the side of the building. It wasn't clear if the bolts still held it securely in place, but there was only one way to find out.

Picturing the broken Spitfire, Ruth made for the stairs.

Charles grabbed her arm.

She turned back. "It's fine. You stay here."

"Too dangerous." Charles didn't release her. "I'll do it."

"No, you won't," Ruth insisted. "I'm lighter." When Charles still didn't let go of her arm, she added, "Look, if I fall and die, Margaret will blame me and say I was stupid." Ruth smiled. "But if you fall and die, or even so much as graze a knee, Margaret will blame me for the rest of my life. I'll never hear the end of it." She let out a slow breath. "Given the choice, I prefer the former if something goes wrong. At least that way I can rest in peace, rather than be slowly tortured to death by my sister." She pulled free of Charles' grasp, squeezed his shoulder, and then headed on up the spiral staircase before he poked holes in her logic.

Ruth placed each foot with care and gripped the railing, while also keeping a close eye on the rusty bolts that held the staircase to the wall.

Up and up she climbed, higher and higher, making a point to not look down as she passed the rotten remains of each floor.

The staircase let out a groan and wobbled.

Ruth grabbed the railing with both hands.

"Come back," Charles shouted. "We'll find another way."

"Carter really didn't want anyone getting to this easily." Ruth looked up. "I'm nearly there." The last floor with the lantern was only a few feet above her head. However, debris blocked Ruth's path.

She moved as slowly as possible and lifted aside rotten planks. "Get clear," Ruth shouted down to Charles.

Once he'd stepped clear of the first floor, she hoisted a plank over the railing. It plummeted through the empty interior and slammed into the debris below, sending a plume of dust into the air.

Ruth repeated this process two more times before she'd cleared a path. "Okay. Safe now," she called down, and then muttered, "Safe-ish." Ruth worked her way up.

A section of the stairs broke free of the wall. Ruth screamed as two steps fell from under her feet, but she leapt forward, grabbed the railing, and hauled herself onto the remaining floor.

She cowered by the wall, breathing hard, blood pounding in her ears.

Charles reappeared, coughing and waving his hand in front of his face. "Are you alive?"

Ruth gave him a thumbs-up.

He then spotted the missing stairs, and his eyes widened.

"It's okay. I'll be fine. I can step over the gap." Ruth muttered, "That is, as long as the remaining steps can hold my weight."

"Be careful. I'll watch you from outside." Charles descended the stairs and vanished through the door.

Ruth straightened and gathered herself.

A thick layer of dust covered each of the lantern's glass panes, and paint peeled from the metalwork, but as far as

Ruth could tell, not being an expert in such matters, it all looked intact.

She edged around the circular walkway until she made out the remains of the model Spitfire on the other side of the windows. Ruth unfastened a window latch, swung a pane forward, and slipped onto the iron balcony.

Wind whipped at her coat and threatened to snatch away her scarf, but she held on to it and tucked it back into the coat.

Now Ruth was up here, with a view over the entire island and beyond, it seemed even higher than she'd anticipated. The mansion looked like a scale model, and Carter's cottage nothing but a small block next to the forest.

She took a step toward the railing and peered down.

The path below stopped at the cliff's edge, and then a set of wooden steps descended to a cobbled beach, flanked by more sheer cliff faces on both sides, and isolated from the rest of the island.

Charles waved.

With her back pressed against the lighthouse windows, Ruth inched her way over to the remains of the Spitfire.

The impact to the railing had folded up and broken the wings off, exposing the wood and wires beneath. However, the fuselage was mostly intact.

Opting not to try and move the model, Ruth knelt and examined the canopy covering the cockpit. She undid the catch and peered inside.

There was no sign of a pilot, but in the seat, held by an elastic band, was a rolled-up piece of paper.

"Yes. Vindicated." Ruth was glad something was finally going her way.

She lifted the scroll out, then keeping a tight grip on it, she stood and backed into the building. Once she'd secured the glass pane, she called down to Charles, "Got it." Ruth pocketed the note and headed on down the iron staircase, taking her time and careful to watch her footing.

At the gap, she held the railing and stretched her right foot down to the next stair. Solid. Secure. With her heart in her mouth, Ruth traversed the missing stairs, and continued down.

The moment she reached ground level, Ruth let out an enormous sigh of relief, and she handed the paper to Charles with a grin.

"I can't believe it. You were right." He unrolled it so they could both see.

On yellow paper with a jagged top edge, a handwritten scrawl read:

I start as I end, in a room with no windows or doors.
Remember you're alive, even though they're dead.

Going up when it comes down.
Up and down, and yet I can't move.
Get under my skin, you'll be sure to cry.

What do you never want to have, but once you do, never lose?

When spoken to, I will always answer.
You'll find me in a puzzle, not in a riddle, and in you, never him.

Finally, smile at me, and I'll return the favour.

Ruth gaped at it. "Henry was not messing about."

Charles scratched his chin. "No. He wasn't."

"I guess by your expression, none of it makes sense?" Ruth asked. She couldn't figure out any of the lines.

"I'm afraid not." Charles handed the note back. "Then again, as I said before, I was never any good at solving my father's riddles."

"I don't know why Margaret thinks I'll be any better at this than either of you two," Ruth said.

"You've already gotten a lot farther than us." Charles looked up at the lighthouse. "We wouldn't have thought to come here."

"We'll work on it together." Ruth pocketed the riddle and pressed the stud down on the pocket flap. "At least we have it now. It's something to start with."

"Carter did take it," Charles murmured. "I'm still in shock. How could he?" He squeezed Ruth's arm. "Thank goodness you're here."

"Don't thank me yet. We've still got a long day ahead of us. It's far from over. Let's get back to Margaret and Greg."

Ruth hoped one of them could figure out the riddle.

She stepped from the lighthouse, and as Charles closed the door, Captain Barney marched up the hill, toward his house. The red blotches covering his face and neck were clear despite the waning light.

Charles called to him, "Something wrong?"

However, Captain Barney threw open the door to his house and stormed inside.

Ruth tensed. "This doesn't look good."

A minute later, Captain Barney reappeared, clutching a canvas shopping bag and a torch. "Have something ye should see." He gestured for them to follow, and then marched back down the hill.

Charles leaned in to Ruth and whispered, "What were you saying about the day being a long one?"

She winced. "Sorry, jinxed it." And they hurried after him.

9

Captain Barney followed a path along the clifftop, then down a slope until they came out at the familiar pontoon with the cliff elevator and steps.

"Where's his boat?" Charles looked about.

At the end of the pontoon, Captain Barney dropped the canvas bag at his feet and then stripped—removing his shoes, socks, jumper, shirt . . .

Ruth stared in stunned silence as he then took off his jeans, leaving nothing but his underpants remaining.

Captain Barney switched on the torch and dove into the ice-cold water.

As he vanished beneath the surface, Ruth turned to Charles. "Does he normally act this way?"

"Not in all the years I've known him," Charles said, his eyes wide. "The fellow is normally laid back. Can't imagine what's gotten into him."

Seconds turned into a minute, and then two minutes, and still Captain Barney didn't return from the murky depths of the Atlantic Ocean.

Ruth wrung her hands, and her anxiety grew with every

passing moment. She took several steps forward, staring at the water with a sense of helplessness, and considered calling the coastguard.

However, she let out a massive sigh of relief when Captain Barney's head reappeared above the surface.

He swam to a metal ladder and hauled himself back onto the pontoon. He then set the torch down and removed a beach towel from the canvas bag and dried himself off.

"I give the dive a nine out of ten," Ruth said. "What it lacked in style, you certainly made up for in shock value."

Charles crossed his arms. "Would you like to share with us mortal folk exactly what that was about?"

Captain Barney nodded to the torch.

Ruth picked it up, stepped closer to the edge of the pontoon and shone the light into the water. She gasped. "Is that your boat?"

Although the water was cloudy, and the sun had almost completed its descent, at the right angle she could discern the deflated outline of a hull on the rocky bottom.

Charles looked too. "What in heaven's name happened, man?"

"Ye tell me." Captain Barney slipped back into his jeans and fastened the fly. "I found her like that. The polis didnae have their own boat, so I collected the pair, and then took them back. When I returned, I moored up, and went to the scullery for a bite." He pulled on his shirt and jumper. "Cannae have been gone twenty minutes. Got back 'ere and spotted what had happened. Then . . ." He gestured to the path. "The rest ye know."

Ruth shook her head in disbelief and looked out at the calm water. "Not a storm."

"Most definitely not." Charles ran fingers over his moustache. "Very odd. Punctured?"

Captain Barney sat on the pontoon and pulled on his socks and shoes. "Sabotaged."

Charles blinked at him. "Come again?"

Captain Barney's eyes narrowed. "Nae doubt aboot it."

"Is that why you dove into the water?" Ruth asked.

Captain Barney stood. "I wanted to see the cause with mah own eyes. Mah suspicions were right. Someone's got it in fer me."

"And what is the cause?" Charles asked. "What did the saboteur do to your boat?"

"Cannae know for certain," Captain Barney said. "Best guess is a cordless drill 'n' cutter. They went right through the solid hull in two spots, and once at the inflatable part. Drilled from the inside, then clambered oot before it sank."

Ruth eyed the moorings. "They untied those too."

Captain Barney slung the towel over his shoulder and looked between them. "At least we know one thing's fer sure."

"Which is?" Charles asked.

"It could only have been someone on this island," Captain Barney said. "No other boats." He snatched up his canvas bag. "I wud have heard an engine approaching."

"Would you, though?" Ruth said. "You were at the house, grabbing lunch."

"You can hear when boats get close to this island from up there." Charles pointed in the direction of the house.

Captain Barney nodded. "I wasn't gone long enough fer them to come in, do the deed, 'n' hurl off intae the sunset, so to speak."

"In that case . . ." Ruth faced Charles. "It's now doubly imperative I have a word with your staff."

His expression darkened. He stared at the water for a few seconds, and then shook himself. "Don't worry, Barney.

We'll not only catch the person responsible, but have your boat recovered and repaired."

Ruth and Charles went to leave.

"Brother."

They turned back.

"Sorry?" Charles said.

"Yer brother," Captain Barney said. "The Aussie."

"Oh, right. Yes." Charles' forehead wrinkled. "What about him?"

"I was supposed to collect him from the mainland," Captain Barney said. "Cannae do that now."

"Of course," Charles said. "A valid point."

"I'll let him know," Barney said. "I've got his phone number at mah cottage. I'll speak to Fred. He's fishing at the moment, but when he returns to the mainland late afternoon, he can collect the fellas and bring them here. Shouldn't hold them up at all."

"Thank you." Charles nodded. "We'll speak again later."

As Ruth walked with Charles back along the pontoon to the shore, she pondered why the killer would have wanted to sabotage Captain Barney's boat if someone else on the mainland could simply ferry them across.

She thought about her late husband, John, and how he'd react to the situation.

Over forty years prior, John had bought his own sailboat, and Ruth had gone with him to sail it to a marina farther down the coast. But after almost drowning when the thing had capsized, she'd sworn to never climb on board the death trap again.

She would have died if she had.

A mere two weeks after purchasing the boat, John had struck upon the fantastic idea of sailing it around the Isle of

Wight. Solo. He'd checked the tide forecasts, along with the weather, and at seven in the morning, off he'd gone.

Ruth remembered standing on the dock, waving, and trying desperately to shake off a foreboding feeling. She'd told herself there was nothing to worry about. After all, John was one of those indestructible type of men who escaped even the direst situations with nothing more than a few bruises and a scrape or two.

So when John didn't return at the stated time, Ruth didn't worry. This was pre–mobile phone days, and he'd always been kind of free and easy when it came to time-keeping.

Ruth had found a cafe in the marina and drank tea while she waited.

Four hours and seven teas later, anxiety had finally kicked in, and then when night fell, and the cafe closed, Ruth's concern had turned to full-on panic.

She'd known John would be cross, but she'd had no choice but to call the coastguard.

Two hours later, they'd returned John in a weather-beaten condition, with a ripped shirt, one shoe missing, and half a trouser leg torn free.

Turned out, he'd run aground on a rocky outcrop, ripped an impressive hole in the boat's hull, and the impact had thrown him overboard. Somehow, John had managed to clamber back on board, but that was where he'd remained. Even he wasn't stupid enough to attempt the mile swim ashore through a strong tide.

Thank goodness.

Despite what had happened, John had insisted on the boat's recovery and subsequent repairs. He'd then gone out on it plenty of times after, and on each of those occasions

Ruth had worried, but he'd always returned safe and sound, and buzzing.

John had simply loved that boat.

Ruth could empathise with how much Captain Barney's vessel must have meant to him, and she vowed to not only solve Henry's riddles and flush out the murderer but also get to the bottom of why they had sunk that boat.

"Do you still avoid tight spaces with locked doors?" Charles asked.

Ruth snapped out of her thoughts. "Sorry?"

Charles pointed to the cliff elevator. Its lights glowed in the twilight. "You know, it's perfectly safe. As a young man my first job was working for a lift repair company."

"I bet that had its ups and downs." Ruth grinned.

Charles waved a hand at the stairs. "Guess we're going this way."

They were now lit by lanterns, and seemed even more steep and imposing than before.

Ruth sighed, "Sure," and off they trudged.

Twenty minutes later, Ruth staggered into Amgine Hall, panting, lungs on fire, legs burning. She removed the riddle from her pocket and threw off the coat. "It's official. I hate those stairs." Then she headed to the study. At the door, she stopped dead in her tracks.

Charles almost slammed into her. "What's going on?" He sounded out of breath too.

Ruth moved to one side.

Margaret had placed several bath towels on the floor, and scattered over them were hundreds of pieces of wood.

She stood over them with her hair tied back, and a hammer in her hand.

Greg sifted through the debris. "Still nothing."

Ruth's gaze drifted up to the shelves on the top balcony. They now sat empty—all the puzzle boxes removed. She looked back at the carnage. "You broke them open?"

Margaret waved the hammer about. "I'm finding it quite cathartic." She roared and smashed one of the remaining puzzle boxes. "Who knew it could be such fun?"

Ruth glanced at Charles, but he didn't seem the slightest bit bothered. "Weren't some of those valuable?" she asked.

He shook his head. "None were antiques, if that's what you mean." Charles dropped into a chair with a heavy sigh.

Ruth crossed her arms. "Even so, you're okay with this?"

"Of course he is." Margaret placed another puzzle box on the towels and offered the hammer to Charles. "Would you like a go, darling?"

He held up his hands. "All yours, my love."

Margaret held the hammer out to Ruth.

"I'm good. Thanks." Ruth eyed a nearby table. There were only two puzzle boxes left intact.

"Don't look so scandalised." Margaret grabbed one of them and placed it on the towel. "It's the quickest way. I'm sure as hell not spending days trying to open all these." She swung down with the hammer and smashed the puzzle box to bits.

Greg sifted through the debris of this one too. "Still nothing, Aunty Margaret."

"One more try." She grabbed the last box and bashed that open.

Greg sighed. "Nothing." He folded the pieces into the towels and slid them aside.

"Well, that was a waste of time." Margaret tossed the

hammer onto the table. "Whatever Carter was searching for, it's clearly not here." She looked between Ruth and her husband. "Any luck on your end?"

Ruth held up the folded paper. "We found the riddle."

"You did?" Greg scrambled to his feet.

Ruth was about to show him when the study door opened and the head housekeeper—in her mid-sixties, dressed in a black skirt and tights, with a white blouse— wheeled in a serving cart.

Following her with a second cart was the same manservant and maid from lunch. He had slicked-back red hair, whereas she wore her bleach blonde hair tied up.

"I thought," Margaret said, "given the circumstances, we'd have dinner in here. Heaven knows I've worked up an appetite."

Sure enough, the carts were full to bursting, with everything from cheeseburgers for Greg to salad bowls for—well, Ruth wasn't sure who those were intended for because she had her eye on a roast chicken and fries.

Charles cleared a nearby table, and the manservant set out the cutlery.

Ruth scanned the rest of the offerings and couldn't hide her disappointment.

"What?" Margaret asked.

"No steak and ale pie?"

A hint of a smirk twitched the corners of Margaret's mouth. "You'll never figure it out."

Ruth poked out her tongue.

When they were done setting the table, the housekeeper, servant, and housemaid left.

"I thought they were supposed to stay in their rooms?" Ruth eyed all the food.

Margaret brushed off the comment with a flick of her

wrist. "We all must eat. Besides, they're sticking together. No one is to be left alone. And they're going straight back to the kitchen and their quarters. No deviation."

Ruth thought there were only four house staff, and if three had served them . . . *Doesn't that mean they left the cook alone in the kitchen?* However, she decided not to argue the point.

Margaret, Charles, and Greg sat down.

Ruth made for the door. "Back in a minute."

"For goodness' sake," Margaret called after her. "Where are you going now?"

"Merlin."

"No need," Margaret said. "I took care of him half an hour ago. The same time I fed Billy. They're both fine."

Ruth winced and turned back. "Please tell me you didn't put them in the same room."

"Of course not." Margaret swept her hand at the carts of food. "Shall we?"

They helped themselves, and after gulping down half a roast chicken and fries—and half a handful of mixed salad, plus several glasses of fruit juice to offset some of the junk food—Ruth strode to the blackboard. "Greg, come help me."

He swallowed the last mouthful of a chocolate pudding and hurried over to her.

They wheeled the blackboard to the other side of the room and faced it away from the door and windows so as to avoid prying eyes.

Ruth handed Greg the riddle. "Dictate, and I'll write it out on here so we can all see clearly."

He flattened it out and cleared his throat. "I start as I end, in a room with no windows or doors."

"What room has no windows or doors?" Margaret frowned. "That would make it a box, no?"

Ruth had absolutely zero idea.

"Remember you're alive," Greg continued, "even though they're dead."

Margaret looked over at Charles, eyes narrowed. "Nice to see your father still loves to confound people, even in death."

He raised a glass of wine.

Ruth motioned for Greg to carry on.

"Going up when it comes down. Up and down, and yet I can't move. Get under my skin, you'll be sure to cry."

Ruth found herself a little dismayed at the fact the riddle made no more sense the second time around.

"What do you never want to have, but once you do, never lose?" Greg said. "When spoken to, I will always answer. You'll find me in a puzzle, not in a riddle, and in you, never him." He let out a breath. "Finally, smile at me, and I'll return the favour."

Ruth finished writing it out, and stepped back to appraise the result.

"Please tell me at least part of that makes sense to you," Margaret said, exasperated. "This is your forte, after all."

Ruth pulled up a chair and dropped into it with a heavy sigh. "I'm afraid not."

10

Ruth spent several minutes pondering various parts of the riddle, but nothing leapt out at her. They really didn't have time for this. She looked over at Charles. "When Henry gave these to you in the past, was anything similar between them? A common link? Any context at all?"

Often, people revealed commonalities with their works, whether or not they realised it. There were experts dedicated to the field, sifting through documents, discerning patterns. None of which Ruth was any good at.

"The first riddle was only ever a line or two." Charles nodded at the blackboard. "Never this long-winded or complicated. He's outdone himself."

"And when you solved them, what did they say?" Ruth asked.

"Invariably, they'd lead us to another part of the house or island," Margaret said. "A location. The one Henry left last year for Charles' birthday took us to a bureau in the reading room."

"Locations." Ruth stared at the blackboard. "Do you still

have that last birthday riddle?" she asked, hoping to compare it to this one.

"I never kept them." Charles smoothed his moustache, and his gaze wandered to the ceiling. "From what I can recall, it talked about wearing clothes on the inside."

"It was ridiculous." Margaret rolled her eyes.

"What was your present?" Greg asked.

Charles pulled back his jacket sleeve to reveal a gold watch.

Greg's eyes almost popped from their sockets. "Seriously? I'd gladly spend a day hunting for that."

"Hide it for him, Charles," Margaret said.

"How about you take the watch and hide with it," Ruth said to her. "We promise to come find you." She winked at Greg.

"Behave yourself, Ruth." Margaret lifted her nose into the air. "Sibling rivalry has its place and time. This is not it. You're disturbing everyone here."

"You're the disturbed one," Ruth muttered, and focussed on the blackboard again. "I think we can assume these must be several riddles combined into one. Perhaps it would be best to break it down into its component parts." Ruth circled the first line of the riddle. "I start as I end, in a room with no windows or doors."

Everyone's expressions glazed over.

"A room with no doors," Margaret murmured.

"Mushroom," Greg said. All eyes moved to him. "A mushroom has no windows or doors." He looked extremely proud of himself.

However, Margaret frowned. "That can't be right."

"It is." Charles checked his watch. "I saw the lad look it up on his phone."

Greg's cheeks flushed, and he held up the smartphone so they all could see the display.

"No shame in that." Ruth wrote the word *mushroom* in the margin. "Now look up these others." She circled the other individual parts of the riddle, nine in all.

Greg typed the riddles into his phone and searched the internet. However, twenty minutes later, he'd only found one more: the answer to *What do you never want to have, but once you do, never lose?* Which was *lawsuit*.

Greg pocketed his phone. "It's all I can find."

"It's an excellent start," Charles said. "Better than we could've done with no help."

Ruth stepped back and considered the results. "If we're right, we already have two parts of the riddle solved. Two answers out of nine." She checked the time on her phone—it was six forty-five in the evening. She let out a slow breath. They were unlikely to get much sleep.

"Mushroom and lawsuit?" Margaret scowled at the blackboard as if it had just called her a nasty name. "Whatever could they mean? It's nonsense." She looked over at Charles. "Your father was losing his mind a bit at the end."

Charles didn't look convinced.

"You'll find me in a puzzle, not in a riddle, and in you, never him." Ruth frowned. "*You* but never *him*?" And then it dawned on her. She groaned.

Margaret sat forward. "You've figured it out?"

Ruth wrote a single letter *U* on the blackboard. She tapped it. "There's a *U* in *puzzle*, not in *riddle*."

Margaret rolled her eyes and sat back again. "And also in *you* but not *him*."

Charles' lips moved as he read through the remaining parts of the riddle. Then he muttered, "Going up when it comes down. Going up when it comes down. What goes up when—"

"*I know,*" Greg shouted.

Margaret jumped and grabbed her chest. "Don't do that."

Greg thrust a finger at the blackboard. "What goes up when it comes down?" When this received three blank stares in reply, he smiled. "An umbrella. I've heard that one before."

Ruth wrote the answer. As far as she could figure, they now had four answers out of a possible nine. Good progress, but a long way to go with little time to get there.

The door to the study burst open, and the head housekeeper hurried into the room. "Quick. Emergency."

Charles stood. "What emergency?"

"Hurry." She waved her hands about in a frantic manner. "Hall. Stairs." She ran from the room.

"This can't be good." Ruth followed Charles from the study, with Margaret and Greg bringing up the rear.

In the main hallway, the four of them ground to a sudden halt, eyes wide.

"What on earth?" Margaret shrieked.

Greg gaped like a koi carp watching a silly human woman fall into their pond.

And speaking of water . . . it cascaded down the stairs and across the marble floor, filling the hallway, already half an inch deep.

Ruth picked her way across, careful not to slip, and peered up the stairs. A section of the plastered ceiling above the landing had fallen away, and water poured through it.

Margaret spun to Charles. "A burst pipe?"

Ruth imagined that could well be the case at this time of year, but somehow, given recent events, she doubted it.

Charles made his way up the stairs.

"Be careful you don't fall," Margaret warned him.

Ruth motioned for Greg to stay close as she followed Charles. When they reached the landing, she scrutinised the exposed beams showing through the plaster. "What's up there?"

"Guest bathroom." Charles gestured to the next flight of stairs.

The three of them continued up and then along a corridor.

Charles stopped at a door and tried the handle. "It's a bathroom. Someone has pulled the bolt across from the inside." He banged on the door. "Open up."

"Maybe we can break it down," Greg suggested.

Ruth ran her fingers over the door and rapped with her knuckles. It appeared to be a solid wood construction, at least a hundred years old, with cast iron hinges holding it securely in place.

Water poured from underneath, soaking the rug, and disappeared through the gaps in the floorboards.

"If we don't do something, the house will soon become the world's worst swimming pool." Charles thumped a clenched fist on the door. "Hello? Who's in there?"

Ruth eyed a transom above. The small window was open a crack. "Oh, Gregory?"

He followed her gaze, and grumbled, "I can try, but I'm not Jackie Chan."

Ruth inclined her head. "Who's she?"

Greg stared at her. "Sometimes, I can't tell if you're joking." He looked about. "Need a stool or a chair to stand on."

"Here you go." Charles pressed his back against the door, bent his knees, and made a stirrup with his hands.

Greg put his foot inside, and Charles hoisted him.

Ruth hopped from foot to foot. "What can you see?"

"Can't make it out." Greg pressed against the window frame, and it swung further open. "There's no one in here."

Ruth tensed. "Try not to break anything."

"There's nothing to break," Greg said. "It's all tiles and porcelain."

"I meant you," Ruth said. "Bones. Skull."

"Oh. Sure. Good tip." Greg hauled himself through, and once he'd reached halfway, with his legs on the hall side, head and torso in the bathroom, he stopped wriggling.

Ruth peered up at him and whispered, "What's wrong?"

"I really didn't think this through. It's a long drop."

Charles grabbed his ankles. "I'll help lower you."

Greg pulled himself through, while Charles did his best to arrest his fall, and a moment later Greg's feet disappeared through the transom, shortly followed by a heavy thump and a muffled, "Ouch."

A few seconds later the door opened.

Ruth and Charles raced into the bathroom.

Both sets of bath taps and the sink taps were on full.

Ruth rushed to the sink and turned those off, while Greg dealt with the bath. Someone had stuffed handkerchiefs into the overflows.

"This is a clear act of vandalism." Charles' eyes narrowed with anger. "Someone did this on purpose." He turned back to the door. "As I suspected, locked on the inside. How did they get out?"

Ruth yanked out the sink's plug so the water could drain, and then she examined the bolt on the door. "If you have a screwdriver, you could lock this from the outside."

Someone stormed down the corridor—wet thuds of their footfalls on the soaked rug.

Ruth's stomach tensed.

Margaret stepped into the doorway and looked around at the carnage. "They've caused thousands of pounds' worth of damage. Why on earth would someone do this to us?" Then her gaze moved to the wet handkerchiefs in Greg's hand.

They were monogrammed with AH for Amgine Hall, and embroidered with the Andrews family crest.

"Where would someone get those?" Ruth asked.

"Any of the guest bedrooms," Margaret said.

Ruth stepped back into the hall. All the doors were closed, except for one ajar at the far end. She pointed to it. "Is that a guest bedroom?"

"What's that doing open?" Margaret took a step toward it, but Ruth stopped her.

"Wait here." Ruth didn't want Margaret to go clomping into the guest bedroom and lose any potential evidence, so she gestured for her sister to stay put, but for Greg to follow her. Ruth wanted Greg nearby in case there were any assailants ready to leap out and murder her to death.

However, Greg gave her a look as if to say, "*If anything happens, I'm outta here.*"

To be fair, a weak eight-year-old could snap the scrawny teenager in half, let alone anyone with more than a modicum of muscles.

At the door, Ruth held her breath and turned an ear to the gap. No sounds coming from within, she nudged the door open with her foot, and stepped inside.

The guest bedroom stood twenty feet square, with a double bed, bedside tables, a wardrobe, and a sideboard.

Greg went to step into the room, but Ruth held up a hand. She circled a rug and knelt. Several muddy shoe tread marks went in both directions, faint but unmissable.

Ruth took several photos with her phone, and checked the photos. It appeared the person wore trainers. Her gaze then moved to a set of French doors that led to a veranda. They too stood ajar.

Margaret stepped beside Greg. "What's going on?"

Ruth pointed to the French doors. "Are these normally locked or unlocked?"

"Locked," Margaret said. "Always locked. There's a key on a hook." She indicated the curtain.

Ruth edged her way over. A hook on the frame behind the curtain sat empty, and the key was in the lock, but on the outside of the French doors.

Mindful not to touch anything, Ruth opened them and stepped onto the veranda.

She hugged herself as an icy breeze cut through her blouse and thin cardigan. Although the view wasn't as impressive as the one from atop the lighthouse, especially as it was dark outside, it still commanded her attention—a sweeping vista of the island and ocean beyond under a moonlit sky.

Spotlights around the grounds lit the house and trees.

Ruth steeled herself and peered over the railing to the garden below, then made her way to the far end of the veranda. A trellis scaled the three floors.

"Surely not." Ruth's gaze drifted to a broken crossmember, about halfway up. "Either brave, stupid, or desperate." She pulled back and headed inside. "Someone climbed up here, and then left the same way."

Margaret's pencilled eyebrows lifted.

Ruth ushered them back into the hallway and closed the door. "I need to grab my coat and look outside."

Ruth marched back down the corridor, across the landing and down one flight of stairs to her suite. She checked in on Merlin, and then grabbed her coat before meeting the others back downstairs.

The head housekeeper and a maid used mops to soak up the worst of the flood.

Ruth turned to Charles, Margaret, and Greg. "Wait here a minute." She strode down the corridor.

"Is that wise?" Margaret called after her.

"Probably not." Ruth marched along the short hallway, and through a back door to the garden.

She circled the house until she found the correct veranda, and knelt by the trellis and border. Sure enough, there were several trampled plants and shoe prints in the soil, heading in both directions. They overlaid each other, and Ruth couldn't make out whether they'd belonged to a male or a female.

She stood and looked about. A path continued on, lit by electric lanterns, and then it forked: one way heading around the house, while the other ran alongside a seven-foot-tall bush. That path then terminated at a shed.

Ruth considered going back for Greg or Charles, but time was of the essence.

She took a deep breath, jogged along the path toward the shed and activated the torch function on her phone. She stopped in front of it, braced herself, and threw open the door.

Inside sat a lawnmower, a chainsaw, a hedge trimmer, a couple of folding chairs, various tools, and a potting bench with plants in containers. In the far corner of the shed, caked in soil, was a pair of Wellington boots.

Ruth had taken a step toward them when someone called her name. She spun around.

Margaret stood by the house, frantically waving at her.

"What now?" Ruth shut the shed door and raced down the path.

"It's gone," Margaret panted. "All of it."

Ruth's brow furrowed in confusion. "What's gone?"

"Come see." Margaret led the way back through the house and into the study.

Ruth's mouth dropped open. Someone had erased the riddle and answers from the blackboard. Stunned, she turned to Greg. "Please tell me you have the original note."

He shook his head and pointed to the table. "I left it there."

Ruth pinched the bridge of her nose and let out a low groan. "Someone's tricked us."

11

Margaret paced the study, fists balled, wearing her best scowl. "Who is doing this to us?"

Ruth removed her coat, draped it over the back of a chair next to the fireplace, and sat. She placed a cushion on her lap, interlaced her fingers, took a calming breath, and ignored her sister as she pondered their next move.

Charles sat opposite.

Greg dropped into a chair at the table and picked at the remains of the food.

"You didn't happen to take a picture of the blackboard?" Ruth asked him.

He swallowed and shook his head.

"Check the search history on your phone." Margaret noticed Ruth's surprise and added, "What? I know things."

"Can't do that," Greg said. "I've set it to automatically clear itself."

Ruth's eyes narrowed to slits. "Why would you do that?"

His cheeks flushed. "We know none of the staff accidentally took the riddle because they haven't cleared away yet."

Greg motioned to the plates and grabbed a handful of French fries.

Ruth screwed up her face. "Aren't those cold?"

"Yep."

"I need to speak to Betty and Maddie," Margaret said through clenched teeth. "They were in the hall mopping up. They must have seen something."

"How come they spotted the flood at all?" Greg helped himself to slices of beef.

"They were on their way to clear this." Margaret waved a hand at the food.

They could have put the riddle going missing down to an accident, but someone had also wiped the blackboard clean, which put paid to that idea.

Ruth closed her eyes. "Let's take this back a step. We can now assume with some certainty that Carter knew about the will's existence." Which wasn't surprising given all the years he'd worked at the house, and his closeness to the family. Ruth tried not to picture his body stored in a coal shed. "He took the riddle, presumably sometime after Henry passed, then hid it, most likely at his cottage, and followed the clues at his convenience." Ruth opened her eyes. "Judging by what's happened today, he must have told another member of staff, or they found out by some other means."

Charles let out a slow breath. "Precisely."

"Why steal the riddle?" Greg asked. "Why didn't Carter just take a picture of it?"

Margaret stopped pacing. "He might have done. We found his phone, but it's password protected." She dropped into a seat opposite him, looking deflated. "Can you hack it?"

Greg's eyebrows shot up. "Me?"

"Aren't you a computer whiz?"

"Not really." Greg looked at Ruth. "Like I said, if he took a picture, why not leave the riddle in the hidden office?"

He had a good point. If Carter had done that, no one would have realised he'd taken it. *Unless* . . . Ruth sat up. He hadn't wanted Charles and Margaret to find it. Carter had wanted to stall them while he figured out the clues. Then he'd hid it at the top of the lighthouse. Which meant the killer didn't have the riddle. "Well, not until we practically handed it to them on a silver platter," Ruth muttered to herself. She sighed and shook her head.

Charles got up, walked to a drinks cabinet, and poured himself a whiskey. "Anyone else care for a drink?"

"I could murder a tea," Ruth said.

Margaret glared at her. "Poor choice of words."

Ruth inclined her head. "So now you believe me when I say someone murdered Carter?"

"I don't know what to believe. I simply want this whole ghastly nightmare to end."

Greg stood. "I'll get you a mug of tea," he said to Ruth. "Aunty Margaret. Want anything?"

She got to her feet too. "I'll come with you."

Once they'd left, and Charles had sat back down in the armchair opposite, Ruth said, "Have you any idea who might have taken the riddle?"

He gulped his whiskey and swallowed. "I thought everyone here was above reproach. I'm shocked by what's happened."

Ruth could understand his unease.

Charles wiped his moustache. "I suppose we must speak to the staff. Demand answers."

"We'll get to that soon enough." Ruth took a calming breath. "Charles, have you thought of any way another member of staff could have found out about the will and riddle?"

"I've been racking my brains, but unless my father told them without my knowledge . . ." He shrugged. "I suppose it's possible, but highly unlikely. My father had no problem keeping secrets his entire life." He nodded to the shelves. "Only showed me that office because he moved his desk in there. I have no idea what he used the room for before that."

Ruth pursed her lips. Carter could have told someone else. *But why?*

She sat back, steepled her fingers, and tried to come up with a way to flush the killer and riddle-stealer out from under their rock. However, even if she could think of something smart, that might take days. Ruth looked at the time on her phone. They now only had twenty-one hours until Noah arrived. She yawned. "Brilliant."

A few minutes later, Margaret and Greg returned with hot drinks.

Margaret handed Ruth an extra-large mug of tea. "As you like it: way too much milk, and enough sugar to support an ant colony for a year."

Ruth took a gulp of tea and savoured its sweet, caffeine-rich goodness as it slid down her throat. "Ah." She smacked her lips. "Thank you, Margo."

Margaret tutted, and then paced the room.

"What are we going to do now?" Greg asked.

With her tea in hand, Ruth stood and examined the blackboard. However, not even the faintest trace of what they'd worked on remained.

Margaret clomped past.

"Please sit down," Ruth said.

"We have to speak to the staff."

"And we will. Once I know what I'm going to ask. I am

trying to think." Although Ruth would never admit to Margaret that things now looked bleaker than before. "It's not as if they can leave. Well, not unless they ask someone on the mainland to come collect them."

"Why would they have to?" Greg asked.

"Some kind soul sank Captain Barney's boat," Ruth said,

"What?" Margaret gaped at Charles.

"Oh, that's right," he said with a pained expression. "We forgot to tell you. Someone drilled holes in Barney's boat.

Stunned silence greeted this.

Ruth asked Charles, "What about that Fred guy he mentioned?"

"He's out fishing most of the day, and he'd tell Barney if someone requested a trip."

Ruth motioned to the blackboard. "Let's focus and have a crack at this while it's still fresh. We'll deal with everything else in a little while." She pointed Margaret to the nearest chair. "Please."

Margaret hesitated, and then dropped onto it. She folded her arms. "We're in your hands. Whatever you think is best."

Ruth faced the blackboard. "What answers can we recall?"

"Mushroom," Greg said.

Ruth wrote that word at the top.

"Greg's other one was *umbrella*," Margaret said.

Ruth jotted that underneath, and remembered one part of the riddle. "What do you never want to have, but if you do, never lose?"

"A lawsuit," Charles said.

Ruth added it to the list. "What else?" She pursed her lips.

"There was that ludicrous line about finding it in puzzle, not riddle," Margaret said.

Greg clicked his fingers. "The letter *U*."

Ruth wrote that too. "Okay, I think that's the four we had solved: Mushroom, Umbrella, Lawsuit, and the letter *U*."

"Back to where we were," Charles said. "Sans the other lines. We've lost five."

While she thought about it, Ruth slipped her phone from her pocket and took a picture of the blackboard, which was what she should have done in the first place. She then looked round at the others. "Can you remember other parts of the riddle? Any part at all?"

They all stared at the blackboard, frowning and muttering under their breaths.

"Wasn't there something about getting under the skin?" Greg asked.

Ruth didn't recall that one, but she jotted it on the blackboard anyway, and the four of them resumed their frowning.

Charles slapped his hands together, and they all jumped. "Up and down but can't move. I remember because it was such an odd thing to say."

Ruth added that line to the blackboard.

Margaret's eyes widened. "Stairs."

Ruth glanced over at her. "Sorry?"

Margaret waggled a finger at the part she'd added. "Up and down but can't move. It's stairs. They go up and down, but they don't go anywhere. They're stationary." Her eyes darkened. "And today they acted as a waterfall."

"She's right," Greg said. "Well done, Aunty Margaret."

She lifted her chin.

Ruth added the word to their list. "That makes five. Over halfway. What about the rest of the riddle? Looks like we have four words remaining."

This resulted in another round of furrowed brows.

Margaret stood. "We're wasting time. We won't remember the rest of the riddle." She strode toward the door.

"Where are you going?" Ruth called after her.

"To fetch Billy. He must think I've abandoned him."

"Not alone, my love." Charles hurried after her, and they left.

Ruth looked at the time on her phone. It was a little after seven thirty. "I'm going to check on Merlin."

"I'll come with you." Greg followed her out.

In her room, Ruth found Merlin asleep on her bed. He opened his eyes and stretched.

"Sorry I've neglected you today." She sat beside him as a wave of exhaustion washed over her.

Merlin brushed up against Ruth's arm, back arched, and he purred.

"I envy you. Ignorance is bliss." Ruth's anxiety eased as she stroked him.

Greg remained by the door, arms folded. "I envy him too. He has a pampered life."

"He deserves everything." With effort, Ruth extricated herself from the bed, refreshed Merlin's water bowl, cleaned his litter tray, and plumped his pillow. However, Merlin seemed content on her bed. He curled up and went back to sleep.

Merlin had a knack for falling asleep quickly.

She shuddered.

With a distinct nip in the air, despite the fact she'd only opened the French door an inch, Ruth pulled it closed, and was about to leave when something caught her eye.

A notepad sat on a side table by the door. She stared at it as a memory rushed forward of a twelve-year-old Ruth running into a fairground, only to have Margaret grab her arm and drag her straight back out again. "Of course." Ruth raced from the room.

"Grandma?" Greg hurried after her.

Back in the study, they found Margaret and Charles clearing the dinner things, loading plates back onto the carts, while Billy sniffed the floor where Carter's body had once lain.

"Charles, your father wrote the riddle on a sheet of notepaper, right?" Ruth asked.

He wiped his hand on a napkin. "Yes."

"And where's the notepad now?" She pointed to the shelves. "In there?"

"I'm not sure." Charles strode over to them, flipped the hidden latch, and pulled the shelves aside.

Greg rushed over to join them.

Ruth slipped into the office. "When I was twelve, a fairground rolled into town." She circled the desk. "I begged my parents to go, but they refused to take me." Ruth lowered her voice. "Of course, Margaret wasn't bothered, she didn't like exciting rides, so she was no help."

"I heard that." Margaret appeared at the door.

Greg peered around the room. "This place is awesome."

Ruth sat behind the desk. "It was the last day of school term, and my parents were taking us away that evening to their cottage in Devon."

"I remember that place," Margaret said. "It was beautiful."

Ruth rolled her eyes. "Same thing every year." She opened the top left-hand drawer of the desk and riffled through paperwork—mainly bills. "So with no hope of going to the fair before we left, I had no choice. I couldn't miss out, so I did the only thing I could think of." Ruth closed the drawer and opened the next one down. This one only held boxes of stationery. She closed it again.

"What did you do?" Greg asked as he examined the mechanical Ferris wheel.

Margaret glared at her with obvious disapproval. "Something nefarious."

"I snuck downstairs early that morning," Ruth said. "Found my mother's chequebook." She opened the upper right-hand drawer and smiled.

"How did a cheque help?" Charles frowned. "Did you cash the money?"

"No, she forged a note from our mother," Margaret said. "Excusing her pending absence from school that day."

Billy let out a yap, and Margaret went to fetch him.

Ruth lifted three jotter pads from the desk drawer and held them up. "I traced Mum's signature impression from the chequebook and copied it to the note for school. Worked a charm. They suspected nothing."

The pads had the same yellow paper as the riddle.

Charles stared at them, and then his eyes widened.

Ruth flicked on the desk lamp and angled the notepad under the light. Sure enough, there were impressions in the paper. "You know your father's handwriting best." Ruth beckoned Charles over. "Help me work these out."

Together they examined the notepad, but all they could discern was a jumble of meaningless words like, "may, attention, drenching, funds," and so on.

Ruth removed a pencil from a pot and then rubbed the side of the graphite across the page.

Words formed:

To whom it may concern,
It has been brought to my attention that a proposed drenching

operation is slated to commence next month. I propose that with inadequate funds, the work carried out will not meet the standard . . .

Ruth set the first notepad aside and tried the second—rubbing the pencil across the page until words formed there too. When it revealed a shopping list of odd jobs that needed attending to around the house and grounds, she put it with the first and tried with the final one.

After only a few times back and forth with the pencil, Ruth knew she had the right one. "This is it."

Greg beamed. "Genius."

"What's genius?" Margaret reappeared at the door, clutching Billy.

Ruth held up the notepad. "We have the full riddle again."

"Why on earth didn't you do that in the first place?" Margaret said. "Would have saved us a lot of bother."

Billy yapped, as if agreeing with her.

Ruth grumbled and copied the riddle out on a fresh sheet, plus she made extra copies, and handed them to Charles, Greg, and Margaret.

Next, Ruth took a picture of the riddle with her phone for good measure, then pocketed both. "Let's see them try and get them all."

Greg read from his copy. "We have these four lines left to figure out: Remember you're alive, even though they're dead. Get under my skin, you'll be sure to cry. When spoken to, I will always answer. Finally, smile at me, and I'll return the favour." He looked around at them. "Anything?"

All three shook their heads.

"We need a break from the riddle." Ruth returned everything to the desk drawer and stood. "Now it's time to speak to the staff before it gets too late."

As they headed across the study, Greg leaned in to Ruth and whispered, "Why are we doing this now? Shouldn't we solve the riddle first? Whoever flooded the bathroom and stole it from us is hardly about to admit it, are they?"

"Oh, I don't know," Ruth said as they picked their way across the slick hallway. "Five minutes with Margaret is enough to make anyone confess to absolutely anything." Although, come to think of it, a false admission would do them no good.

Margaret scowled over her shoulder. "I heard that."

"Carter's murder is rather important," Charles said.

"How many house staff members do you have?" Ruth asked.

He glanced at the ceiling. "Seven. Well, six now that poor Carter has left us. That includes the two groundskeepers."

"It would take at least a day to interview them all thoroughly," Ruth murmured. "Maybe longer. We'll have to speak to them in two batches."

"Is that wise?" Margaret said. "Alone they're more likely to spill the beans."

"I don't think there's going to be much bean spilling," Ruth said. "Whoever took the riddle from us knew exactly what they were doing. They now think we don't have it. That gives us a slight edge."

"How so?" Charles asked.

Ruth let out a slow breath. "They want to blackmail you, not kill you, so as long as we're careful, that's not a worry." She looked about and lowered her voice. "As far as the murderer knows, they now have the only copy of the riddle and want to figure it out for themselves. They plan to get to the will first."

"And you're betting they won't figure it out before us?" Margaret asked.

"I'm hoping they can't," Ruth said. "We don't have any choice but to try. If the killer is now hunting for the will, they'll have to sneak about. That increases their chances of getting caught."

"Why does it?" Greg asked.

"If they're on the same trail as us, they could leave evidence behind." Ruth gave her sister and brother-in-law a sympathetic look. "We want to know who murdered Carter, right? And who caused thousands of pounds' worth of damage to your beautiful home. Who fooled us."

Margaret let out a slow breath. "What do you suggest?"

"That we get these interviews over quickly and return to the riddle. Of course, our priority is to catch the killer and have them brought to justice, but the best way is to beat them to the will. Then their game is over." Ruth faced Greg. "Grab a notepad and pen from somewhere. Anywhere other than Henry's office."

"I can find those," Charles said.

"Thank you." Ruth addressed her sister. "I'll see the house staff first, and then the two gardeners."

Margaret pointed to a reading room. "In there?"

Ruth hesitated. "Somewhere they feel relaxed."

"The kitchen," Margaret said. "There's a table and chairs that's suitable."

"Perfect."

Margaret didn't move. "I want to hear what they have to say."

Ruth cringed inside. "You're too intimidating." And that was an understatement.

"I most certainly am not." Margaret set Billy down. "I have a right to know what's going on."

Ruth took Margaret's hands in hers. "I promise we will figure it out, but you're too involved. You're upset about Carter, and that's understandable. His death, coupled with the missing will . . . It's a traumatic time. I can keep some level of detachment and get to the bottom of it. Will you let me do that for you? Please?"

Margaret seemed taken aback by this display of fondness and sincerity. She stared at Ruth for a few seconds, and then her shoulders relaxed. "Fine."

Ruth forced a smile. "Thank you."

"But the moment you find out who did this, I'm throwing them off a cliff." Margaret marched across the hallway, with Billy trotting at her heels.

Greg watched her go. "I don't think she's joking."

"I can assure you she isn't." Charles rested a hand on his shoulder. "Now let me find you that notepad and pen."

12

Ruth hurried after Margaret, through the house, along a narrow and winding corridor, and then into the east wing. Somewhere Ruth had never ventured.

The kitchen stood thirty feet long by fifteen wide. An Aga dominated the far wall, with cupboards and worktops lining each side of the room, and a table down the middle, flanked by a mismatch of old chairs.

At the other end of the kitchen stood a further two doors. The first, made of worn oak, had part of the original castle stonework on either side, and a crow within a triangle carved above. The other door was a modern white addition, surrounded by red brick.

"I'll fetch them as soon as Charles gets here." Margaret stood by the latter door.

Ruth sat down. As she waited, her thoughts drifted back to one of the last interviews she'd conducted as a police officer. The perpetrator had leapt across the table and grabbed her by the throat.

Ruth only hoped this evening wouldn't be so eventful . . . and painful.

A few minutes later, Greg slipped into the kitchen.

Charles closed the door behind them, and then followed Margaret.

Ruth gestured at the chair to her right. Greg sat and placed a pad in front of him, pen poised.

"Note all the key details." Ruth straightened creases in her skirt. "Start with their name, position within the household, and then we'll ask them what they know." She checked the time on her phone. It was eight thirty in the evening. Ruth sighed. At this rate, they were in for a long night. "Pay attention to everything I ask, and their answers. You might pick up on something I miss." She rubbed her eyes and yawned.

"What's the Tammy Radcliffe incident you and Aunty Margaret mentioned?" Greg asked.

"A mistake I made when we were kids," Ruth said. "Margaret has never forgiven me." She took a deep breath. Now there was a real possibility of finally putting it in the past where it belonged. A chance to atone.

Greg leaned in. "What happened though?"

The white door at the other end of the room opened again, and Margaret marched into the kitchen, head held high. She motioned behind her. "The house staff."

Three bewildered-looking people filed in after her. The first was the head housekeeper, with her black hair cut into a neat bob, deep brown eyes, and wearing a serious scowl.

She was followed by the man who had helped serve lunch and dinner. He appeared to be in his forties, but Ruth guessed he could be at least a decade older. It was clear he took care of his appearance, with his deep red hair slicked back, smooth skin, and Hollywood teeth. He wore a black suit, white shirt, and black bow tie. The man walked with a slight limp, as though carrying an old knee injury.

Last through the door was a slim woman in her early fifties, with dyed purple hair, dressed in a grey skirt and blouse, wearing an apron. No doubt, the cook.

Margaret thrust a finger at the chairs opposite Ruth and Greg. "Sit. Please."

They did as she asked.

Charles remained by the door.

Margaret turned her attention to Ruth. "The housemaid, Maddie, thought now would be the perfect time to take a bath. It's like she hasn't got a care in the world."

"Okay," Ruth said. "We'll speak to her at the same time as the gardeners."

"Groundskeepers," Margaret said.

The manservant shuffled in his seat, glanced at Greg, and then he stared at the table.

Margaret spun on her heel and marched from the room.

Charles nodded at Ruth and followed his wife out, closing the door behind them.

Ruth smiled at her three nervous interviewees, but flashing her teeth didn't seem to ease their wariness.

The cook clasped her hands on her lap in an apparent attempt to hide their trembling, whereas the head housekeeper gripped her knees and stared straight ahead, unflinching. It was as though enemy soldiers had captured them on the battlefield and they now faced the real possibility of a firing squad.

"My name is Ruth Morgan," she said, keeping her tone soft and relaxed. "I'm Margaret's sister, and I'd like to ask you a few questions." She cleared her throat and studied their faces. "How about we start with your names and then confirm your positions within the house?" Ruth nodded at the eldest lady.

She puffed out her chest. "Betty Miller. Head housekeeper." Betty gestured to the man on her left. "This is Ray. Ray Gibson. He's a servant, and the house's Mr Fixit."

"Oh really?" Ruth leaned forward. "You're handy with a screwdriver?"

"What about plumbing?" Greg asked, deadpan.

Ray kept his gaze lowered, and tugged an ear.

Even though she wanted to ask why Ray hadn't leapt into action during the flooded bathroom incident, Ruth's focus moved to the remaining lady with the purple hair.

"H-Helen Wood," she said in a shaky voice. "Cook."

"Nice to meet you all." Ruth sat back. "I gather you're aware of what happened to Mr Carter?"

This resulted in downcast expressions.

"It's terrible," Helen mumbled. "Really terrible." She sniffed.

"Horrible," Betty agreed. "Tragic. Stanley was a good man. Wouldn't hurt a fly."

Ruth's eyes narrowed. It was something in their reactions that seemed off. *Forced? Crocodile tears? Had Carter not been a good man at all?* And the way Helen had said he wouldn't hurt a fly: *why would he have ever been in the position to warrant hurting anyone?*

"We'd like to figure out why Carter was in the study," Ruth said. "So as to better understand what led to the tragic event."

Greg scribbled down notes.

Ruth focused on Ray. "What about you?"

His gaze rose to meet hers. "What about me?"

"Were you close to Carter?"

"No. I mean, well, we worked together." Ray clamped his jaw closed.

"Did you like him?" Ruth asked, sensing there was more.

Ray crossed his arms over his chest and shrugged one shoulder.

Ruth studied him for a few seconds longer, and then her gaze returned to the ladies. "Did you know him well?"

"Of course." Betty flattened creases in her skirt. "I've known Stanley for many years. We often dined together."

"Here?" Ruth asked. "In private?"

Ray's lip curled.

"At Stanley's cottage." Betty didn't notice his reaction. "Cook graciously allowed me to prepare a meal on Wednesday evenings, and I'd take it to him." She smiled and her expression turned wistful. "Stanley would provide the wine. He had such great taste." Then her face dropped as sadness took over. "I can't imagine how the house will run without him."

"It'll be just fine," Ray murmured.

Ruth inclined her head. "You didn't get on with Mr Carter?"

Ray sneered. "He was rude and arrogant."

"He most certainly was not," Betty snapped.

Helen the cook looked between them with an anxious expression—forehead wrinkled; mouth open as if she wanted to interject, but she closed it again.

Ruth kept her focus on Ray. "Would you care to elaborate?"

"Carter never liked me, and never hid the fact either." He looked away and muttered, "According to him, nothing was right. Nitpicked everything I did."

"Stanley was a perfectionist." Betty's nostrils flared. "That's all. You didn't give him a chance or try to get to know him."

"Did he seem out of sorts today?" Ruth asked the three of them. There clearly had been tension in the work environment, but that didn't warrant murder. "Notice anything out of character?"

"He scolded me for not putting the sitting room candlesticks back in the exact spot I took them from," Ray grumbled. "Can't ever do anything right, even when I do it right." He rolled his eyes. "Same old, same old."

Betty glared at him. "How dare you speak ill of the dead."

"It's the truth," Ray shot back. "She's asking, I'm telling." He waved a hand in Ruth's direction. "Or should I lie?"

Helen buried her face in her hands and sobbed.

"Did any of you spot suspicious behaviour from Mr Carter before he died, or anything unusual since?" Ruth asked. "Anyone acting strange?" She looked between them. "Think carefully." Ruth studied their reactions. "It's important. Any detail, no matter how small or insignificant, could be important."

"You don't think it was an accident?" Betty asked with a look of incredulity.

Helen gasped and dabbed at her eyes with a tea towel.

Ray seemed unaffected by the news.

Ruth held up her hands. "We're only trying to understand if any unusual events surrounded Carter's death. As I say, I'm asking a few questions to make sure we fully comprehend what transpired, and to prevent it happening again."

"And figure out what he was doing in the study," Ray said.

Betty's eyes narrowed to slits. "What are you suggesting?"

"Why was he in there?" Ray turned in his chair to face her. "Touching Master Henry's personal belongings? He had no business doing that."

"He had every right to be in there," Betty shot back. "How dare you suggest otherwise." Her cheeks flushed. "What business is it of yours? Master Henry gave permission for Stanley and Master Charles to be inside the study whenever they saw fit."

Ray fixed her with steady eye contact. "Yeah, but Master Henry is dead, isn't he? Did Master Charles give Carter permission to be in there? I bet he didn't." Ray bared his teeth, and he looked at Ruth. "Anyway, what gives you the authority to ask us questions? Why should we talk to you? It's the job of the police, and they weren't interested."

"Why wouldn't you talk to us?" Greg retorted. "If you've got nothing to hide, there shouldn't be a problem. Right?"

Ruth rested a hand on his arm and kept her focus firmly on Ray, wanting to bring the temperature back down a notch. "You don't have to do anything that makes you uncomfortable. I'm only asking that you share what you know."

"Grandma used to be a police officer," Greg said.

Ray scowled at him. "Still doesn't give her the right to throw accusations about the place."

"I've not accused anyone of anything." Ruth looked between the three of them. "I'm sure you all cared for Carter in—" She cleared her throat. "In *your own ways*."

Betty lifted her chin and her shoulders rolled back.

"Now you come to mention it," Helen said in a small voice. "He did seem a bit out of sorts." She glanced furtively at Betty.

"How so?" Ruth asked.

Finally, they were getting to something.

"He was being his usual rude self, if you ask me," Ray said.

"I mean . . ." Ruth took a steadying breath. "How was he acting differently from normal?"

Betty glanced at the white door. "I suppose Stanley's had a lot on his mind with your visit. We all have."

"Not that it's been a bother," Helen said with a weak smile.

"Mrs Andrews wanted everything to be perfect for your stay," Betty lifted her chin. "We were all feeling the pressure."

"I understand." Ruth pictured her sister fussing about the place and barking orders prior to their arrival. "Did Mr Carter say what was bothering him?"

"He's been on and off the boil for the past couple of months," Helen said. "Master Henry's passing seemed to make things worse."

Betty shrugged. "I told him to take a break, but he dismissed me. Today, he did seem particularly solemn, though."

Ruth considered their answers for a few seconds, and then asked, "Is there anything else you can add?"

Helen and Betty shook their heads.

Ray resumed staring at the table, and muttered, "He had a phone."

Ruth's eyebrows lifted. "Sorry?"

"This morning." Ray sighed. "He had a mobile phone on him."

"He did not," Betty said in a haughty tone. "They're banned from the house while we're working."

Ray shot her a nasty glance. "I know what I saw." His attention moved back to Ruth. "He had a mobile phone in his pocket."

"Did he use it?" Ruth pictured the smartphone back at Carter's cottage.

Ray hesitated, and then murmured, "Not sure. Maybe."

If he was holding something else back, Ray wasn't about to share that information. Ruth would have to try again with him, if she got the chance, alone. Pressing about any awkward work relationships would need to be tackled individually, without fear of rebuke or chastisement from the others.

"One more thing before you go," Ruth said. "When was the last time you each saw Carter?"

Helen looked to Betty. "Luncheon?" When this received a nod in reply, she turned back to Ruth. "Right before we served lunch at midday."

"And you didn't see him again after that?" Ruth asked.

"No."

Ruth pursed her lips as she thought through the timeline. They hadn't found Carter in the study for quite a while after that moment. Given the fact she'd also checked in on Merlin before heading to the study, Ruth gauged it had to be over an hour later.

"How did no one notice he was missing for so long?" Greg asked.

A valid question.

"Mr Carter doesn't serve or clear away," Betty said. "That's not his job. We wouldn't likely see him again until around two."

"What does he usually get up to during those couple of hours?" Ruth asked.

"It varies." Betty's eyes lifted to the ceiling. "I suppose today he would have gone to the wine cellar."

"Thank you." Ruth forced a smile at them in turn. "That's all for now. I may have more questions for you later."

The three of them stood and went to leave the kitchen, but Ruth added, "Oh, one more thing. Did any of you venture into the study earlier today?" She watched their reactions closely. "When we were upstairs dealing with the flood, I mean."

"Maddie and I fetched mops and buckets," Betty said. "And Helen was in here."

"What about you?" Ruth asked Ray.

"I stayed in my room," he said in a rough tone. "As the mistress ordered."

"You didn't leave?" Greg asked with a dubious look. "Not even to use the toilet?"

Ray shook his head.

Ruth motioned to the door. "Thank you. You've all been very helpful." Although, she wasn't sure they had been.

Once they'd left, Greg leaned in to his grandmother and whispered, "My money's on Ray."

Ruth smirked. "I thought it might be."

A minute later, the door opened again, and Margaret swept into the kitchen with Charles. "I've sent Maddie to the head groundskeeper's cottage. Do you know where that is?"

"I know." Greg stood. "It's the one you can make out from the conservatory, right? On the other side of the wall. The stone building with the slate roof?"

"Next to the vegetable garden," Charles said.

Margaret checked her watch. "I need to settle Billy down for the night, or he'll have a tantrum."

"We won't be long," Ruth said.

"Meet you in the study with a cup of tea?" Margaret asked. "Then you can tell us all about it."

"Sounds perfect." Ruth got to her feet and muttered, "The tea part, that is." She followed Greg from the kitchen, along a hallway, and through the back door. Ruth shuddered as the cold night air cut through her cardigan and blouse. "How far is it?" Perhaps she should go back for her coat.

Greg pointed to a gate between tall bushes. "Just beyond that."

Ruth hugged herself as they hurried along the path, through the gate, then around the corner until they came out at a small cottage topped with blue slate.

The front door stood open.

"Hello?" Ruth called.

"Come in," a gruff voice replied.

Ruth stepped over the threshold into a sitting room with a low ceiling, and a lit fireplace with a mantelpiece filled with family photos; grown kids, and grandkids, all smiling at the camera.

Seated in a tatty armchair covered with dishevelled blankets was the man they'd seen tending to the garden when they arrived: seventies, with white hair jutting out at impossible angles from the side of his head, beneath a tartan flatcap.

Alec also wore an oversized lumberjack shirt, and tartan slippers that matched his cap.

Perched on the edge of an old wooden chair covered in paint splashes to his left was a scrawny, pale young woman in her late teens, with wet mousy blonde hair, wearing jeans and a bomber jacket.

At first glance, Ruth didn't recognise her, but this had to be Maddie, the housemaid. Her appearance was vastly different with her hair down and without makeup.

"Good evening." Ruth dropped onto a sofa, and Greg joined her. "Thank you for seeing me. I won't take up too much of your time."

Maddie beamed, and Alec nodded.

The chair to his right sat empty.

Ruth was about to ask where his assistant had gotten to when the front door opened, and a man stepped through.

"Sorry I'm late," he murmured.

Ruth's mouth dropped open.

Greg looked up. "No way. It's him."

13

The last member of the group to enter Alec's wee cottage was a familiar man with a weathered face and grizzled red beard—the very person Ruth had "hit" with her motorhome earlier that day: Josh Green.

When Josh laid eyes on Ruth and Greg, his steps faltered. He half turned back to the door, as if considering making a break for freedom, but then he clearly realised it would do him no good on an island with zero means of escape at present.

Greg balled his fists and glared at him.

Josh shuffled into the room, head bowed, shoulders slumped, attempting to make himself invisible.

It didn't work.

Ruth contained a smirk as he sat, and then she gave her grandson a hard look, signalling him to bite his tongue.

Greg straightened his face with obvious reluctance. He snatched up his pen and made angry notes—the nib scratching the page back and forth.

Josh wore tatty jeans with soil stains, an equally grubby

denim shirt, and a wax overcoat, plus Wellington boots. He sat in the remaining chair and stared at the floor.

A few thoughts flashed through Ruth's mind, chief among them being: *Seeing as this guy is a con artist, immoral, able to ruin people's lives for money, could he be the killer? Is he after Henry's will? Is Josh capable of blackmail?*

Ruth answered a probable *yes* to all those questions but worked hard to remain neutral. At least in outward appearance.

She gathered herself. "Thank you for agreeing to see us on such short notice. We've already spoken to Helen, Betty, and Ray, so we want to ask you the same questions, which chief among them are: Did you notice anything odd about Mr Carter before he died? And have you seen anything unusual either prior or since?"

Silence greeted her, with the only sounds coming from the crackle of wood burning in the fireplace, and the insistent tick of an oversized clock on the wall.

Maddie blurted, "I overheard an argument."

Both Alec and Josh looked at her in surprise.

"Who was arguing?" Ruth asked. "And what was it about?"

"Well, a one-sided argument, at least." Maddie bounced her feet and spoke in a rush. "I heard Mr Carter shouting at someone. They were in the dining hall. I didn't see either of them, so I don't know who the other person was. Only Mr Carter spoke, and I recognised his voice." She took a breath. "I was on my way to dust the billiard room. And sweep the floor. And other things. Tidy."

"When did this happen?" Ruth asked.

"This morning."

Greg made notes. "What time exactly?"

Maddie stared into space. "Hmm. We'd cleared the

breakfast things. So around eight thirty. I think. Yes. About then." She smiled.

Ruth pursed her lips and sat back. "Did Carter usually frequent the dining hall at that time of day?"

"No," Maddie said with a vehement shake of her head. "He maintains the silverware and makes sure everything is tidied away, but normally waits for us to bring it to him. Today was different."

Ruth considered the timing. Not only had Carter been in the study after lunch, when he should have been in the wine cellar, but now somewhere else out of place before that too.

Betty and Helen hadn't mentioned this, so Ruth assumed Carter could not have been gone long enough for them to miss him.

Ruth cleared her throat. "And what was Carter shouting about?"

"I didn't catch all of it." Maddie sat bolt upright. "But Mr Carter said Victor's fortunate to safely enter." She screwed up her face.

"Who's Victor?" Ruth looked at the men in the room, but they shrugged. "Safely enter what? The house?"

Maddie shrugged too.

"Could he have been on the phone?" Greg asked. "Apparently, he had a mobile."

"I don't think so," Maddie said. "I was already in the billiard room when the door to the dining hall banged open, and someone marched off. By the time I peeked into the entrance hall, they'd gone. I only saw Mr Carter leave a short while after. He looked very upset."

Ruth glanced at Greg to make sure he got all this down. "Can you describe the first set of footfalls? Male? Female?"

Maddie gave her an apologetic look. "I don't know."

"Any idea which direction they went?" Ruth asked.

Again, Maddie shook her head.

If that other person had been either Helen, Betty, or Ray, it meant they'd lied.

Ruth addressed her next question to Alec and Josh. "Did you hear about the flood?"

"Yeah," Alec said in a gruff voice. "Odd happenings."

"What flood?" Josh mumbled.

"Maddie only just told me about it before you arrived," Alec said to Ruth. "The bathroom flooded some time before seven, right?"

Ruth checked the time on her phone. "I'd say about then." She looked up. "Where were you both?"

Alec pointed to the chair he was seated in. "Letting my dinner go down." He then pointed at a small television in the corner of the room. "Watching my programs."

"What about you?" Ruth asked Josh.

His eyes darted to the front door. "Shower."

Ruth didn't bother to ask whether someone could corroborate his alibi. "Anything else you can tell me?"

Maddie lifted a hand high into the air.

Ruth smiled at her. "Yes?"

"I was the one who found the flood," she said with pride in her voice. "I told Mrs Miller right away. Before that, Mrs Miller had asked me to fetch another stack of tablecloths from the laundry room. As I left, that's when I spotted water pouring down the stairs. I hurried to tell her what was happening." She looked eagerly at Greg as he scribbled all this down.

"She let you go off on your own?" he asked.

Maddie hesitated, and then nodded.

Ruth remembered the door to the study bursting open

and Betty's pale face. "When we went upstairs to the guest bathroom, what did you do?"

"Fetched mops and buckets," Maddie said.

So far, it all tallied up.

"You can see the study door from the entrance hall, right?" Ruth asked. "A clear vantage point from the bottom of the stairs?"

"Yes."

"And you didn't spot anyone going in there?"

Maddie shook her head.

"It appears we have a poltergeist," Ruth muttered to Greg.

Maddie gasped. "The phantom."

Josh snorted and looked away.

However, Alec nodded in sage agreement. "Could well be."

Ruth inclined her head, and although she knew what they were talking about from her conversation with Charles, she feigned ignorance. "Phantom?"

"Take no notice of her," Josh said. "Maddie's talking crazy."

She blinked at him. "The phantom is real."

"It's not."

"Now there." Alec shuffled in his seat. "We've all had experiences with the phantom. It doesn't do well to dismiss such things."

Greg's forehead wrinkled. "You believe in a phantom?"

"Of course." Alec gripped the arms of the chair and leaned forward. "Too many strange things have happened over the years not to believe." He winked and sat back again.

"Like what?" Greg asked.

"Lots of things," Alec said. "Hundreds of strange goings-on. Food missing. Stuff moving about. Not only at the house, but on the grounds too. Tools vanishing and then reappearing days later." He looked at Josh. "You can't deny you've noticed."

Greg glanced at his grandma, as if confirming he should write this down too.

She nodded, and then an image of the light in the cave from over thirty years ago appeared fresh in her mind. *Could that have been the phantom too?* She shook herself back to the present. "Does anyone have photographic evidence of the phantom? Any solid proof?"

"Of course they don't," Josh said. "It's all in their heads."

"It's not in our heads," Maddie retorted. "Explain why things move or go missing? Locked doors miraculously unlock themselves. The footsteps on the floors above, and yet when someone checks it out, there's no one there."

"Exactly." Josh rolled his eyes. "No one's there."

If her time as a police officer had taught Ruth anything at all, it was that every unexplained occurrence had a foundation in truth. Sure, people exaggerated, made up stories, embellished events to suit their own narratives and beliefs, sometimes flat-out lied, but there was always a logical explanation at the heart of it all.

"When was the last time something went missing?" Ruth asked the three of them.

"Only last week," Maddie said. "Food taken from the fridge. Half a pork pie, a pickle sandwich, and a bottle of ale."

"Could someone have helped themselves to a midnight snack?" Greg licked his lips, obviously picturing every item she'd listed.

"That's what happened," Josh said. "Ray went down in the middle of the night and—"

"He said he never does that." Maddie refocussed on

Ruth and wrung her hands. "Cook asked everyone about it, and we all denied taking anything." She shot Josh a look. "If Ray said he didn't, then that's the end of the matter."

Ruth couldn't help but think of the cave and how there could be a connection. "Returning to the subject of Carter, did any of you know him outside work? Did you socialise with him at all?"

Maddie and Josh shook their heads.

"Stanley and I sometimes played poker on a Friday," Alec said. "Had a whiskey or two with it. Or three." He grinned, revealing several missing teeth, including one at the front.

"Did he ever mention anything out of the ordinary to you?" Ruth asked. "One of the others mentioned he seemed glum recently. Perhaps he had something on his mind?"

"Never really spoke about much at all," Alec said. "Although I must admit he did seem downcast recently. I asked him if he was okay, and he told me it was nothing to worry about. I'd assumed it was grief, with Master Henry's passing."

"Did you see Carter at any other times?" Ruth looked between Alec and Josh.

"Don't fraternise with the house staff," Josh muttered.

"Right," Alec agreed. "We keep ourselves to ourselves for the most part." He gave Maddie a sidelong glance. "Stay out of all the bickering and nonsense."

"They argue a lot?" Greg asked.

"No, we don't," Maddie said with a pained expression.

Alec shrugged.

"What about at lunch time?" Ruth asked the groundskeepers. "You must have to go into the house then."

"They take their sandwiches and leave," Maddie said. "Barely say a word."

"That's true." Alec stared at her. "Wouldn't want Cook's nice clean kitchen floors all muddied up, would we?" He looked back at Ruth. "Josh and I eat lunch in the tool shed."

"Ah, yes, about that," Ruth said. "I saw a pair of Wellington boots in there earlier. Maybe a size ten?"

This resulted in frowns.

"Shouldn't be," Alec said. "Mine are outside the front door."

Ruth thought back, but couldn't remember seeing them. "There definitely was a pair in the shed earlier today."

"Have you not cleaned up?" Alec asked Josh. "What have I told you about leaving your boots lying about?"

Josh pointed at his feet. "These are mine. Don't know whose the other ones could be."

"Would you mind putting on a pair of gloves and fetching them for me?" Ruth asked.

"I'll do it." With some effort, Alec extricated himself from the armchair and left the cottage.

The four of them sat in silence.

Ruth stared at the fire as she processed the day's happenings.

Several pieces of the puzzle were missing, although the sequence of events had become somewhat clearer. That morning, Carter had seemed downcast. Perhaps something had weighed on his mind, other than the recent passing of his longtime master.

After breakfast, he'd gotten into an altercation in the grand hall. And then, during lunch, Carter had entered the study, and that was when he'd met his untimely end.

Ruth's gaze moved from the flames to Josh. "Where were you at lunchtime today?"

"Already told you," he said in a gruff voice. "In the tool shed with—"

The front door opened, and Alec slipped back into the room. However, he was empty-handed.

"They've gone," he said to Ruth as he dropped back into his armchair. "Those boots you mentioned."

"You didn't see them at all?" Ruth asked. "Earlier in the day? A pair by the back wall?"

A flicker of a frown crossed his features. "No." He looked at Josh. "Not yours?"

"I don't have a spare pair." He pointed at his boots. "All I own."

Ruth let out a slow breath. Maybe there was a phantom after all. One that required Wellington boots. "Okay. I think that will do for now."

Josh leapt to his feet.

Ruth stood and blocked his path before he could make a beeline for the door. "Can we have a word on our way back to the house?"

"I've got to phone my Mum." His eyes followed Maddie as she left.

"Would you mind escorting us anyway?" Ruth asked him. "We're heading in the same direction, no?"

"Can't." Josh stepped round her. "I'm late." He rushed from the cottage without a backward glance.

"Don't mind him," Alec said. "He's a funny lad, but harmless enough."

"He's far from harmless," Greg said. "He is a menace."

Ruth stepped outside and glanced down at Alec's Wellington boots by the front door. "Guess they were here all this time."

Greg leaned in to her and murmured, "And *funny* is not the word I'd choose to describe Josh. He's evasive about answering more questions. Will you tell Aunty Margaret and Uncle Charles about his con?"

Ruth pursed her lips. "Not yet."

"Why not?" Greg said. "Surely they need to know one of their staff members likes to scam people."

"Because I don't want Margaret flying off the handle. I need more time to mull over what they've told us." Ruth motioned down the path. "Shall we?"

In Ruth's bedroom suite, she refreshed Merlin's water, then dropped to the sofa and sank into the cushions. The sleek cat curled up on her lap.

Greg walked in. He and Merlin glared at each other, both watching with deep suspicion and pure loathing. Greg lowered himself onto the other end of the sofa.

After all, any sudden moves may trigger an angry flurry of fangs and claws, and that would be from Greg, never mind Merlin.

Ruth yawned and looked at the time on her phone: 9:45.

She groaned.

Normally Ruth would have been tucked up in bed with a warm milk and her copy of *Mrs Beeton's Book of Household Management.*

"Do you still think someone murdered Carter?" Greg asked.

"The same person who flooded the bathroom." Ruth rubbed her eyes as she fought to stay awake. "The muddy footprints upstairs, the broken trellis, and the missing Wellington boots from the potting shed."

"How do they all point to murder, though?" Greg flipped through the pages of the notebook. "And why didn't you ask any of the staff about the will?"

"Because the ones who know of its existence would most

probably lie," Ruth said. "And the ones who don't know, would then know of its existence."

Besides, some avenues of enquiry were pointless to pursue without pertinent evidence to back them up.

Greg sighed. "What about the puzzle boxes? Do you think Carter was close to finding the will? There was something in that one he took, but the killer now has it?"

"We can't know for sure, but it's a possibility." Ruth stroked Merlin, and he purred, sending soothing vibrations through her weary legs. "Although, from the fact they wiped the blackboard and stole the riddle from us, I suspect it was a dead end."

"But there's no evidence of foul play in the study," Greg persisted. "Otherwise, the police would have found more clues, wouldn't they?"

Ruth tipped her head back and closed her eyes. "Carter was missing for at least an hour between anyone last seeing him at lunch, and then us finding his body in the study. Anything could have happened during that time, and it did." She remembered his lifeless form crumpled on the study floor.

Greg scanned the notepad. "Now what?"

"We follow the riddle as far as we can," Ruth said. "Whatever path Carter was on, we must do the same." Again, with a lack of hard evidence, the riddle was their best shot. She still felt the killer might make a mistake and reveal themselves along the way. "It's a chance to figure out what happened to him."

Greg's eyebrows lifted. "And get murdered."

"Well, hopefully not," Ruth said. "The killer also has the riddle and therefore is on the same trail. Likely ahead of us. Even so, we must endeavour to beat them to the will. We can't risk them destroying it."

"What about Captain Barney's boat?" Greg asked. "Why would someone want to sabotage it? I mean, we can call for another one from the mainland, right?"

That was correct. However, calling for a friendly fisherman would mean waiting for some time for them to turn up. Enough time for the killer to escape via another method. With Captain Barney's boat out of commission, there was no way to chase after the murderer when they decided to flee.

Thumping footfalls approached the door.

Ruth tensed.

Margaret stomped into the room, wearing her customary frown. She thrust a mug of tea into Ruth's hands. "You were supposed to meet us in the study when you were done with your interviews."

Ruth sipped the sugary goodness and sighed. "Sorry. Came to check on Merlin."

Margaret hurried back into the hallway and returned with a malt drink for Greg.

"Thanks, Aunty Margaret."

She put her hands on her hips. "So, what did you discover?"

"Not a lot," Ruth said. "Apart from Maddie overhearing Carter shouting something."

Greg flipped through his notes. "He said, *Victor's fortunate to safely enter.*"

Margaret's brow furrowed into a deep line, which threatened to cleave her head in two. "Victor? Who on earth is Victor?"

"We don't know," Ruth said.

Margaret motioned to the door. "Come on, then. Let's recommence work on the riddle."

"I need a good night's sleep." Ruth yawned. "Can't think

straight. Want time to digest. We'll pick up with the riddle first thing in the morning."

"How can you sleep at a time like this?" Margaret said in a shrill voice. "Noah will be here tomorrow."

"We drove all the way from Vanmoor." Ruth closed her eyes. "I'm tired. We'll get up at first light."

"Talk some sense into her, Greg. This is ridiculous."

Ruth opened one eye and peered at him.

"Grandma's right," he said. "If we want to stand a chance at solving the riddle, we need to be fully awake and on form. I'm tired too."

Margaret huffed. "Fine." She marched to the door. "Are you coming down for supper?"

Greg leapt to his feet and ran past her.

"Lock your bedroom door tonight," Ruth called after him.

"Well, Ruth?" Margaret asked. "Are you coming too?"

She waved a limp hand. "I'll give it a miss."

"Seven a.m. sharp," Margaret said with a stern look, and then left.

Ruth closed her eyes again. "Seven thirty."

14

After completing her nighttime ablutions, and now wearing a fetching cucumber-and-lavender-scented face mask, Ruth sat up in bed, with her trusty *Mrs Beeton's Book of Household Management* open on her lap; a delightful tome over a hundred years old, packed full of recipes and advice on running a home to its maximum potential.

The latest recipe was *Sardine Pasties*.

Ruth screwed up her face.

Mrs Beeton had once again taken her exuberant love for cooking a little too far.

Ruth couldn't help but read on.

The recipe required a tin of sardines, puff pastry trimmings, and an egg.

Inspired.

The method involved not only skinning the sardines, and removing the backbones, but also placing the halves back together again, as though nothing had been done to the poor fellows. Ruth assumed the heads and tails were optional. Then one simply, and lovingly, wrapped each sardine in pastry, brushed with beaten egg, and threw them into the oven for fifteen minutes.

Ruth scanned the suggestion of only serving one per person. "Is that all?" She closed the book. "Well, I certainly won't be trying that, Mrs Beeton." She set the hefty tome on the nightstand and lay down. "However, I wonder if Margaret would exchange that recipe for her steak and ale pie." Ruth yawned, "Worth a shot," and approximately two seconds later, she was dreaming of Captain Barney's happy sheep jumping over a fence, and the one lucky tup chasing after them.

After a hearty breakfast of eggs, bacon, beans, sausages, black pudding, mounds of buttered toast, and not a single sardine in sight, Ruth considered herself refreshed and ready to tackle almost anything. She sat at the table in the dining hall with Greg, and polished off her second mug of tea.

The door burst open, and Margaret hurried in, out of breath. "Mirror."

Ruth looked at her phone. "Seven forty-five? What time do you call this?"

"I've been up for hours and was in the study, pacing up and down, waiting an excruciatingly long time for you to finish your darned breakfast. Anyway"—she threw her hands up—"it struck me."

Ruth cocked an eyebrow. "A mirror struck you?"

"Don't be ridiculous. That would be absurd. Can we be serious, please?"

Ruth winked at Greg. "My mistake. Go on."

Margaret gripped the back of a chair opposite. "That

infernal riddle. Kept me up all night. The part banging on about 'smile at me, and I'll return the favour.'"

"A mirror," Greg said. "The answer is a mirror."

Margaret lifted her chin. "Precisely."

Ruth got to her feet. "Come on."

They hurried to the study, and she added the word "*mirror*" to the blackboard, beneath the others on the list. Ruth took a picture with her phone to be extra cautious this time, and then angled the blackboard further away from the windows too.

They now seemed to have solved six out of the nine parts. So that left them with the remaining three lines: "When spoken to, I will always answer," "Get under my skin, you'll be sure to cry," and "Remember you're alive, even though they're dead."

Ruth dropped into a chair at the table, opposite her sister, and drummed her fingers on the house's blueprint as she considered the remaining riddles.

Greg attempted another search via his trusty smart-phone but drew a blank.

Charles sauntered into the room, rubbing his hands together. "Good morning one and all. How are things?"

"Awful," Ruth and Margaret said in unison.

Charles frowned at the blackboard for a few seconds, and then shrugged. "I give up." He sat in a chair by the fire-place, sighed, and crossed his legs. His gaze drifted to the patch of floor where Carter's life had ended abruptly. Charles shuffled in his seat and looked away.

Margaret glared at him. "You do realise your nefarious half-brother is arriving today? We only have eight and a half hours remaining."

"I'm as eager as you are to solve this nonsense, my darling." Charles swept two fingers across his moustache. "I simply know my limitations." His gaze moved between them. "But I must say I have faith in each and every one of you."

"What has gotten into you this morning?" Margaret frowned. When her husband didn't answer, she addressed Ruth. "It would be nice to solve this before lunch. That could leave us some breathing space to prepare for Noah's arrival." She glanced at the door. "Which reminds me, Ruth. I've asked Cook to prepare a meal for Merlin too. It will keep her busy. A tuna fish blend. High on nutrition, low on salt and calories."

Ruth smiled in surprise. "That's kind of you. I'm sure he'll love it."

"Merlin won't appreciate that," Greg said. "Sounds way too good for him. Better slap the tuna between a couple of slices of bread and let me have it instead." He beamed.

"That's fine," Margaret said. "Whatever you want. I'll ask Cook to throw away your steak sandwich and chunky chips." She inclined her head. "What shall I tell her to do with the slice of five-layer chocolate cake? Feed it to the pigs?"

Greg's smile faded.

"You've got pigs?" Ruth asked.

Margaret folded her arms. "We'll buy some."

Greg swallowed. "I— I really appreciate you, Aunty Margaret. Anyone tell you how young you look today?"

She waggled a finger at him. "Flattery will get you everywhere in this world, Gregory. Don't let anyone tell you otherwise."

"Speaking of steak." Ruth cupped a hand around her mouth and lowered her voice. "What about adding ale and pastry to it, and telling me what—"

"If you're once again attempting to extract my delicious

recipe . . ." Margaret's eyes narrowed. "Then forget it."

Ruth huffed and sat back. "Does Cook know how to make it?"

"Only I know the secret ingredient," Margaret said. "And I'll take the recipe to my grave."

Ruth muttered a few choice words, got up, and sauntered over to the blackboard. "These answers somehow relate to locations, right?"

"Given experience with my father's past riddles, I would say so," Charles said. "However, we don't know which of the answers relate to the first location."

Ruth focussed on the remaining lines of the riddle. "Remember you're alive, even though they're dead. Remember you're alive, even though they're dead." She peered at the others. "Any ideas? Anything at all?"

The others shrugged and shook their heads.

"Helpful. Thanks," Ruth murmured. "Get under my skin, you'll be sure to cry." She sighed. "Sounds like most of our childhood, Margaret. All our bickering."

"And adulthood."

Ruth took several more steps back, as if the riddle were a Magic Eye poster and the answer would suddenly pop out at her in glorious three dimensions.

It didn't.

Ten more excruciatingly exhausting minutes later, and they were no closer to solving it.

Ruth was about to walk away, get some fresh air, or leap off the nearest cliff, when an idea struck her. "Charles, your father usually only gave you one riddle at a time, right?"

"Correct."

"And to be clear about this—they would lead to one location within the house? A hiding place where you'd find your present?"

He nodded. "Or somewhere on the grounds."

"Henry didn't give you any other hints along the way?" Ruth asked.

"Nope."

"Don't feel too sorry for Charles," Margaret said. "He always had help from either his mother or me. Although . . ." She frowned at the blackboard. "This riddle is the longest I've seen Henry compose."

"Must have wanted to go out with a bang," Charles said. "If I didn't know there was a will hidden somewhere on the premises, I'd think it was a joke. An unsolvable puzzle to confound and annoy."

Ruth pinched the bridge of her nose as a tingle of a migraine threatened her grey matter. The day hadn't started out any easier than the previous, despite a good night's sleep, and she considered going back to bed as a viable alternative.

However, Ruth took a deep breath, and relaxed her thoughts. She cleared her mind as best she could, and focussed on the blackboard.

It all must mean something, but what?

Think, Morgan. Think.

"If these words are a clue to a location," she murmured, "perhaps they combine somehow."

However, taking them at face value, four words were physical objects; lawsuit was used as a noun; and the *U* was a letter of the alphabet.

Ruth groaned.

None of this helped her.

However, another one of the most important things her time on the force had taught her was that the simplest explanation was often the correct one.

Human nature was to overthink and make events more

complicated than they ought to be. Like a missing person had never simply walked off, but they'd been abducted.

In Ruth's experience, the best investigators always reduced crimes to their essence.

So, what's the simplest form of this riddle?

She scanned the list again. It still made little sense. Perhaps, if—

Ruth's eyes widened. "Wait."

Greg stood. "Have you found something?"

Ruth looked over at Charles. "Your father was fond of word games too?"

"Obsessed with them," Margaret said before he had a chance to answer. "Forced us to play most birthdays and Christmases, didn't he, Charles? Drove us insane. Watched that daily TV game show with something bordering religious fervour. The one with all the letters? Anagrams?"

Charles nodded wearily.

"And you didn't think to bring this up earlier?" Ruth said.

Margaret stared at her.

Ruth snatched up the chalk. "So what if all these seemingly random answers point to a bigger one? Combine them into a location." She took the first answer in the riddle, mushroom, and wrote the letter *M*. Then she left a blank space for the unsolved line that said, *Remember you're alive, even though they're dead*, and continued on with what they had: umbrella, stairs, blank, lawsuit, blank, letter *U*, and mirror.

The result was:

M_US_L_UM

Greg inclined his head. "That's a real word?"

Ruth's lips moved as she worked through various permutations, and then she landed on the only word she could think of that could possibly fit.

She smiled. For once in her life, and much to her surprise, Ruth had solved a word puzzle. More by fluke than skill, but she'd take the win.

Charles smiled back at her. "You have it?"

Ruth filled in the blank spaces on the blackboard and spelled out:

MAUSOLEUM

Greg's brow furrowed. "Mausoleum? As in a tomb?"

"Our family's mausoleum," Charles said. "We placed my father there. God rest his soul."

Ruth set the chalk down and rubbed her hands together. "A room without windows and doors." She pointed to that first part of the riddle.

"It doesn't have a door?" Greg asked.

Charles got to his feet. "A gate. It's open to the fresh air. All our family have lead-lined coffins. A tradition going back centuries." He motioned. "Shall we take a look?"

Greg screwed up his face. "Seriously?"

Margaret stood too, and as they left the room, she whispered, "Well, done, Ruth. Great progress."

Ruth beamed at her.

Perhaps the rest of the day would turn out fine after all.

She winced at the wayward thought and crossed herself.

After gathering their coats, the four of them headed outside.

To the left of the house, a low moss-covered stone wall

surrounded an area fifty feet on each side, with oak trees beyond, creating an enclosed space, perfect for quiet reflection.

An iron grate let out a long high-pitched screech of protest as Ruth pushed it open and stepped into the Andrews family graveyard.

Greg, Margaret, and Charles followed her along a brick path as it wound its way past tombstones, stone angels, and crosses.

Everyone was here: the entire Andrews clan stretching back generations and hundreds of years.

"Grandmama." Charles indicated a tombstone etched with a jigsaw pattern. "That's where my father inherited some of his unusual obsessions. My grandmother used to spend most Sunday afternoons playing games with him. Even in adulthood. It was how they remained close. Most memories I have of her are of the two of them laughing and arguing over a board."

"Trained from an early age to enjoy riddles." Ruth stopped in the far back corner, in front of a mausoleum, fifteen feet at its peak, with a portico held aloft by pillars.

A brass plaque bolted to a baroque gate declared it to be the final resting place of the more recent Andrews family members.

Ruth looked back at the grave marker with the puzzle pieces. "Why isn't your grandmother in here?"

"She had a thing about the dark." Charles pulled a bunch of keys from his pocket. "Grandmama wanted to rest outside, in the sunshine."

Ruth squinted up at the overcast grey sky. "Makes sense. Scotland's renowned for its year-round sunny days."

Charles unfastened the lock and swung the gate outward. "I'll wait here."

"Me too," Margaret said. "Holler if you need us."

Although Ruth would have preferred all of them to search inside, especially seeing as she didn't know what they were looking for, she opted not to press the issue.

Besides, Charles had only laid his father to rest a month prior, so that likely had something to do with his reluctance.

"Would it have been possible for Carter to gain access?" Ruth asked him.

"These keys remain hanging in the boot room," Charles said. "Anyone can go in. It's more than possible."

"Alec and Josh sweep the mausoleum out once a month during the winter," Margaret said. "As well as maintain the graveyard at other times of the year."

Ruth looked about. Although most of the tombstones were weathered from decades, if not hundreds of years of Scottish island weather, the lawn between them was manicured, weeded, and free of detritus.

Charles handed her a torch.

Ruth examined the gate, making sure there was no way it could accidentally slam shut with them inside. Again, the tight space didn't bother her, but Ruth's cleithrophobia gave her pause in most such situations.

Once satisfied she could escape the mausoleum should she need to, Ruth motioned for Greg to follow her inside. She took a deep breath and stepped over the threshold. However, Greg hung back.

Ruth furrowed her brow. "What's the matter?"

He swallowed. "Maddie said that Victor guy is fortunate to safely enter. Do you think he meant this place? It's booby-trapped? And the riddle? All that talk of 'Remember you're alive, even though they're dead.'"

Ruth tensed.

He had a point.

15

Ruth took a few minutes to examine the mausoleum gate and its frame, but it looked ordinary. No mechanisms. She also recalled the lines in the riddle that said, "Going up when it comes down, up and down, and yet I can't move," and there was no harm in being extra cautious.

She shone the torch at the wall, above and around the entrance—nothing but solid stone. Although never having had personal, hands-on experience with a real-life booby trap, Ruth couldn't make out any devices or contraptions.

However, given all the homemade devices in Henry's hidden office, it wouldn't have been off-brand for him to install something here.

Ruth addressed Margaret. "Just so you know, I'm doing this part specifically to make up for the Tammy Radcliffe incident."

Margaret lifted her chin. "Duly noted."

After another sweep of the torch to make sure, Ruth waved Greg inside. "Come on. I need your eyes."

With obvious reluctance, he followed her in, and Ruth muttered a prayer under her breath.

The mausoleum's interior was as she'd expected: alcoves on the left and right, stacked four high, in three columns, most blanked off with granite plugs, and with plaques affixed.

The beam of the torch scanned a few of the names: Thomas Andrews, 1922–1943, *"died serving his country"*; Brianna Andrews, 1925–1998, *"missed by many, loved by all"*; and Malcolm Andrews, 1885–1956, *"one whiskey too many."*

Ruth walked to the far end of the mausoleum, to a stone altar. Placed on top were two candlesticks, sans their candles; a golden cross on a stand; and a Bible with a mother-of-pearl cover, inlaid with gold.

She handed Greg the torch, picked up the Bible, and riffled through as he aimed the beam at the pages. No folded notes or torn leaves tumbled out.

"Would have been too easy," Ruth muttered as she set it down.

"Grandma?" Greg's expression had turned downcast. "Who do you think murdered Carter?"

Ruth sighed. Truth was, she had no real idea, and that was rare for her. Usually in these types of situations, she had a suspicion, right or wrong, and at the very least an inkling. "I'm not sure. It was someone close to him because they were both in the study, on that balcony together."

Greg glanced at the entrance to the mausoleum and lowered his voice. "If they hadn't finished with the riddle yet, why did someone kill him? I mean, it doesn't make sense."

Ruth rested a hand on his shoulder. "We'll find the answers. I promise."

"Uncle Charles and Aunty Margaret are relying on us. What if we fail? They'll lose everything."

Ruth stepped back. "The road to success is littered with the bodies of failed attempts."

Greg shivered and glanced round at all the crypts.

Ruth forced a smile. "We won't give up. Together, we'll find Henry's will and bring the killer to justice." She looked across the mausoleum, toward the entrance.

"You don't think Uncle Henry hid it in one of these alcoves?" Greg asked. "Behind a coffin or something?" He grimaced. "Maybe *in* a coffin."

"I hope not," Ruth said. "Anyway, it's too exposed out here." And too gruesome to think about. Although, Henry coming to pay his respects to past family members would've been an excellent time to access any hiding places. It wasn't such a terrible idea. "The ghosts could guard the valuables." Ruth raised her hands and waggled her fingers. "Woohooo."

Greg gave her a disgusted look. "You're not funny."

Ruth stuck out her bottom lip. "Comedy is subjective."

"Really subjective," Greg said. "Because you're the only one who finds you amusing." He shone the torch around the crypts. "Can we go now? There's nothing here."

"Not until we find something of use," Ruth said. "There's a reason the riddle spelled out the word."

"Find what, though?"

Ruth took the torch from him. "I'll let you know when it shows up." Ruth edged down one wall, scanning the plaques.

There was Jeremy Andrews, born 1817, died 1878, and next to him was "*his loving wife,*" who'd lived from 1823 to 1899. Then a lad who'd died at sixteen, during World War I, and a girl who, judging by the dates, was his sister, and had died at six years old, a decade earlier, of scarlet fever.

Ruth shook her head. "So sad." She moved down the

other wall, scanning the rest of the plaques, and she stopped at the freshest of the bunch: Henry Andrews.

His epitaph read,

A long game, played well.

"He really was obsessed." Ruth was about to continue on when something caught her eye. "Greg?" He hurried over to her, and she pointed. "Look at this." Ruth ran the tip of her finger over several raised bumps beneath the inscription. "It's braille."

Greg frowned. "Did Uncle Henry go blind?"

Ruth handed him the torch. "Angle it across the dots. I'll see if I can get a picture of them." She removed her phone and, after a few attempts, got a clear shot.

Ruth examined the result. "Definitely braille, and not morse code. They're in cells of six dots." She squinted. There were five cells in total. The first one comprised a backward *L* shape, then the next was a single dot, followed by a group of four, another four, and a single dot again.

"Can you read it?" Greg asked.

"Yes, Gregory. I learned braille at the same time I mastered Tai Chi and competitive duck herding." Ruth rolled her eyes and pointed to the exit. "But I'm a little rusty, so let's see if my sister and brother-in-law know anything about this." Ruth stepped from the mausoleum and blinked in the daylight.

Margaret and Charles stood a little way away, huddled together, talking in whispers. When they spotted Ruth, they stepped apart.

She strode over to them. "What's going on?"

"Nothing," Margaret said in the least convincing way imaginable.

Charles looked at a spot on the ground.

"This is not the time for more secrets. My heart can't take extra surprises right now." Ruth glanced at Greg as he joined them, and she folded her arms. "If you want us to find your father's will, we need to be open and honest with each other." She looked between her sister and brother-in-law with what she hoped came across as a serious expression. "Spill it."

Charles took a breath. "We have a misgiving."

"*You* have a misgiving," Margaret corrected. "I think you're being silly. It was nothing."

Ruth's chest tightened. "What was nothing?"

"Well, with everything that's happened"—Charles straightened his tie—"it completely slipped my mind." He focussed on Ruth and whispered, "Yesterday morning, before breakfast, as I was about to come down the stairs, I found the horse statue missing."

Greg's brow furrowed. "The one on the landing? But it was there earlier."

"That's the thing," Charles said. "I went to speak to Carter—"

"You talked to him right before he died?" Ruth said, incredulous. "And you didn't mention this before?" She couldn't believe what she was hearing.

Charles held up a hand. "I couldn't find Carter at the time. So, I sought out Betty and Maddie. They denied knowing anything about the missing horse. They didn't seem to believe me, so I insisted one of them should go and confirm it for themselves. Maddie went." Charles brushed a couple of fingers over his moustache and looked sheepish. "However, she returned and said the statue was there, as it always is. Astonished, I went back to see for myself, and the girl was right." He shrugged. "Utterly baffling."

Charles offered Ruth an apologetic look. "So that's why I'd forgotten all about it until a moment ago. Totally slipped my mind."

"Could you have been mistaken?" she asked. "Missed it somehow?" After all, he'd been under an enormous amount of stress, and with a house filled with so many valuable objects, he could be forgiven for mistaking the placement of things.

"Someone might have removed it to clean," Greg suggested. "Then put it back." Although, he didn't look convinced by this explanation.

Charles shook his head. "The staff were all working on breakfast, as they do each morning. The statue is far too heavy. It's dusted in situ by either Betty or Maddie, which is why I went to them next."

Ruth blew out a puff of air. "What's your misgiving?"

Charles opened his mouth to respond, hesitated, and closed it again.

"He suspects Maddie wasn't telling the truth," Margaret said.

"It was something in the way she reacted," Charles said. "At first, neither Betty nor Maddie seemed to believe me, and then when she checked for herself, Maddie came back white as a sheet. She wouldn't look me in the eye, and when she spoke to Betty, it was as if she thought I'd lost my marbles. Maddie is usually so sweet and happy-go-lucky. Totally out of character."

"And an hour or two later, Carter was dead," Ruth muttered. "Odd."

Maddie had also been the one to overhear Carter shouting at someone.

"She has something to do with Carter's death?" Greg asked, as if reading Ruth's mind.

"We'll have to check out that statue, and speak to her about it."

Perhaps Maddie had broken the statue while cleaning, glued it back together, and then returned it, hence her reaction.

Margaret nodded to the mausoleum. "Did you find anything of use?"

Ruth held up her phone and flicked through the photos. "Can either of you two read braille?"

"Braille?" Charles' eyebrows lifted. "No. Why?" He squinted at the images. "Is that what those dots are?"

"They're on your father's plaque," Ruth said. "You didn't know about them?"

"I had no idea." Charles glanced at his wife, and she shook her head. "Father made all the arrangements. Margaret and I have no acquaintances who are visually impaired."

"Did Henry?" Ruth asked.

"Not that I know of." Charles stared at the sky. "He donated to a care home on the mainland with some degree of frequency, but never mentioned anyone blind. I suppose it's possible."

"Part of his game, no doubt," Margaret said. "Probably has some deep meaning only known to Henry."

Greg brought up a site dealing with braille on his phone and navigated to the section with the alphabet.

"Let's do this in the study." Although they seemed to be alone, Ruth felt a twinge of unease deciphering the next clue out in the open. She addressed Charles. "On our way back, I'd like to check out that horse statue you mentioned."

He locked the mausoleum gate, and then the four of them returned to the house.

In the entrance hall, Ruth stopped at the bottom of the

stairs and pointed to the study door. "Margaret and Greg, feel free to make a start on decoding the braille. We'll catch up to you."

"I'll fetch us some hot drinks," Margaret said. "And check on the staff." She marched off. "Come along, Gregory."

He eyed the study door, then traipsed after her.

Ruth and Charles headed upstairs.

On the first landing, Ruth examined the statue of a horse on a plinth. It stood eighteen inches high, had a long mane, and appeared to be cast in bronze. Although Ruth's knowledge of sculpture started and ended with, "Ooh, *I like that.*"

An octagonal base formed part of the statue, but there were no inscriptions, and certainly no cryptic phrases, riddles, or braille.

Once she'd examined the horse from all sides, Ruth stepped back, her lips pursed. "I think someone took this for a reason, and then returned it once you'd noticed it missing."

"Part of the riddle?" Charles asked.

"Perhaps, but the question is what could anyone hope to gain by moving it?" Ruth waved a hand. "Can you pick the statue up, please? I'd like to look underneath."

"It's heavy," Charles said. "But I can manage. After all, I put it here in the first place."

"You did?" Ruth said. "Why?"

"My mother had a ghastly giraffe statue here for my entire life. Gave me nightmares as a child. When my father passed, I—" Charles swallowed. "I disposed of the giraffe and replaced it with this fine horse. It was hers too, so I'm sure she wouldn't have minded." He heaved the statue from the pedestal. "Yep. Just as heavy as I remember."

"Meaning someone can't have taken it far." Ruth peered underneath. "Nothing. Not even an artist's mark."

Charles set it back down. "Why on earth would they go to all the trouble of removing it, only to replace it again? Surely if they wanted to look underneath, as we did, they could set the statue on the floor. Why take it somewhere?" He scratched his head and looked up. "Light is perfectly adequate here, and if they were careful, they could angle the statue back enough to see."

Ruth examined the pedestal, but it appeared unremarkable. "How long ago did she die?"

Charles blew out a puff of air and stared at the ceiling. "Got to be coming up on twenty-six years now. Seems like only yesterday."

Ruth had met Jean Andrews a handful of times, and recalled her as a kind-faced, poshly spoken woman, who had a fondness for boiled sweets and poetry.

"Do you know anything about this piece?" Ruth asked. "The artist? Anything that might help us? Its provenance?"

"I'm afraid not. Horses were my mother's thing." Charles smoothed his moustache. "As I say, it belonged to her. After she died, Dad sold my mother's livestock. The stables have stood empty ever since. These statues and her awards are all that's left of her legacy."

"Statues?" Ruth said. "There are more?"

Charles glanced along the nearest corridor. "Down there you'll find Mother's old sewing room, a spare bedroom now used for storage, and the horse room." He waved a hand to the second door of three. "See for yourself."

Ruth strode down the corridor and opened the door.

For a few seconds she remained frozen on the spot as her mind tried to catch up with her eyes.

Charles leaned through the doorframe and flicked on a bank of switches.

Lights sprang to life, illuminating display cabinets that took up three of the four walls, full of silver trophies, medals, and shields.

Ruth's chin hit the floor.

"Mother was quite the competitor," Charles said. "Dressage and jumping."

What must have been a thousand rosettes of varying colours filled the remaining wall, most declaring first place.

Ruth strode over to a table overflowing with silver-framed pictures. Each one followed a theme: they showed a horse, Charles' mother, and various podiums. She picked up an image of Jean accepting a large trophy. "Your mother looked happy."

Charles smiled. "She was born to ride, so to speak."

Ruth set the photo frame down and turned to three octagonal plinths in the middle of the room. All three had statues; the ones at the ends were of horses in standing poses, but the one in the middle was an almost exact copy of the bronze statue on the landing, only this one appeared to be made of porcelain and painted in fine detail.

"That's where I took the bronze statue from." Charles motioned to the pedestal. "Put this one in its place."

"We need to speak to Maddie and find out what spooked her." Ruth was about to suggest they go look for her when a scream made her spin back to the door. "Who's that?"

The two of them ran from the room and down the stairs in time to meet Margaret and Greg in the hallway.

"Where did that come from?" Margaret said, her eyes wild.

"We were about to ask you the same thing," Charles said.

Hurried footfalls drew their attention to the right. The

four of them ran, with Ruth in the lead, and she raced into the dining hall.

Alec and Josh stood by the door.

"What on earth is going on in here?" Margaret said. "Who screamed?"

Josh pointed to the far end of the hall.

A small group had gathered. Helen the cook sat in a chair, and Betty rubbed her back, while Ray stared.

Laid at his feet, facedown, was Maddie, with a medieval axe embedded between her shoulder blades.

16

R uth stood rooted to the spot as the full weight of the situation crashed down around her. Someone had now killed Maddie, and there was no pretending it was an accident this time.

"I can't believe this is happening." Margaret clapped a hand over her mouth and staggered back.

"Poor girl." Charles screwed up his face and looked away. "What kind of animal would do this?"

Ruth faced her sister and brother-in-law. "Leave." Neither of them moved. "*Leave,*" Ruth repeated, more insistent this time, and she stepped into their line of sight. "Call the police."

Charles snapped out of his trance, put an arm around his wife, and guided her from the grand dining hall.

Ruth indicated for the groundskeepers, Alec and Josh, to do the same.

"We'll go straight to my cottage and remain there until called for," Alec said as he steered Josh out.

Ruth took a breath. "Wait." They turned back to her.

"You were in the garden when someone screamed?" She glanced over at Helen, Betty, and Ray.

Alec pointed down the hallway. "Right there. Just outside that door. About to tend to the borders. We came running the moment we heard. You got here a few seconds after us."

"You have a key to that door?" Ruth asked.

"No," Alec said. "We don't have keys to the house. Betty opens the doors every morning, and locks them at night."

Josh nodded his agreement. "We— We only go in the k-kitchen."

"Did you see anyone else?" Ruth asked them.

Alec and Josh looked at each other, but both shook their heads.

"That's all, thanks." Ruth faced the room again while the two of them left via the back door.

"I feel sick." Greg dropped to a chair and bent forward, breathing hard.

"Don't look at the body, but stay here if you can. I might need you." Ruth marched to the other end of the dining hall.

Ray continued to stare at Maddie's body, his face pale.

Ruth composed herself. "What happened?"

Betty swallowed. "We found her like that." She motioned toward Maddie's lifeless form but avoided looking at her.

Ruth eyed all three of them in turn. "Describe what you did and what you saw."

Although they were clearly in a state of shock, it was imperative she got their accounts before recollections became fuzzy. In other words, the quicker she got their statements, the closer they'd be to the truth.

Carter falling to his death was one thing, but a young girl like this . . . Ruth balled her fists.

"Helen and I came through the door." Betty pointed to the far end of the room. "Walked down there." She indicated the other side of the table. "Carrying those." Betty nodded at a silver platter. "Setting the table for lunch."

Ruth looked at the time on her phone: 10:22 a.m.

"Helen and I were talking." Betty continued to rub the cook's back. "When I noticed Ray standing there, and I asked what he was doing." She shook her head. "We circled the table, and that's when we saw . . . Maddie." Her eyes filled with tears.

"Who screamed?" Ruth asked.

"Me," Helen said in a weak voice.

"And why are you all in here?" Betty opened her mouth to answer, but Ruth held up a hand. "I mean, after what happened yesterday, you were supposed to remain either in your rooms or the kitchen."

"We thought it was okay, as long as we stuck together," Betty said.

Ruth looked at Ray. "You found Maddie first?"

His gaze hadn't moved.

"Ray?"

"What?" he said in a hoarse voice. He snapped out of it. "Oh, yes. Yes, I found her."

"Why was she alone?"

"I—" Ray squeezed the back of his neck. "I was only in the bathroom a couple of minutes."

Ruth studied him. "You left her alone? How long was it before these two arrived?" She indicated Helen and Betty.

"We were apart for five minutes at most," Betty said. "Ray and Maddie brought in those." She pointed at trays with stacks of cutlery, napkins, and plates.

"I didn't do it," Ray murmured. "I swear." His face had

drained of colour, and sweat glistened on his brow, sticking strands of red hair to his face.

"Then who did?" Ruth asked in a calm tone.

After all, that was exactly what a killer would say.

"I don't know." Ray mopped the sweat with a handkerchief.

Ruth's attention returned to Helen. "Why were you in here?" After all, she was a cook, and her domain was the kitchen.

"We were staying in pairs," Helen said. "Also discussing the surprise and setting up for this evening."

Ruth's brow furrowed. "What surprise?"

"Your birthday," Betty said.

"My birthday's not until June," Ruth said, incredulous.

Betty nodded. "The mistress told us last week she wanted a feast in your honour. Said she'd not celebrated a birthday with you since you were kids."

This news took Ruth aback, and now she came to think of it, Margaret was right; they'd not spent any birthdays in each other's presence since their teens. They always sent cards and presents without fail, but her sister had never shown the slightest inkling of wanting them to do something together.

Even though a twinge of guilt gnawed at Ruth's stomach for not having suggested they meet up for their birthdays once in forty-eight years, it somehow never came up.

Besides, now was a terrible time to celebrate, what with two murders in as many days, and a hidden will to locate.

Ruth shook herself. "Who was the last person to see Maddie alive?"

"She was helping us." Betty pointed to the corner of the table and a stack of linen. "Maddie came in here with Ray.

They were supposed to have it all set up by the time we got here."

Helen put her head in her hands and sobbed.

Ruth motioned to the door, and she softened her tone. "You two should go. Have a lie down. Don't leave the house, though. Stay close to each other."

Betty helped Helen to her feet, and they traipsed from the room.

Ruth stepped beside Ray as he stared down at Maddie's lifeless body again.

"I liked her," he said. "She was funny." His gaze rose to Ruth's. Sadness twisted his face and his eyes welled with tears.

"I'll do everything I can to find the person responsible." Ruth steered him away, and as they headed to the door, she asked, "Is there anything you can tell me?"

"I— I'm not sure what you mean."

Ruth gestured for Greg to remain seated. When she and Ray reached the doorway, Ruth faced him and lowered her voice. "You went to the bathroom?"

He pointed to a door father down the corridor. "I was only gone a few minutes, I swear."

"You came straight from the kitchen with Maddie?"

"Yes."

"Did you see anyone else?"

"No."

"Hear anything?"

"No."

Ruth pictured Maddie walking into the grand dining hall with an armful of linen. "She went ahead? Didn't wait for you?"

"Maddie was supposed to make a start setting the table-cloths." His expression glazed over. "I thought she'd be fine."

"What mood did she seem to be in this morning?" Ruth asked.

"Her usual bouncy self." Ray's voice cracked. "She— She was shook up about Carter, of course, but we all were. I mean, *are*. When it came to Maddie, she was always happy. Tried to cheer us up." A flicker of desperate sadness crossed his features, and then he looked Ruth dead in the eyes. "I don't know why someone would want her dead. She wasn't a threat to anyone. It's not fair."

Ruth studied him. "And to be crystal clear, you didn't pass anyone on your way? Not another living soul?"

"No."

Ruth signalled for Ray to remain where he was, then she walked past and looked to the left. At the end was the door to the garden—the one Alec and Josh had used. She strode over and peered out.

Beyond stood the courtyard, with a wheelbarrow, a spade, and a mound of soil on a tarpaulin next to the border. Clearly, this was the spot where they'd been working when they heard Helen's scream and came running.

The timing may need some clarification, but everyone appeared to be accounted for. For a brief moment she thought about Captain Barney. *Could he be the murdering type?* Somehow, she doubted it, but couldn't rule out anything at this stage.

Ruth did an about-face, marched back down the corridor, past the dining hall door, and stopped in the main hallway. She looked about. There were several more doors. If Maddie's killer had been fast enough, a few minutes was plenty of time to murder her and escape without running into anyone else. He, or she, could have gone in any direction, other than to the courtyard or heading to the kitchen, where they would have bumped into the others.

Ruth hurried back to Ray. "Where are the staff quarters?"

"Above the kitchen and pantry."

"They have their own staircase, right?" Ruth vaguely remembered a tour of the house Margaret had given her decades prior, before Henry banned Ruth and John from the island. They'd not gone inside that wing, but she recalled peering through a window at the side of the house.

"There's another way up," Ray said. "But it's an emergency exit. An alarm triggers if that door's opened."

Ruth tried to get a grip of her thought process before the police arrived. "Please make sure everyone remains in their quarters and stays there for the time being. No one is to leave, understood?" She felt like she was repeating herself from the previous day. Ruth thought she'd been clear enough then. "If you want food and drinks, that's fine, but again, the three of you must go down to the kitchen together. No exceptions."

"In case one of us is a murderer," Ray muttered.

Ruth sighed. "Unless the killer is hiding out somewhere on this island, it must—" She stopped as a thought struck her—a figure in a cave.

Is there someone else hiding in this house? The phantom?

Ray frowned. "Something wrong?"

Ruth straightened her face. "Thank you." She waved a hand. Ray traipsed off toward the kitchen, and as soon as he was out of earshot, Ruth hurried back to Greg. "How are you feeling?"

He looked up at her. "Do you ever get used to it?"

"Not even a little bit," Ruth said. "It's more a case of tolerating the ugliness in the name of doing what's right. Uncovering monsters." She glanced over at Maddie's body.

As a police officer, she'd used the horrific crimes as a

way to galvanise her resolve. It always angered her, but that only increased Ruth's determination to uncover the culprit.

"What about the police?" Greg asked.

"We will touch nothing," Ruth said. "So there's zero chance we'll contaminate the crime scene. Some of our fingerprints will already be in here from earlier."

Greg shook his head. "I mean, it's their job to catch a murderer, not yours."

Although Ruth agreed, her deep sense of justice would not allow her to simply turn her back and walk away. "You can stay here." She strode down the dining hall and stopped at Maddie's body.

The poor girl lay on her front, rolled a fraction to one side as though she'd attempted to reach behind her back.

Ruth's gaze moved to the wall. There were two empty hooks where the axe had once rested. Given that, and the limited time involved, it meant the killer had likely acted on the spur of the moment, grabbing the nearest weapon, rather than anything premeditated.

Kneeling by Maddie's body, Ruth scanned the girl from head to toe, but found nothing out of the ordinary. Well, apart from the aforementioned axe, of course. There were no bruises or scrapes, no signs of a struggle.

Maddie had been facing away from her attacker when they struck, so that, coupled with no defensive wounds, indicated a surprise from behind. Therefore, it was someone she knew and felt at ease with because she would have heard their footfalls on the stone floor.

"Definitely someone living on this island." Ruth straightened and looked over at Greg.

He stared at the wall. "I don't think that's a good thing. Makes it worse."

Ruth shrugged. "It keeps our list of suspects down, but also puts us directly in harm's way."

"And we can't leave because someone sank Captain Barney's boat."

"We *can* leave anytime we want," Ruth said. "In theory. All we have to do is call for someone on the mainland to come and pick us up. Margaret and Charles mentioned they know a 'Fisherman Fred'. Although, he's not back until late afternoon. We could find someone else to ferry us home."

"Should we go?" Greg asked.

Ruth gave him a sympathetic smile. "I don't think the police would be very happy about that. We're suspects."

"I'd be happy," Greg said. "Very happy. I don't ever want to come back here."

Ruth hadn't expected to return to Ivywick Island either, and yet here she was. Her memory drifted to John, the cave, and the shadow of a person they'd seen on the other side of the wall.

Who was that? And, more importantly, do they have anything to do with what's happened here?

Although, Ruth dismissed the idea because, for one, that had been decades ago. That person may be long gone. Especially with the cave crumbled and off-limits. And secondly, Maddie had clearly known her killer, which forced Ruth to remain with her current hypothesis that it was a fellow staff member known to all of them, rather than the elusive phantom.

She eyed the axe handle. The police would dust it for fingerprints, and hopefully the perpetrator would swiftly be brought to justice.

Ruth took a step toward Greg but froze midstride.

Another hook on the wall sat empty. "What was here?" Ruth stared at it.

Greg's brow furrowed. "I don't know. Can't remember."

Ruth turned on the spot, and her gaze scanned every inch of the walls, over each of the swords and armour, hunting for anything else she might have missed, but nothing seemed out of place or absent.

"Police are on their way." Charles appeared at the door with Margaret.

Ruth edged over to the wall and squinted at the empty hook again.

"I don't feel so great," Greg murmured.

"Go with your aunty Margaret," Ruth said. "Charles and I will meet you in the study."

Greg shuffled off with Margaret.

Charles stared at Maddie's lifeless body for a few seconds, then cringed and looked away. "It's a tragedy." He focussed on Ruth with a serious expression. "Any suspects?"

"Everyone is a suspect right now."

"Please tell me you have someone particular in mind."

"Well, the only people we know for sure didn't kill her are you, me, Margaret, and Greg. Everyone else is fair game."

Charles' eyes narrowed. "A devil among us. How do we flush them out?"

"I'm working on it." Ruth pointed at the empty hook. "What was here?"

Charles' eyebrows knitted. "Family coat of arms." He glanced about. "Has someone taken it?"

"Can you describe what it looks like?"

"Around ten inches high, the same wide: a shield shape painted in gold, black, white, and blue, with a carved relief of a horse ridden by a knight." Charles looked about again. "I have no idea why someone would remove it. Been in that exact spot since before I was born. Passed down through the generations. Family names on the back. Mine now must be added, to keep up the tradition."

"Is there anything special about it?" Ruth asked. "Any reason someone would take it?"

"Not that I can think of. Not unless someone wants to prevent my name from being included."

Ruth let out a slow breath.

"You think it has something to do with the riddle?"

Ruth pursed her lips. "Without seeing it for myself, I don't know."

"Shall we go?"

Charles went to leave but Ruth called, "Was there anything else written on it?"

He turned back. "Only the Andrews of Ivywick family motto across the front."

Ruth inclined her head. "Which is?"

"Victrix Fortunae Sapientia." Charles lifted his chin. "Wisdom, the conqueror of fortune."

Ruth gasped in realisation. "Say that again."

"Wisdom, the conqueror of fortune."

"No, not the translation." Ruth waved a hand in Maddie's direction. "She overheard Carter arguing with someone. Maddie recalled him shouting, 'Victor's fortunate to safely enter.'" Ruth thrust a finger at the empty space on the wall. "What he really said was—"

Charles' eyebrows lifted. "Victrix Fortunae Sapientia."

17

In the study, Ruth added the words, *"Victrix Fortunae Sapientia"* to the blackboard.

Greg sat at a table and watched her.

Ruth stepped back as a renewed urgency coursed through her limbs, driving her on with single-minded determination.

After the terrible events of the past two days, she refused to allow the killer to beat them to the will's hiding place, and certainly not to take another life along the way.

They had to solve this puzzle, and fast.

Margaret stomped into the room with Charles. "The staff are terrified and paranoid in equal measure. So am I."

"Can you blame them?" Charles said.

Margaret folded her arms. "Helen refuses to come out of her room. She's locked and barricaded the door. I tried to explain the three of them are better off sticking together, but she will not listen to reason. There's no getting through to her. Figuratively or literally."

"Did you tell Betty and Ray to at least stay together?" Ruth asked.

"I reminded them," Margaret said. "But if the killer is one of those two, I don't see how that will be of any help. They're better off following Helen's lead—locking themselves in their rooms until the police arrive and sort out this mess." She huffed. "Which reminds me, we got a call from the detective with some bad news."

Charles sighed. "Haven't we had enough?"

"Indeed, we have," Margaret said. "But with Captain Barney's boat out of commission, they have no way to get here."

"What about old George?" Charles asked.

"He's in the Maldives."

Charles' eyebrows rose. "Good for him. He's the palest person I know."

"When he returns," Margaret said, "he'll be the reddest person you know."

Greg stifled a laugh.

Margaret sat opposite him at the table. "Unless we expect the detective to row across, or hire a novelty paddleboat in the shape of a swan, they'll have to wait until Fred returns from his fishing trip." Margaret addressed Charles. "I told Detective Murray we've already arranged for Fred to collect your half-brother and the lawyers at four, so they will hitch a ride at the same time."

"From now on, I don't want you wandering off on your own," Charles said in what he clearly thought was a firm tone.

Margaret cocked an eyebrow at her husband. "The killer is welcome to take their shot."

"If they know anything about you"—Ruth pictured her sister punching them square on the nose—"they'll steer well clear."

"Precisely." Margaret cleared her throat. "What should we do with Maddie?"

"She'll have to stay where she is," Ruth said.

"For five hours?" Margaret blew out a puff of air and studied the blackboard.

"What about Captain Barney?" Greg asked. "Who's watching him?"

"I've spoken to Barney on the telephone," Margaret said. "And I have explained the tragic events. He was blissfully unaware. Still ranting about his boat."

Charles brushed his moustache. "How did the fellow take it?"

"As to be expected under the circumstances." Margaret adjusted her blouse sleeves. "With shock and dismay. I suggested he stay with Alec and Josh until the police sort out this mess, but he didn't want to do that. Said he couldn't trust anyone but himself. So he agreed to remain in his cottage until otherwise called for. Captain Barney has plenty of dinosaur programs recorded. Will keep him occupied for days."

"Dinosaurs?" Greg asked.

"He's mad about them," Charles said. "If Barney had his way, he'd dig up half the island hunting for fossils."

"Greg would join him," Ruth said.

Charles let out a slow breath. "It's not as if Barney's needed right now. Not with his boat on the bottom of the sea."

"Agreed," Margaret said. "Barney is still angry about that, so I think it's best he tends to the sheep and takes some time off."

"While we're on the subject," Ruth said. "Why did you let the staff out earlier? I thought we agreed to keep them where they were until we get to the bottom of all this?"

"I didn't give them the all clear," Margaret said. "They took it upon themselves. Thought that with Carter's body in the coal shed, and you having interviewed everyone, they could go about their business, as long as they stayed in pairs." She rolled her eyes.

Ruth chose not to bring up the fact she knew why Maddie, Ray, Betty, and Helen had been in the dining hall, for fear of triggering her sister into thinking Ruth blamed her for Maddie's death.

Margaret frowned at the blackboard. "What's the Andrews family motto doing on there?"

"Someone stole the crest from the dining hall," Charles said. "We figured it's the same person who's done poor Maddie in."

Margaret's eyebrows rose. "Why would they take it?"

"One thing at a time." Ruth studied the picture of Henry's grave plaque on her phone. "Do we have the translation from the braille?" she asked Greg. Ruth hoped they hadn't missed any other important clues with all the distractions.

"I've checked out a couple of websites." Greg held up his phone with the internet open. "I think the backward *L* part could be a numeric indicator. Which means the dot, four dots, four dots again, and then another single dot are the numbers: one, seven, seven, and then one."

Ruth wrote them on the blackboard.

"Is that a PIN?" Greg asked.

Margaret faced Charles. "Ring any bells?"

He shook his head. "The bell tower is well and truly empty, I'm afraid."

"Any safes? A combination lock?"

"None."

Ruth stared at the four-digit number, then she scanned

the list of words, and then back to the number again. She let out a breath. "In plain sight."

A memory rushed forward, one from Ruth's time as a Metropolitan police officer, serving central London.

On one sunny July day, with the temperature so high that even air-conditioning on full blast struggled to keep up, they'd gotten a call Ruth always dreaded: that of a missing person. For they seldom turned out to have a happy ending.

Ruth and another officer, Constable Miles Baker, arrived at a block of flats. They'd gone in to find the elevator out of order, which at first Ruth was glad of, but then they'd had to climb eight floors.

By the time Ruth had reached the top, sweat soaked her uniform and she wanted to pass out.

Baker leaned against the wall, breathing hard. "That's your fault."

She cocked her head at him. "How do you figure?"

"You jinxed us," Baker said. "You grumbled in the car about this call being in a block of flats, and how you'd have to avoid the lift and climb floors." He panted. "You jinxed that elevator and made me have to climb with you."

Ruth cracked a smile. "Now you know how I feel."

Baker pointed down the hallway. "Let's go."

When they found the right door, he went to knock, only to find it open and a distraught woman in her thirties pacing, crying, on the verge of a nervous breakdown. Her ninety-year-old father with dementia had gone missing.

While Baker interviewed her, Ruth checked that all the windows were locked, and looked inside cupboards and under furniture in all the rooms, which included two bedrooms, before returning to the sitting room.

Coats hung from hooks by the front door, above a pair of

men's shoes and a walking cane. Next to those were a pair of women's black leather shoes.

The daughter, a nurse working double shifts, had come home to find her father in his usual spot—his favourite armchair in front of the TV. However, after making herself a cup of tea and relaxing on the sofa, the overworked, exhausted nurse had fallen asleep. She guessed only for twenty minutes, but when she'd awoken, her father had vanished.

She was understandably distressed, given his state of declining mental health and the current heat wave, plus he'd never wandered off before.

Ruth eyed her cold mug of tea. "What's his name?"

"William. William Clarence." The nurse explained her father had seemed down for the past few days, and kept talking about his childhood in the countryside.

"The front door was open when we arrived," Baker said.

The nurse nodded. "When I called you, I opened it."

Ruth looked back. "Was it locked before?"

"Only from the outside."

"William can easily open it?" Baker asked.

"He can, but he's never done that before." The nurse dropped to the sofa and sobbed.

Ruth checked the old man's room again. William had taped pictures to the walls: wild birds, forests, fields, blue skies with scattered clouds.

"You think he's headed to the country?" Baker asked from the door.

Ruth looked back at him. "Does he have a bus pass?"

"Hold on." Baker disappeared for a moment and then returned. "He does, but she has it in her handbag."

Ruth stared at the pictures. "He's wearing slippers. Walking shoes and cane are by the door."

Baker looked. "He could have forgotten them."

Ruth shrugged.

"But you don't think so?"

She faced him. "One more floor, right?"

"Of this building?" Baker screwed up his face. "I think so. Nine storeys. Yes. Why?"

"Be right back." Ruth hurried from the bedroom, gave the nurse a sympathetic smile, and rushed from the flat.

In the stairwell, she hesitated, and then headed on up.

Another couple of flights of stairs later, she'd passed by the ninth floor and reached a door to the roof. Someone had pushed the emergency bar down, and it stood ajar. Ruth stepped through.

An elderly gentleman sat with his back pressed against the wall, eyes closed, and a smile on his lips.

Ruth let out a sigh of relief. "William?"

He opened his eyes, and the smile faded once he took in her uniform. "Am I in trouble?"

That incident, and countless others during her time on the force, had taught Ruth a couple of valuable lessons: the simplest explanation was the most likely, and answers were usually staring you in the face.

She eyed the numbers on the blackboard, and her mindset shifted. All the answers to the riddle were in plain sight, starting with the mausoleum and the braille. That was the start of the trail Henry had left behind. Her attention drifted to the word *mirror* in the list. "I know what it means."

"The number?" Margaret's face brightened.

"They're all linked. One leads to another. As you'd expected, Henry's left a path to follow." Ruth broke her gaze, and with a wave of excitement coursing through her veins, she practically skipped across the study.

Margaret, Charles, and Greg jumped to their feet and rushed after her.

"Where are we going?" Greg asked.

Ruth headed up the stairs with renewed determination and hope.

On the landing, she hurried into the corridor and stopped outside her bedroom door. Ruth waited for the other three to catch up, and said to Charles, "I believe your father is using parts of the house, and objects you recognise, tied into the riddles. He wants you, and only you, to find the will." Ruth waved at her bedroom door. "What did this used to be before you turned it into a guest suite?"

When she'd visited the house with John all those years prior, they'd stayed in a room on the next floor up.

"That used to be my bedroom," Charles said. "When Margaret and I married, my father had the second master suite decorated and furnished to our taste. We moved in there." He motioned over his shoulder. "Father turned this one into a guest suite."

Ruth opened the door and beckoned them into the vestibule. She faced the baroque mirror. It was six feet high, including all the elaborate scrollwork, and four wide. Ruth only had a passing interest in antiques. "Who's this?" she asked her grandson, and pointed to a section of the frame's carving depicting a woman's head wearing a plumed helmet.

"That's a bust of Minerva," Greg said. "The Roman goddess of wisdom."

"A little ostentatious for my taste," Margaret said. "But stunning nonetheless. What's your point, Ruth?"

She pointed at a date at the bottom of the frame.

Margaret leaned in. "1771."

"Seems about right," Greg said.

However, Margaret's eyes widened. "The number you transcribed from the braille."

Ruth examined the lettering in close detail. It was slightly out of line and raised, with a different tint of gold leaf. The change was subtle, but unmistakable. "This is a recent addition. Not part of the original design." She straightened up and ran her hands around the edge of the frame.

"What are you looking for?" Greg asked.

"Guess I'll know when we find it." Ruth touched the glass, but it didn't shift under her fingertips. "Something unusual." She scrutinised the filigree, looking for any inconsistencies, as well as the bust of Minerva, then Ruth pressed her cheek to the wall and peered down the side of the frame.

Nothing else, apart from the numbers, seemed out of the ordinary. Ruth ran her fingers over them too, but they remained in place—Henry had bonded the numbers to the frame, and they were a solid addition.

Ruth stepped back. "Has this mirror always been here?" she asked Charles.

"Ever since we moved to the other suite," he said. "Father added this as part of the refurbishment."

"It used to be in the reading room, as I recall." Margaret looked at Charles, and he nodded in agreement.

"He wanted you to see this, but why?" Ruth let out a breath as she recalled that part of the riddle. "Smile at me, and I'll return the favour. Smile at me, and I'll return the favour." Ruth forced a tremulous smile at the mirror, but as expected, nothing happened.

"Shall we remove it from the wall?" Charles asked. "Perhaps Greg and I could—"

Ruth raised a hand. She motioned for the three of them to step aside. After a brief hesitation, they complied, and as they did, the oil painting on the opposite wall of the vestibule appeared in the mirror's reflection.

Ruth faced it and pointed.

A striking woman with long red hair and a flowing white dress stood at the bottom of a flight of stairs, her dainty hand on top of the newel post, while a faint smile played on her lips.

"My great-grandmother," Charles said. "She and her second husband bought Ivywick Island. If it wasn't for them, we wouldn't be here now."

Margaret sniffed. "In more ways than one."

"That's not the entrance hall." Greg frowned. "It looks similar, but the stairs are on the wrong side."

"You know what . . ." Charles' brow furrowed too. "I have never noticed that."

"Why would they paint it backward?" Greg asked.

Ruth faced the mirror.

Of course, in the reflection, the oil painting was now orientated the right way. Ruth strode over to the painting and leaned in. "Ah. That explains it."

Charles moved beside her.

"This is a print." Ruth stretched out a finger and touched the surface. "Smooth. Not the original."

Charles stepped to the side and peered at it. "You're right."

"Do you know where the original is?" Ruth asked him.

"No idea," Charles said. "I thought this was the original." He sighed. "I must confess I paid it little mind. I'm sorry I didn't spot it being reversed. Should have been obvious to me, but I seldom step foot inside this suite."

"Don't blame yourself, darling," Margaret said. "I hadn't noticed either."

In a house filled with hundreds of paintings, that wasn't a surprise.

Ruth examined the frame, then lifted it away from the wall by an inch and peered behind. "Nothing here." She set the painting back as frustration built. "What are we missing?" Ruth tapped her chin and faced the mirror again. "Something in plain sight." Her gaze moved to the woman's hand resting on the newel post. "Part of the riddle was about stairs, wasn't it?"

Greg removed the notepad from his pocket and read, "Up and down, and yet I can't move."

Ruth jogged from the room.

18

R uth hurried along the corridor and onto the landing. "Grandma?" Greg called after her.

With her heart hammering in her chest, she raced down the stairs.

Once the others had caught up with her in the entrance hall, she pointed. "This is where your great-grandmother stood, right here." Ruth got into position, faced the door, and rested her hand on the newel post. "This is the exact pose, right?"

"Looks about right," Charles said. "But I fail to see a connection to the riddle."

Ruth spun back around and was about to examine the newel post when movement caught her eye.

At the end of the corridor, through the glass of the back door, her eyes met Josh's.

He scampered off.

"Be right back." Ruth raced after him. "Greg. Quickly." She ran down the corridor, burst out the back door, and glimpsed Josh hurrying through an stone archway in the wall. "Hey. Stop." Ruth jogged after him, with Greg hard on her heels. "Why am I always having to run places?"

On the other side of the wall, Josh made a beeline for a gate at the far end of a vegetable garden.

"Stop right there," Ruth shouted. "You can't hide forever. We're on an island, and the only boat sank."

"He probably sank it." Greg went to sprint after him, but Josh stopped when he reached the door.

His shoulders slumped, and he turned back.

Ruth panted. "Thank you. I hate running." She thrust a thumb over her shoulder. "Can we have a word, please? Won't take up too much of your time."

Josh hesitated, as though he still considered making a break for it. Clearly realising Ruth was right and he had nowhere to go, he bowed his head and traipsed over to her.

Greg folded his arms. "Why are you on your own?"

Ruth agreed that Josh had looked suspicious by himself, especially when he and Alec were supposed to be sticking together.

Josh mumbled something about Alec fetching a bag of tools. He pointed through the gate.

"While we have you, I want a word," Ruth said.

They followed the path back to the house, with Ruth leading the way and Greg bringing up the rear, sandwiching Josh between them in case he had a change of heart.

As they rounded the corner, Ruth motioned to the conservatory. "Ten minutes, and then you can get back to working with Alec." She opened the door, Josh stepped through, and Ruth and Greg followed him in.

Josh dropped to a chair, looking defeated.

Ruth sat on the sofa opposite.

Greg remained standing by the door.

For a moment, Josh looked as though he may rip off the well's glass cover and jump in.

Greg's eyes narrowed as he pulled a notepad from his pocket, and he sat next to his grandmother.

She crossed her legs and straightened the creases in her skirt. "It's certainly was a shock seeing you here."

Josh squirmed in his seat. "What are the odds?" His face dropped at Greg's expression. "I don't want any trouble."

"You started it by trying to scam us," Greg snarled. "You could have killed someone."

Josh looked scandalised. "I've killed no one, ever, and I'm not about to start." He eyed the door to the house and lowered his voice. "You're not suggesting I had anything to do with Carter and Maddie's deaths, are you?"

He was certainly a lot more chatty now, away from Alec.

"Why did you try to fool us?" Ruth pursed her lips. "I mean, you work here. Charles and Margaret must pay you for your services. You live on the island rent-free."

Josh's gaze lowered to the floor.

It was clear he wasn't about to explain his thinking, and Ruth didn't want to press him too hard on the matter. Well, not yet anyway. She didn't have the time for an interrogation.

"Let's get down to it," she said. "What time did you arrive yesterday?"

Josh's eyes rose to meet hers. He took a breath and composed himself. "Captain Barney picked me up an hour after you. Got here not too long after you."

"When we were either in the sitting room with Margaret or having lunch," Ruth said. *And right about the time someone murdered Carter.* "How did you get to the island?"

"Fred," Josh said. "On his way to his fishing spot."

"Where did you go after you arrived?" Ruth asked.

"Straight to my room. I got freshened up, changed, and then sought out Alec. He wanted to work on the borders in the tulip garden." He pointed through one of the conservatory windows. "We started that before lunch."

Ruth inclined her head. "When you say *room*, what do you mean? Where is it?"

"East wing," Josh said. "Down the hall from the house staff."

"You say you're not friends with any of them, but what about Alec?" Ruth asked.

Josh's face turned sour. "We work together. That's all."

Greg made notes. "Did you see the butler yesterday?"

Josh shook his head.

Ruth thought it may be likely, given the other timings and staff movements, Carter was already dead by that point. Although, she could not be sure, so Josh remained a suspect at the top of her list.

She took a breath and looked back at him. "What then?"

"I helped Alec with the border and then swept the paths for about an hour before we went to lunch."

"Where did you have lunch?" Ruth asked.

"In the tool shed. Like always."

"Can anyone else corroborate that?"

"Alec—" Josh swallowed. "Cook Helen made us both sandwiches. I collected them."

"Alec didn't go with you?" Ruth asked.

"He went back to his cottage and met me at the shed later."

Although Ruth couldn't force the staff to stick together, all this wandering off made accounting for their whereabouts troublesome. "And after lunch?"

"We sorted out the bulbs ready for spring planting."

"What time?" Greg asked.

"Some point after one. I'm not sure."

Which would have been around the time we discovered Carter's body, Ruth thought.

Greg looked at her askance and jotted it down.

"When did you last see Carter?" Ruth asked.

Josh looked at the ceiling. "A couple of days ago. Before I left for the mainland."

Ruth leaned forward. "Did he seem odd? Out of sorts?"

"Carter was always a little off with me."

"In what way?"

Josh's gaze dropped to the floor again. "We didn't see eye to eye on a few things."

Ruth sat back. "Such as?"

"Only minor stuff," Josh said. "He moaned about me wearing my boots in the house. Things like that. They were honest mistakes."

Ruth's attention moved to his wellies. "Did you take them off at lunchtime yesterday?" She pictured the Wellingtons in the tool shed. "When you collected your sandwiches from Cook?"

"I left them by the back door."

"What about this morning?" Ruth asked. When she received a nod in reply, she said, "What time did you have breakfast?"

"I don't have breakfast in the kitchen," Josh said. "I have cereal in my room and start work at eight."

"In the garden?" Greg asked.

Josh stared at him. "Where else?"

Greg opened his mouth to retort.

"And what were you and Alec doing this morning?" Ruth asked before they got into an argument.

"Alec was taking care of the borders at the front, and I was trimming the hedgerows along the east lawn."

"Until when were you doing that?"

"Ten fifteen."

That meant Josh was on the opposite side of the house from the dining hall. She pictured the route he could have taken, which meant passing Alec working outside to reach Maddie. However, there had been a small window of opportunity, only a few minutes while Ray used the bathroom.

"So, at quarter past ten, you did what?" Ruth asked.

"Met Alec by the tool shed."

Ruth made a mental note that next time she saw Alec, she'd ask him to corroborate Josh's movements.

Greg's eyes narrowed. "When was the last time you saw Maddie alive?"

Josh baulked. "Yesterday. I told you I don't have breakfast with the others, and I was trimming the hedges this morning. I was nowhere near Maddie when—"

"We only have your word for that," Greg said.

Josh glared at him. "You want to see the clippings?"

"I might," Greg shot back.

Ruth cleared her throat, and kept her tone level. "Someone murdered Maddie, and by the time we got to the dining hall, you were already there with Alec."

Greg glared at Josh. "Exactly. *Inside* the house. The corridor."

"I told you I was with Alec in the tool shed."

"How long after you arrived at the shed did you hear the scream?" Ruth asked.

"Only a minute or two."

"But you said you were trimming the hedge," Greg said. "Why did you go to the tool shed?"

Josh's jaw muscles flexed. "I came back to get some more petrol. As I was filling the tank, that's when someone in the house screamed."

Greg frowned and made a note.

"What was Alec doing?" Ruth asked.

"Sharpening a pair of secateurs." Josh watched Greg as he wrote this down. "You can check with Alec."

"We will," Greg muttered.

Josh's gaze moved to Ruth. "You think someone murdered Carter too?"

"Keeping all options on the table." Ruth smiled. "Thank you for your time, Josh."

He stood.

As Josh headed to the door, Ruth called after him, "Try not to throw sandbags in front of any other moving objects. We don't want you arrested, as may need to talk to you again."

Josh left, and once the door clicked shut, Greg faced his grandmother.

"What do you think?" He scanned the notes. "Josh could have murdered Maddie, right? Killed her and then went to the tool shed to meet Alec. He had plenty of time."

Ruth's eyes glazed over. "Perhaps."

"Shouldn't we speak to Alec now?" Greg asked. "Corroborate his story?"

Ruth let out a long breath. Nothing definitive seemed to tie Josh to the murders, no solid piece of evidence, and she did not currently know how to find something that did. Ruth hoped the police would discover fingerprints, a strand of hair, a thread of fabric, anything to tie someone to Maddie's death.

The door to the house opened.

"There you are." Margaret huffed and held on to Billy. "What have you been up to? Charles and I have waited for your return like a pair of idiots."

"Well." Charles joined her. "That's not the term I'd use."

Ruth refrained from making any smart comments.

"Lunch is almost ready," Margaret said. "We saw to it. The three of them will fetch it together."

"You coaxed Helen out of her room?" Ruth asked.

"Ray did," Margaret said. "He convinced her they should remain together and prepare lunch. To carry on as normal."

"Carry on as normal," Ruth murmured.

If Ray was the killer, it would certainly benefit him if he could move about freely again.

Right now, Ruth considered Ray the primary suspect.

After all, he didn't hide his disdain for Carter, and seeing as Ray worked in the house, he could've easily slipped into the study when Carter was looking through puzzle boxes.

Were they *in on the scheme together? Does Ray know about the riddle and the will?*

Despite his alibis, and the distinct lack of any evidence to prove otherwise, Ray still could be the one who'd wiped the blackboard and stolen the riddle. After all, flooding the bathroom and locking the door would be no big deal to "Mr Fixit."

And what about poor Maddie?

Ray had been the closest to Maddie at the time of her death, and yet he'd heard and seen nothing.

"So?" Margaret said. "Lunch?"

Greg got to his feet. "Don't have to ask me twice."

Charles smiled. "That's the spirit, young fella."

Ruth snapped out of her thoughts and stood too.

Margaret's face brightened. "But before that, Charles has made a discovery he's eager to share with you."

Charles' smile broadened.

The four of them headed on through the house, and into the entrance hall.

Charles stopped at the foot of the stairs, now beaming

from ear to ear. "Wait until you see this." He grabbed the cap of the newel post, twisted it, and lifted it off. "Ta-dah." Charles pointed to a hole in the newel post. "Look inside."

Ruth peered into it.

The entire newel post was hollow, with mirrored sides all the way down, and light streamed in from the bottom, revealing a multicoloured starburst pattern that reflected a hundred times over up the sides. "It's a kaleidoscope."

"Let me see." Greg looked into the hole. "Wow. That's incredible. Where's the light coming from?"

"Down here." Charles knelt and indicated several horizontal slits in the base. "I've not noticed them before. One of my father's additions, no doubt." He straightened. "A clever man."

"What are these?" Greg pointed at the inside lip of the hole.

Ruth looked. There were two metal plates opposite each other. She motioned to Charles. "May I see that?" He handed her the newel cap. Sure enough, it too had metal plates on either side. Ruth fitted the newel cap back to the post and turned it, so they lined up.

There came a small crack of electricity.

Greg's eyes widened. "It's a switch."

"For what?" Margaret looked about.

"Do it again, Ruth," Charles said.

She turned the cap to the off position, paused for a couple of seconds, and then turned it back again, but no lights came on or sirens sounded.

Greg's eyes lit up. "What's it for?"

Not knowing the answer, Ruth erred on the side of caution and turned the newel cap to the *off* position.

In her mind's eye, she pictured the switch activating the

lighthouse, or perhaps a giant laser beam, signalling aliens to come take Margaret back to their home planet.

Footfalls drew Ruth's attention to the other side of the hall as Betty, Helen, and Ray strode toward them, each carrying a silver tray loaded with food and drinks.

"Ah, here we go," Margaret said. "We must keep our strength up."

Billy yapped in agreement and tried to leap from her arms.

"That reminds me," Ruth said. "I need to check on Merlin."

"We have prepared his lunch too." Ray nodded to a bowl of cat food on his tray. It seemed to comprise chicken and vegetables.

"In that case, how about we take lunch in Ruth's suite?" Margaret's expression darkened. "Seeing as the dining hall is off-limits."

The house staff headed upstairs.

Ruth stared at the newel post, eager to figure out what it meant, but she had no immediate answer and needed a break to clear her head, so she followed them up.

Twenty minutes later, having eaten, drunk four gallons of tea, and now feeling ready to tackle the rest of the day, Ruth sat with Merlin on her lap, trying to figure out what the newel post clue meant.

Margaret was seated on the sofa opposite with Billy, who looked as though he'd like nothing better than to leap across and chase Merlin about the house. Little did he know that would be a terrible idea, and he was bound to wind up worse off in such a reckless scenario.

Margaret seemed to have also come to this conclusion because she held on to the micro pooch with both hands.

Ruth stared out the window to the horizon. Somewhere in the back of her mind, she'd seen that kaleidoscope pattern before, but couldn't recall where exactly.

She pulled her phone from her pocket, navigated the photos, and found the latest one of the blackboard. Ruth then studied the riddle for what felt like the billionth time, and the list of words, searching for anything that stood out to her.

Charles sipped a coffee. "I told you my father spent his life in civil engineering. He worked as an apprentice and joined the design department."

"Hence all the little contraptions in his office," Ruth muttered.

"He must have been very clever," Greg said.

Charles set the mug on one of the trays, and sat back. "My father always tinkered. Even during retirement and later life, his creativity never waned, not for a second."

Despite their history, Ruth admired Henry. He'd followed a passion, exactly like her late husband.

When she'd met him, John had enough income from renting out land on his family estate to never have to lift a finger, but despite this, he'd followed his passion too—cats. In a few short years, John had built up a reputation as one of the country's, if not the world's, most respected breeders.

Ruth had already joined the police force before they started dating, and she came from a working-class family. They couldn't have been more opposite, but John's passion and energy shone like a bright flame, and she was the moth to it.

Merlin climbed from Ruth's lap and slinked over to Charles.

"Watch out," Greg said. "He doesn't like men. Sit on your hands, otherwise he'll bite and scratch you."

Merlin leapt onto Charles' lap and curled up. "We seem to get on fine." Charles massaged the cat's ears.

Greg stared. "What the actual—?" He leaned across to stroke the cat, but Merlin hissed and lashed a set of claws at him. Greg pulled back and glowered. "That makes no sense."

Ruth gasped and sat bolt upright.

Billy let out a high-pitched bark of excitement and tried to leap from Margaret's hands, but she reined him back. "What on earth is wrong now, Ruth?"

"I know where I've seen that starburst pattern." She leapt to her feet.

"Where?" Greg asked.

"The gable end of the roof." Ruth waved in that general direction as a renewed flood of adrenaline washed through her veins. "I spotted it when we first arrived."

"Of course." Charles lifted Merlin from his lap. "The attic."

19

Ruth, Greg, Margaret, and Charles stood at the foot of a set of narrow wooden stairs, on a landing at the highest level of the house. At the top of those stairs was a closed door. Paint peeled from its wooden surface, and cobwebs hung across the corners.

"If you think for one moment I'm going up there . . ." Margaret sniffed. "You have another think coming." She folded her arms. "I'd rather take my chances with the murderer."

"We could arrange that." Ruth grinned.

Margaret glared at her. "People we know and care about have died."

The grin slipped from Ruth's face. "Sorry." Her sister had a good point. "Just trying to lighten the mood." She faced the stairs. "You and Charles can stay here."

Greg let out a low groan. "Do I have to go with you?" He shuddered. "I hate spiders."

When he was seven years old, Greg had vanished. One moment he'd been playing in the garden with his twin sister, Chloe, and the next he was gone. Ruth and her daughter, Sara, had frantically searched their house and grounds for hours, trying to find him. In the end, as it was getting dark, Chloe had been the one to finally locate the wayward child.

Turned out, he'd gone to a rarely visited shed, hunting for a football pump, and having found it in the far corner, behind a fishing tent and a tub of golf balls, a triumphant Greg had turned to leave.

That was the precise moment a giant spider had chosen to lower itself in front of the door, barring Greg's escape.

A Mexican standoff reaching biblical proportions.

Of course, Greg's definition of giant was relative. The spider was impressive, but hardly any real threat with a leg span under a couple of inches.

Greg had remained paralysed at the back of the shed, shivering and whimpering, evaluating his life choices.

And so, despite his subsequent rescue by Team Morgan, Greg's fear hadn't diminished by a whole lot over the years. He still avoided spiders and would often scream when they so much as waggled a hairy leg in his direction.

"They've got eight eyes. Did you know that?" Greg shuddered again. "Why does anything need that many? I mean, seriously?"

"So they stand a better chance of seeing you coming and can get organised in their attack." Ruth headed on up the stairs. "Don't worry, Gregory, I'll protect you." After all, she knew what it felt like to have a phobia or two. "If the killer's up here, I'm the first one out, though."

The teenager grumbled under his breath as he followed.

At the top of the stairs, Ruth held her breath, grabbed the handle, and opened the door.

She ducked under the cobwebs, and flicked on a bank of switches. Bare bulbs glowed dull yellow in the gloom. The attic had a low, pitched ceiling, with various connected spaces—rooms linked by archways.

On either side of the first were crates, boxes, old furniture, and general detritus collecting decades of dust.

To the left was an antique crib with several porcelain dolls lying within blankets.

Greg screwed up his face. "That's not at all creepy."

He went to step round Ruth, but she thrust out an arm. "Wait. Someone's been up here." She pointed to a stack of paintings on a nearby table, leaning against the chimney brickwork.

The one at the front had broken glass, and someone had disturbed dust on the frame where they had returned it to an upright position.

Ruth knelt and examined it in detail. "They must have knocked it to the floor, and they've left their fingerprints in the dust. Appear to be fresh." She took a picture with her phone and looked about. "Someone was definitely here recently."

"A man or a woman?" Greg asked.

"Hard to tell, as it's only the tips of their fingers, but could be a man." Ruth stood and made her way across the first attic room, careful where she placed her feet. "Follow me but stay close and mimic my movements. We don't want to disturb any evidence."

Greg stepped into the room and did as she asked.

"Look for anything else out of place." Ruth reached the first archway and peered into the next room—another area filled with more boxes overflowing with old linen, and forgotten furniture stacked to the rafters.

Ruth edged through the attic space and into a third. Unlike the other two, shelves lined this room, packed full of knickknacks.

They were worthless ornaments: everything from china rabbits and frogs to grotesque figurines of children with oversized heads, plus toby jugs, brass animals, ornate teapots, plastic flowers in vases, a cheap nativity set, wooden animal sculptures, trinket boxes, and a thousand other items.

Greg looked round at it all, his face twisted with disgust. "What is all this cheap crud? It's awful."

"Hey." Ruth snatched up a metal fridge magnet that doubled as a bottle opener. It declared in large letters, '*I heart London.*' "I bought this for Margaret."

Greg rolled his eyes. "Can't imagine why it's up here, and not pride of place."

"I know, right? Decorative and practical. The perfect gift." Ruth pocketed it and continued scanning the bookcases.

"What are we looking for exactly?" Greg asked.

"Anything that may tie to the riddle."

"So, this is where unwanted presents come to die?" Greg checked out a paperweight with a dead crab encased in resin. "Charming."

"You like that?" Ruth asked. "I'll get you one for your birthday."

Greg set it back. "We should put your ghastly garden gnome up here." He shuddered. "You know, that horrible monstrosity you got from Vanmoor."

Ruth smiled at the image of the drunk gnome with his butt stuck out of his trousers. "A masterful example of premium sculpture." Which is why she had placed it on the dashboard of her motorhome. In fact, if she'd had the time, Ruth would have taken all this clutter downstairs and distributed it in random locations about the house. *Margaret would freak.* "Oh well," she murmured. "There's always next time."

Greg snatched something from a shelf. "Can I have this?"

"I don't believe it." Ruth took it from him." It was a Swiss army knife. "I bought this for Margaret too. A birthday present from a few years ago." She pulled out the biggest blade.

Greg's brow furrowed. "You bought her a pocketknife?"

"This isn't any old knife." Ruth flipped up a corkscrew. "This is a vital survival tool."

"Why would she want that?"

Ruth returned the blade and corkscrew and handed it back to Greg. "She lives on an island. Anything could happen."

"It was a thoughtful gift, Grandma." He slipped it into his pocket. "I'll ask Aunty Margaret if I can have it."

"Tell her to reimburse me."

"While we're alone," Greg glanced over his shoulder. "Are you going to tell me what happened?"

"With what?"

"The Tammy Radcliffe incident."

"Oh that." Ruth turned around and checked out the next shelf full of knickknacks. "When I was fourteen years old, I cycled from a friend's house and spotted my father, your great-grandfather, driving past. I waved, but he didn't see." Ruth glanced about to make sure they were alone, and she lowered her voice. "Dad was supposed to be at work, so curiosity got the better of me. I followed his car to town and glimpsed him turning into the industrial estate." Ruth squeezed her eyes closed for a few seconds as old memories rushed forward. "By the time I found him again . . ." She opened her eyes and picked up a frog ornament. She recognized this as another gift for Margeret. "Dad knocked on the door to a warehouse, and a few moments later, a woman answered."

"Tammy Radcliffe?" Greg asked.

Ruth nodded. "Tammy Radcliffe." She set the ornament back and continued along the shelves.

"Who was she?"

"A friend of my mother's." Ruth swallowed. "Anyway, Dad looked about as if to make sure no one was watching, then kissed Tammy on the cheek, and they snuck inside together."

Greg winced. "Uh-oh."

Ruth's stomach tensed at the uncomfortable memory. "I raced home to tell Margaret. She wouldn't believe me, said no way our father was having an affair, and she was very angry with me for even suggesting it. Demanded I stay out of whatever was going on."

Greg smirked. "Which you didn't."

"Of course not." Ruth picked up a porcelain doll with realistic green eyes that made her suspect it could come to life at any moment. "Anyway, I planned to return after dark. I wanted to go to that warehouse and find proof of their affair. I said Mum had to know. Margaret eventually, and with a lot of reluctance, agreed to go with me." Ruth allowed herself a small smile. "So, later that night, we snuck out and cycled to the warehouse. It had a newfangled lock neither of us had seen the likes of before."

"Electronic?" Greg asked.

"No, a mechanical push-button type. I got past it, though." Ruth waved the doll at Greg. "Want this?"

"Not even a little bit." He motioned. "Go on. How did you know the combination?"

"First of all, four of the numbers showed more signs of

wear than the others." Ruth returned the freaky doll to the shelf. "Now, Tammy might have used any of those numbers more than twice, but I guessed she didn't. Back then, people were less used to having to remember numbers for any reason. PINs were still a few years off. So, I guessed Tammy would use her birth year. She was around Dad's age, so I assumed the first number would have to be a one, second a nine, and then I pegged the third was a three, which left the eight."

"It worked?" Greg asked.

Ruth lifted her chin. "It did. Margaret and I snuck into the warehouse, me wanting to find proof Dad was having an affair, and my sister determined to show he wasn't."

Greg stared at her. "And?"

"I switched on the lights and revealed party balloons, wrapped presents, and a giant banner that read . . ." Ruth gestured with her hands. "*Happy Sixteenth Birthday, Margaret.*"

Greg winced.

"Turns out," Ruth said through clenched teeth, "Tammy was storing all the stuff for Mum and Dad's surprise birthday party. They booked the town hall around the corner."

Greg pinched his nose.

Ruth sighed. "Yeah. Fun times."

"Hold on." Greg furrowed his brow. "Why is Aunty Margaret still mad? That was a long time ago."

"Because that's not where our story ends." Ruth lifted a plastic model windmill from the nearest shelf and examined it. She vaguely recognized this object too, but had never visited Amsterdam, so it couldn't have come from her. "When we got home, Margaret told our mother about what we'd done."

"I still don't get it," Greg said. "You got in trouble? So what?"

"Yes, but it got worse." Ruth set the windmill back and continued scanning the shelves. "A week later, Mum followed Dad to that same warehouse and caught him with Tammy Radcliffe."

Greg gawked at her. "He *was* having an affair?"

"My parents divorced, Margaret went to live with Dad, and I stayed with Mum."

"And Aunty Margaret blamed you?" Greg asked.

"My sister held a grudge." Ruth sighed. "She said if I'd not been so nosey, we would have been blissfully unaware of what my father was up to, and we would have stayed together as a family."

"That's not fair," Greg said, incredulous. "Your Dad was the bad guy."

"Margaret didn't see it that way." Ruth glanced round the cluttered room. "And that's why she hates it whenever I've been determined to solve a mystery. She says I put my obsession above relationships." Ruth let out a long breath. "And yet, here we are now, solving a mystery for her."

Greg nodded. "Now I understand why you want to make up with her."

"Time is short." Ruth stepped through another doorway. "Ah. Here we go."

Between two sets of bookshelves at the far end of the attic was the circular window with the starburst in stained glass.

She checked out the shelves on either side and froze.

On the uppermost shelf of the right-hand unit, in a gap between a novelty mug declaring itself to be for "*Dad's Brew*" and a hedgehog-shaped pincushion, sat a brass mushroom.

Ruth stood on tiptoes to get a better look. "From the

riddle." Her insides jumped with excitement. "I start as I end, in a room with no windows or doors. Each part still refers to a location. Here's the mushroom."

The brass object was about the size of a fist and sat on a metal rail fixed to the woodwork. Someone had recently disturbed a layer of dust, leaving an obvious line going from left to right.

Ruth glanced at Greg.

He shook his head.

She nodded.

"Don't do it," he said through tight lips.

Ruth smiled, and before he could stop her, she grabbed the brass mushroom and slid it along the rail.

A heavy clunk reverberated beneath their feet, and Greg leapt back through the doorway.

Ruth let go of the mushroom, stepped away, and looked about. "What happened?"

"Put it back," Greg said from the other room. "I don't like it."

Ruth reached up, slid the mushroom to its previous position, and the floor vibrated again.

Then everything fell silent.

"Hold on." Greg hurried to the window with the glass starburst. "Do that again."

Ruth frowned at him. "Make up your mind."

"Do it."

She slid the mushroom across.

"There." Greg pointed.

Ruth moved the mushroom back and forth along the shelf, and as she did, a metal rod with a lens mounted inside a hoop appeared from the window frame and snapped into place at the middle.

Greg peered through the clear piece of glass. "What's

that?" He moved out of the way.

Ruth looked for herself. "Hmm."

The lensed part of the rod acted like a sight, which lined up with the transparent section of the window, which also turned out to be lensed, which had the combined effect of creating a makeshift monocular of sorts.

Magnified several times through the viewer was the conservatory. Or, to be more precise, the middle of the conservatory.

"What on earth?" Ruth pulled her phone from her pocket and navigated to the riddle. "Locations, right?"

Greg looked over her shoulder at the display.

"Remember you're alive, even though they're dead. Get under my skin, you'll be sure to cry. When spoken to, I will always answer." She peered through the lens again. "Conservatory, not graveyard, so unlikely to refer to being alive or dead."

"Thank goodness," Greg murmured.

"Get under my skin, you'll be sure to cry." Ruth shook her head. "When spoken to, I will always—" She hesitated for a second, and then a smile swept across her face again. "This is fun. Henry was a genius." Ruth slid the mushroom back to its starting position and marched through the attic with revitalised determination.

"What happened?" Greg asked as he followed her through the door.

"A theory. I'll show you." Ruth hurried down the stairs, but stopped halfway, turned to Greg, and whispered, "Oh, and it was right after Mum and Dad separated, at the ripe old age of fourteen, that I realised I'd like to join the police force. I wanted to hone my detective skills." She beamed at him. "I *love* solving mysteries, and there's nothing Margaret can do about it."

"No need to ask what you two are discussing." Margaret stared up at them.

Ruth winced and hurried down the remaining stairs, back onto the landing.

"My seventieth is in a few years," Margaret said to her. "Charles isn't having an affair, so you can't ruin another relationship."

Charles looked between Ruth and Greg. "Progress?"

"Progress," Ruth said with a fervent nod.

"Well?" Margaret asked. "What did you discover?"

"Give me your steak and ale pie recipe, and I'll tell you," Ruth replied, deadpan.

Margaret's expression darkened.

"Meet us in the sitting room," Ruth said. "We'll bring you up to speed as soon as we've checked out this next part." She slipped past them and headed down the stairs.

Greg followed.

"Shouldn't we stick together?" Charles called. "All four of us?"

"Give us ten minutes." Ruth was eager to solve the next part of the riddle without her sister looming over her.

She and Greg jogged through the house and into the conservatory. Ruth motioned to the well. "When spoken to, I will always answer."

Greg stared at her, unblinking.

"Echo," Ruth said. "When spoken to, it will always answer. This is what the lenses line up with." She bet Henry installed them before the addition of the conservatory.

Together, Ruth and Greg lifted the glass cover clear, set it to one side, and then peered into the depths of the well.

Greg squinted. "There's something down there."

Sure enough, a rectangular object, about the size of a lunch box, was mounted to the inner brickwork of the well.

It was thirty feet below floor level, and metal straps held it in place.

"Wait here." Ruth rushed outside, up the path, and threw open the door to the tool shed. Inside, she found a coil of rope. She snatched it up, and then hurried back to the conservatory. "Hold still." Ruth looped the rope around Greg's waist twice and started tying it at the front. "Double knot for good measure."

He looked from the rope, to the well, and back to the rope. "No way." Greg slapped Ruth's hands away.

She winced and pulled back. "You'll be fine."

"You are insane." Greg untied the rope.

"We need a look at that box," Ruth said. "I can brace my feet on that." She pointed to the brick edge of the well. "And lower you. There's no other way, Gregory."

"Of course there's another way, you lunatic." Greg pulled the rope free, and then tied it around his phone, creating a cradle for it. "I'll set this to record."

"Have it your way. Would be quicker to lower *you*."

Greg shook his head. "Again, can't tell if you're joking or not."

Ruth sniggered.

His idea was a little less risky, though. Well, if Greg's phone didn't slip free of its harness. Ruth cringed. The tantrum that followed would last for days.

"Be careful," she said as Greg hit the record button and lowered his phone into the well.

He'd gotten it halfway down when he froze.

"What's wrong?" Ruth whispered.

Greg gritted his teeth. "We should have used *your* phone."

"Or better still, Margaret's." Ruth gave him an evil grin.

Greg's smartphone reached the mysterious box in the

well and rotated on the end of the rope a few times before he hauled it back up to the surface. "I hope there's enough light down there to still make it out."

However, he needn't have worried, as the image sprang to life, grainy, but still showing brickwork gliding past the screen. The box came into view. Greg hit *pause,* and they both leaned in.

"What is that?" Ruth asked.

"Not sure."

Mounted to the wall by steel straps was a clear plastic box. Inside was a circuit board, a display, and a battery.

Greg squinted at the screen. "That's a very large battery for a small circuit. Whatever it is, I bet it can last months, if not years."

"Which would make sense," Ruth said. "If Henry put it down there for us to find."

Greg rotated the screen. "See that circular black thing in the corner? That's a speaker." He zoomed in. "And I think this thing next to it is a microphone." He pointed to a cylindrical black object filling the left side of the box, with a silver mesh dome protruding from the top.

Ruth stared at the screen. "What words in the riddle do we have left?" She pulled her phone from her pocket and examined the photo of the blackboard. Then she peered into the well. "You said that thing has a microphone, right?"

"Yes. Why?"

Ruth cupped her hands around her mouth and called, "Yoo-hoo."

A couple of seconds later, the speaker in the device blasted out, "Yoo-hoo," in return, and the display glowed.

Greg's eyes widened. "Whatever it is, we just activated it."

20

Greg edged away from the well, his expression panicked, skin pale. "Don't make any sudden moves."

"What's the matter?" Ruth asked, puzzled by his reaction.

Greg whispered, "It's a bomb."

"No, it isn't."

"Yes. It is."

Ruth blinked. "You really think Henry would have planted a bomb in his own house?"

"Maybe." Greg took another step back.

"Ridiculous." Ruth rolled her eyes. "It's not a bomb." She waved him back. "Do it again. Lower your phone. I want to see."

"Are you sure?"

"Positive."

"If we die—"

"You can blame me." Ruth grinned.

With the display on the mysterious box now glowing, Greg lowered his phone back into the well. He let it swing on the end of the rope for a minute, and then pulled it back to the surface.

They huddled together as the camera view turned and the box came into view. On the newly activated screen was a symbol—a crow within a triangle.

"I've seen that before," Ruth said.

"Where?" Greg asked.

"Carved above a door in the kitchen. Part of the original castle."

"I didn't notice it," Greg said. "What's behind the door?"

"Let's find out." Ruth turned to leave, but something on the recording caught her eye. "Wait. What was that?"

Greg frowned.

Ruth motioned. "Rewind . . . there." She squinted.

Under the glow of the device's screen, lines in the brick-work opposite became visible, and as the view rotated, they got a measure of its size—about a foot square.

"Looks like someone cut the bricks," Greg said.

"It's a point of access," Ruth murmured. "Henry must have cut them from the other side, lifted the bricks out, and then fitted that device, before returning everything. No one has replaced the mortar."

Greg nodded. "Would explain how he bolted it to the wall."

Ruth stared at the image. "Which means there's a way down there." Her gaze lifted, and she looked out the conservatory windows, to the vegetable garden and the stone wall beyond. Her breath caught. "How far are we from the clifftop?"

Greg scratched his chin. "I'm not sure. I think it's right behind that wall, isn't it?"

With her heart thumping against her rib cage, Ruth scanned the area, trying to get her bearings. *We must be near the cave.* She looked back at the phone's display, and the image of the access cut into the brickwork. "Huh." Ruth stepped back. "I need to check something out." She tried to sound casual. "I won't be long."

Greg untied his phone. "I'll come with you."

"No." Ruth took the rope from him. "I'll put this back. You stay with Margaret and Charles. Keep them entertained. Go straight there, and nowhere else. I won't be long."

"You keep banging on about us not splitting up," Greg said.

"I'll be only a few minutes." She had to see for herself, and she couldn't risk her grandson getting hurt.

He stared at her. "You think there's a way down to that part of the well, and you're going to check it out, aren't you?"

Ruth shrugged, though her insides squirmed.

"Why do you need to go down there?" Greg asked. "What's the point? The symbol tells us where we need to be next—the kitchen."

Ruth swallowed. "I want to have a quick look. Make sure we haven't missed something. That's all. No big deal."

Greg's eyes narrowed. "Come on. What's so important?" A flicker of understanding crossed his features. "Has it got something to do with the cave you asked Uncle Charles about?"

"We told Margaret we'd only be gone ten minutes," Ruth said. "We've been far longer. She'll come looking for us. Give me another ten minutes to check something out. Please, Gregory?"

In fact, it was a miracle her sister hadn't hunted them down already. Margaret wasn't renowned for her patience.

Greg let out a breath. "Don't do anything reckless."

"Me?"

"You."

Ruth smiled. "I wouldn't dream of it. You know what I'm like: the textbook definition of cautious."

Greg muttered, "Sure you are," and he left.

"Thank you," Ruth called after him. She looked from the well, out the window to the vegetable garden, and back again. Ruth pictured a straight line, bisecting the well, from the device to the hatch, and onward. "It has to be linked." She balled her fists, and hurried from the conservatory, and stepped into the tool shed. Ruth returned the rope to the workbench.

"Where are you?" She knelt and examined the floor, but nothing seemed unusual about it.

Next, Ruth inspected the side walls, lifting tools and the lawnmower aside, but found nothing extraordinary there either.

She faced the back wall.

The planks ran horizontal, from one side to the other, but there were also two vertical lines in the woodwork, spaced a couple of feet apart.

Ruth ran her fingers over the panel, pressed, and it swung inward to reveal a narrow opening, not only in the shed, but the garden wall behind.

Ruth held her breath and peered inside.

To the left was a narrow passageway within the wall, running for the length of it, and disappearing around the corner. "Not at all creepy or dangerous." Now she understood why the garden wall was so broad and tall—to hide this corridor. Ruth hesitated as she weighed whether to fetch Greg, or better yet, Charles.

However, she checked the door hatch wouldn't lock her inside, then activated the torch function on her phone, and stepped into the brick passageway.

As Ruth edged her way along, she brushed cobwebs aside. "Greg would freak."

At the corner of the tunnel a stone staircase descended.

Ruth steeled herself and headed down. The air grew colder with every step, and a salty breeze blew through her hair.

At the bottom of the stairs, she stopped at an intersection. A corridor stretched on both sides, each end terminating in a door.

Ruth got her bearings. The door to the left led back toward the house, so she went that way first and opened it.

Beyond was a room no bigger than a cupboard with metal plates mounted to the bricks, holding a section of curved wall in place. This was clearly where Henry had accessed the interior of the well and placed his elaborate contraption. She would not mess with it.

Ruth hurried down the hallway in the opposite direction.

She turned an ear to the door and, hearing nothing from the other side, opened it and stepped through.

Greeted by darkness, Ruth found a light switch on the wall and flicked it on. She stood still, squinting as her eyes adjusted, and then her jaw dropped.

Ruth now stood in a room, twenty feet wide and long, with a single bed, an armchair, desk, small tube TV and video player, and an old computer. A worktop marked the kitchen area with a sink, and a fridge-freezer to one side.

Pipework and cabling crisscrossed the walls and ceiling, while straight ahead, another door stood open, which led to a bathroom complete with shower and toilet.

Ruth gaped at it all. "Henry built this?"

A curtain covered the left-hand wall.

She pulled it back to reveal a jagged cave wall, held in place by various steel beams and wooden props.

"This is it." Ruth peered through an opening. Sure enough, she could make out the cave on the other side.

Stunned, Ruth replaced the curtain and faced the room.

"No wonder Henry didn't want us to find it. Someone's lived down here all this time." She smacked her forehead. "The phantom."

But why would Henry want to hide someone on the island?

That same someone had made the bed, but it was hard to tell when they'd visited last. It could have been recently, or years ago.

Ruth walked to a nearby bookshelf and scanned the titles. Most were nonfiction books on gardening and sailing. Ruth opened one and found a dedication inside to Henry, from his wife, Jean, with love. Clearly the person living here had stolen them.

There were also around twenty novels, each spine creased, and the pages well thumbed. The selection covered everything from *Animal Farm* to *A Christmas Carol*, but nothing published in the past decade.

Next, Ruth moved to a cupboard and opened it. Inside were piles of newspapers, old and yellowed, and a small leatherbound journal. She rifled through the pages, and her blood ran cold.

Someone had scrawled notes: disjointed conversations between Henry and Charles, Henry and Carter, and then Charles and Margaret. All of them on the same topic: the will.

Henry had told Carter he'd hidden it somewhere in the house.

Ruth frowned. "None with the solicitors?" She supposed

it made sense—by only having one copy of the will, it forced Charles to play Henry's game.

Why had someone burned it down though? Had they assumed a copy resided there and got it wrong? Or was it a massive coincidence? After all, Detective Murray had blamed kids for the fire.

Henry had also said he knew Charles could never solve the riddles on his own, and if it came to it, Carter could help him. Henry continued to explain that the entire estate would go to Charles, but Noah had been harassing him to split the fortune between them.

Having refused Noah's demands, Henry stated Noah's mother had made it clear she'd wanted no contact between them, and that he'd not heard from him in over fifty years.

Noah indeed planned to turn the island into a hotel for the rich and famous. This, according to Henry, would be a disservice to its family heritage.

"So, Carter *was* trying to help?" Ruth muttered, but she still couldn't understand why he hadn't told Charles. She turned over the page and continued to read, when echoing footfalls made her start.

Ruth jammed the journal back into the cupboard and rushed to the door. Sure enough, the stomp of feet grew louder.

With her pulse pounding in her ears, she closed the door, and considered hiding behind the curtain. Realising someone would spot her feet, she ran to the bathroom instead.

Ruth looked about, but there was nowhere to hide there either, only a shower, sink and toilet, and no other means of escape. She pushed the bathroom door almost closed and left a gap of a fraction of an inch, which allowed her to peer out.

The footfalls grew closer, and Ruth held her breath.

Then her heart leapt into her throat.

She'd left the light on.

Ruth swore, and before she knew what she was doing, she ran into the main room again, flicked off the light, and dove back into the bathroom.

The footfalls stopped.

Ruth tensed.

The door to the main room swung open, but the stranger didn't switch on the light.

Holding her breath, Ruth tried to make out the dark figure as they headed to the cupboard, opened it, and placed something inside.

Then as they made their way back, their form was momentarily silhouetted by the light from the corridor.

Ruth stared.

Clearly a man, given his squared shoulders, but who?

She couldn't discern any more details as they closed the door behind them, once again plunging the room into darkness.

Ruth waited in silence for a couple of minutes before daring to switch on her phone's torch function. She then crept into the room and hurried over to the cupboard.

Now lying on top of the old newspapers and journal was the previously missing plaque from the grand dining hall.

The phantom murdered Maddie.

Carved reliefs displayed a crest comprising a horse ridden by a knight, his head turned to the right, a crosshatch patterned background on either side, plus the Andrews of Ivywick family motto across a banner beneath: Victrix *Fortunae Sapientia.*

"Wisdom, the conqueror of fortune," Ruth murmured.

On the back were a list of fifteen names, ending in Henry's—all Andrews family ancestors.

Ruth pocketed the journal and was about to take photos of the plaque when more footfalls sounded from the corridor.

"You have got to be kidding me." She rushed back to the bathroom, pushed the door to, and peered out.

The door to the room swung open, and a tall figure stepped inside. "Ruth?"

She let out an enormous sigh of relief.

Ruth threw open the bathroom door, and raised her phone high above her head, illuminating Charles' face. "Fancy meeting you here."

He held his head and staggered sideways.

Ruth rushed to him. "What happened?" She flicked on the light switch and pocketed her phone.

A red welt formed on the left-hand side of Charles' forehead. "I'm all right." He wobbled.

"Clearly." Ruth guided him to a chair.

Charles dropped to it. "You weren't alone, I take it?"

Ruth examined the wound. "He got you?"

"I came searching," Charles said. "Was at the shed, trying to figure out where you'd gotten to when I heard a noise. Being a stupid oaf, I peered through the side window and spotted someone opening the back wall. I thought it was you. I'd just reached the door, only to have it burst open and slam into me." He motioned to his forehead. "Hurts like hell. I feel like such an imbecile."

"We need an ice pack," Ruth said.

Charles gently pushed her hands away. "I'll be fine. I was very worried. Had to make sure they hadn't walloped you too."

Ruth glanced at the door. "Did you see who it was?"

"Afraid not. By the time I'd turned back, they'd run through the archway. I couldn't even tell you if it was a man or a woman." Charles' wide-eyed gaze moved around the room. "What is this place?"

"I take it from your reaction you didn't know it existed?"

"Absolutely not." Charles looked at the bed. "Someone's living down here?"

"I'm not sure." Ruth opened the fridge-freezer, but it was empty. "Doesn't look like it." She closed the doors and faced the room. "Doesn't seem to be anything that identifies them. No clothes or personal belongings."

"The phantom," Charles murmured. "It has to be." He cleared his throat. "We were worried about you. I volunteered to go see where you'd gone. After our friend escaped, I found the back of the shed still open." His gaze moved around the room. "Incredible to think this place has been here for all these years." Charles screwed up his face. "What other secrets have I overlooked? And why didn't you tell us what you're doing, Ruth? It's dangerous to be alone."

"No one believed John and me about what we saw that day in the cave," she said. "Henry banned us from coming back to investigate, remember?" Ruth tried to hide the irritation in her voice. After all, it hadn't been Charles' fault. In fact, Ruth's brother-in-law had done all he could to change Henry's mind. All to no avail.

The question foremost in Ruth's mind now was: *if Henry knew about this hideout, who was he protecting and why?*

She pulled back the curtain to reveal the rock wall.

Charles' face dropped. "Goodness me." He got to his feet, stepped over, and peered through the gap.

"Careful," Ruth warned him. "It doesn't seem very stable."

"That's why you were so desperate to visit the cave

yesterday?" he asked. "To follow up on your theory? You knew this would be here."

"I wouldn't say desperate." Ruth perched on the arm of the chair. "More like *eager*. Anyway, I wanted to investigate the mystery on my own. Prove what we saw. Then I'd report back once I had evidence." She gestured around the room. "And this is the evidence I needed."

"But it's dangerous to go wandering off on your own." Charles turned back to her. "You should have told us."

"I'm sorry." Ruth swallowed and looked at the floor. "And while we're on the subject of secrets . . ." She muttered, "There's something else." Ruth refocussed on Charles. "The detective said something I think you should know."

Charles blinked. "What?"

"He told me there's a report from four decades ago about—"

"The redheaded boy," Charles finished.

Ruth's eyebrows shot up. "You know about him?"

Charles tugged at his cuffs. "I hate to break it to you, but there are quite a few redheads in this part of the world." He pointed to his own flaming red and grey hair.

"I understand. But what if that missing person never died, but they lived here?" Ruth motioned around the room.

"For all those years?" Charles didn't look convinced. "Is that likely?"

Ruth opened the cupboard and pulled out the plaque. "I think he killed Maddie."

Charles' eyes widened. "And Carter?" He took the plaque from her and examined it.

"How old was the redheaded boy?" Ruth asked.

"Reports at the time were mixed," Charles said. "There were four fishermen on board that boat, and they all gave differing accounts."

"A rough idea?" Ruth asked.

Charles' brow furrowed. "Anywhere between ten and fifteen. They didn't get a clear look at the lad."

Ruth did a quick mental calculation. "Which would put him at somewhere in his fifties now." That person could well be Josh Green. However, Ruth wanted to keep level headed while she considered their next move. If Charles cottoned on to her thoughts, he'd have to tell Margaret, and Margaret would flip. Which, with the police not arriving for over two hours, would do no good.

They'd still need solid evidence linking Josh to the phantom, and then to the murders. At the moment, all they had was speculation and a lot more questions.

Besides, Josh worked on the island, had a room, and a certain amount of job security.

He certainly wouldn't need to steal food and hide down here. Could he really be the phantom?

She was missing a piece of the puzzle.

Charles went to leave with the plaque.

"No." Ruth motioned, and he handed it back to her. "We must return it."

Charles' frown deepened. "It's mine."

"I don't want the phantom to know we've discovered this family crest yet." She examined the plaque one last time, looking for anything out of the ordinary, before returning it to the cupboard.

"What's your plan?" Charles asked.

"Now we finish our hunt for the will." Ruth closed the cupboard doors and faced him. "And set a trap."

21

Margaret paced the sitting room. "What do you mean you're going to set a trap for this squatter we apparently have, and most likely have had for years?"

"Phantom." Greg shuffled his weight and adjusted a cushion on the sofa. "What?" he said in response to her scowl. "They're clearly the person the staff refer to as the phantom. They were right." He looked to Ruth for confirmation.

Seated at the other end of the sofa from him, she sipped a tea and savoured its sugary, milky, caffeine-rich goodness as it slid down her throat. "We think Henry must have known about the phantom too."

"Even if that's the case, it still remains that there is a murderer on the island," Margaret said. "Now we can stop pointing fingers at the staff, and know we have an unwanted guest on Ivywick. We must inform the police."

Ruth couldn't resist a little needling. "What good will calling the police do?"

"She's right," Charles said from an armchair as he

pressed an ice pack to his forehead. "They can't get here until Fred is back from his fishing trip."

"You keep quiet," Margaret said. "You could've been murdered too." She glared at Ruth.

"I know," Ruth said. "My fault. Always my fault."

"Once again your incessant need to uncover each and every mystery gets you, and this time my husband, into trouble." She put her hands on her hips. "Greg said you were supposed to go to the kitchen next. That's where the puzzle was leading, so why the deviation? What on earth is more important than finding a will and avoiding a killer?"

"I had to know about the cave," Ruth said. "Don't you understand? It's all linked."

"How exactly?" Margaret asked.

Ruth muttered, "I'm not sure yet." Even so, she felt vindicated.

"So where did the phantom go?" Greg asked.

"He has to be a member of staff," Ruth said. "A stranger couldn't move about the island for all these years." Her attention rested on Charles. "Who's been here for decades?"

"Apart from Carter, only Captain Barney."

Ruth hadn't considered him as a suspect yet, purely for the fact he seemed unlikely to sink his own boat.

Could that have been a ruse?

"You asked the staff to lock all the external doors, right?" Ruth said to Margaret.

"Yes, I did as you told me." Margaret dropped to another armchair. "Although, I don't see how that helps. The murderer could have a spare set of keys for all we know."

Alec and Josh had told Ruth they did not have keys to the house, but they could have lied. Ruth pictured Josh killing the poor girl and then escaping back to the garden before Alec noticed he was missing. Josh then feigned innocence when Helen screamed, and came running with Alec in tow.

Ruth finished her tea and set it on a tray. "We'd better get to it."

"How are we going to trap him?" Greg whispered.

"It's gone half past two already," Margaret said. "We don't have time to play games with a killer." She sniffed. "Noah arrives soon. We must focus on finding the will. That's our priority."

"We can do both." Ruth looked at Charles. "Would you mind fetching your father's blueprint of the house, please? Take Greg with you."

Charles stood, squeezed Margaret's shoulder, and he and Greg left the room.

Margaret watched them go. "How do we know the squatter is the murderer, and is after the will too?"

"Well," Ruth said. "Yesterday morning we found Carter dead on the study floor. It appeared he'd been on the upper balcony, removing a puzzle box from the shelf, when he fell." She shrugged. "What was he doing?"

"We've been through this," Margaret said. "We can't know for sure that—"

Ruth held up a hand. "But we can know."

"Know what?" Charles returned with Greg and the rolled-up blueprint. He sat down and placed it on the coffee table between them.

"I was explaining how we can know with a degree of certainty that Carter was looking for the will," Ruth said.

"Of course he was," Charles said. "Why else would Carter have placed the riddle inside the Spitfire and shot it up to the lighthouse?"

"I found this in the cave room." Ruth pulled the phantom's journal from her pocket.

Margaret held out a hand. "Show me."

"We don't have time." Ruth pocketed the journal. "Suffice to say, the phantom noted various conversations, but the upshot is, Henry told Carter he'd hidden the will, and then he asked him to help Charles find it when the time came." She took a breath. "If the journal conversations are to be believed, Henry's will has you down as sole beneficiary," Ruth said to Charles. "As you'd anticipated. Meanwhile, Noah pressured your father to sell, but he refused." She took a breath. "I believe Carter thought the puzzle box was the last part of the riddle." Ruth pursed her lips as she thought through the events. "It must be related to a clue we have yet to reach. Somewhere near the end of Henry's trail."

"And the plaque," Greg said. "Maddie overheard Carter shouting the family motto."

Ruth unrolled the blueprint across the coffee table, and placed cups in each corner to hold it down. She then examined the redacted parts: one in the conservatory, another in the attic, yet another section missing over the study and hidden office . . .

"What are you doing?" Margaret asked. "The next part of the riddle points to the kitchen, no?"

Ruth glanced at Greg. "We have something else to figure out before we continue."

Margaret groaned. "Not this ridiculous notion that you're going to capture the murderer? Please, Ruth. I don't want anyone else to get hurt."

Ruth traced her finger over the walls, corridors, and rooms, and muttered under her breath. She needed to pick a suitable spot.

Her gaze halted on the study again. If the killer had overheard conversations taking place in there, he might have another way into the house, but Ruth could see nothing to suggest that. The redacted parts covered the middle of the room, all the way over to Henry's office. He'd clearly wanted to keep it a secret.

"I think Aunty Margaret is right," Greg said. "Let's find the will and let the police deal with the rest."

Ruth sighed at her sister's concerned expression. "I think he's waiting for us to do all the hard work, like he did with Carter, and then he'll pounce."

"And do what exactly?" Charles asked. "There's four of us."

Ruth continued to study the blueprint. "I'm sure he would have made allowances for that." Her attention moved to the other side of the house and the kitchen. Beyond was another redacted section. "We know the plaque figures into the riddle."

"And it comes before the puzzle box," Greg said, cottoning on to what Ruth had in mind.

"The plaque was in the dining hall." She tapped the blueprint. "Here. And the riddle led Carter to the puzzle box . . . here." Ruth indicated the study. "I think there's a chance the puzzle box was the wrong answer. I concede there could have been something inside that the killer took, so we won't know for sure until we get to that point in the riddle. But then why take the plaque?"

"They haven't found the will yet," Greg said.

Margaret stood, sauntered to the window, and stared out toward the front lawn. "How can the murderer know we're close to finding it?"

Ruth pursed her lips. She didn't have an answer to that either. Somehow, they could remain hidden and yet still eavesdrop. Her face fell as she watched her sister. "The study window," she breathed. "It's open all the time."

Charles' eyes widened in realisation. "That means—"

Ruth put a finger to her lips and signalled for Charles to remain silent.

Margaret spun back. "Means what?"

Charles swallowed and whispered, "The killer was outside when they eavesdropped on our conversations."

"Are you sure?" Margaret said. "Risky, if you ask me. Alec and Josh would have seen them." She looked at her watch. "Whatever you're planning, Ruth, let's do it fast. It's ten to three."

Greg pulled a copy of the riddle from his pocket. "There's still a lot more to go."

"Okay. Fine." Ruth stood. "I believe the next part of the riddle leads us to the kitchen." She marched from the sitting room with the others close behind, and on through the house.

A couple of minutes later, Ruth stepped into the kitchen, and her gaze moved to the doors at the end. In particular, the oak one with the crow and triangle carved into the stonework above.

"Is there something I can help with?" Cook Helen wiped her hands on her apron.

Betty and Ray sat at the table with downcast expressions and drawn faces.

"Sorry to be a pain," Margaret said as she strode into the kitchen with Charles and Greg. "We know how hard this has been on everyone, but can we please ask you to go to your rooms?"

Helen hesitated, stared at Ruth, and then bowed and left.

Betty and Ray stood.

"Thank you," Ruth said. "We should only be a few minutes." Once they'd left too, she hurried over to the door and peered up at the carving. "Same one. Right, Greg?"

"Same one."

Ruth opened the door and flicked on a light switch, revealing a pantry lined with shelves, each packed with cans and packets of food, plus plates, bowls, and a range of crockery.

Greg joined her. "What are we looking for?"

Ruth pictured a redacted part of the blueprint. "No idea." At the back of one shelf, something glinted and caught her eye. She moved a can of soup aside.

Behind it sat a round metal object, polished brass, and like the mushroom in the attic, Henry had fixed it to the shelf. Vertical lines were etched into its surface.

Ruth leaned in. "What are the remaining lines of the riddle?"

Greg read from his phone. "Remember you're alive, even though they're dead. Get under my skin, you'll be sure to cry."

Ruth chuckled and waved a finger at the metal object. "Onion. Get under my skin, you'll be sure to cry. It's an onion."

Margaret groaned. "Henry."

However, unlike the mushroom, the onion did not sit on a track.

Ruth reached for it.

Greg grabbed her arm. "Be careful."

Ruth motioned to the metal onion. "Do you want to do it?"

Greg let go of her.

Ruth rolled her eyes. "My brave grandson. Whatever would I do without you?"

"Probably have a lot more accidents."

"Don't tell me she's crashed that tin monstrosity again." Margaret smirked. "What did she hit this time?"

"I haven't crashed since Vanmoor," Ruth said. "I hardly ever do. It's a rare occurrence."

Greg snorted.

"Can we concentrate on the task at hand, please?" Ruth faced the shelf and grabbed the onion.

Nothing happened.

Ruth let out a breath. "See? It's fine." She tried to shift the onion left and right, but it wouldn't budge. Then Ruth attempted to pull it, followed by lifting, but still nothing happened. She let go. "Has anyone mentioned this before?"

"Not to me." Margaret glanced back at Charles, and he shook his head. "Hold on." She hurried from the room and, a couple of minutes later, returned with Helen. Margaret led her to the pantry and pointed at the metal onion. "Any idea what that is?"

"An enigma," Helen said in a sage tone.

Margaret cocked an eyebrow at her.

"It's been here longer than I have," Helen said. "I asked Master Andrews about it once."

"My father?" Charles said. "And what did he say?"

"He told me it was part of the shelves. Keeps them from falling, and that I should leave it be, if I know what's best."

"Wise words," Margaret said. "Thank you."

Once Helen had left the kitchen again, Greg asked, "Could it be another mechanism?"

"That's what I'm thinking." Ruth peered under the shelf containing the onion, but there were no obvious gears, rods, or levers of any kind. And certainly no electronic circuits.

"Try twisting it," Charles suggested.

Ruth did—first clockwise, and when that didn't work, she tried anticlockwise.

A loud clunk reverberated through the wall.

Startled, Ruth glanced over her shoulder.

Margaret, Charles, and Greg had leapt from the pantry, and now stood in the kitchen, peering in at her.

"Oh, thanks a bunch." Ruth let go of the onion, and froze as more loud clunks sounded from the walls around her.

Margaret gasped. "Look."

A panel in the wall slid aside, around a foot square, and a room stood beyond.

"Wait a second." Charles stepped back into the pantry and peered through the opening. "That's the boot room." He stared for a moment and then rushed off.

A minute later, he reappeared on the other side of the wall and gazed back at Ruth.

"Can you see anything out of the ordinary?" she asked.

"I never knew this panel was here." He looked around the room. "Nothing leaps out. Everything seems to be in its place."

"I'm coming round." Ruth turned to Greg and Margaret. "Wait here, in case we need you to twist that onion again." She then squeezed past, hurried out of the kitchen, down the hall, and the next corridor, and finally joined Charles.

The boot room had benches down each side, along with racks to store boots and hats, and hooks for coats and scarfs. A door opposite led to outside, and the walls were wood panelled, with one section slid aside to reveal the pantry beyond.

Greg waved.

Ruth waved back. "What're the remaining words in the riddle?"

Greg pulled the sheet from his pocket. "Umbrella, lawsuit, and the letter *U*. Plus the whole 'Remember you're alive, even though they're dead' bit."

Ruth's gaze locked onto the umbrella stand. First, she examined each umbrella—there were five in total. Four were plain black in both their handles and fabric. The fifth, however, had an ornate handle.

"My father's," Charles said.

Ruth held her breath, grabbed the umbrella, and removed it from the stand. She stiffened as something clicked, but nothing else happened. Ruth examined the umbrella.

Apart from being fancy with its carved mahogany handle, and a solid gold ring holding the ribs in place, it seemed like most other umbrellas.

Ruth unlocked the back door, stepped outside, and opened the umbrella. "Nothing unusual here." She closed the umbrella and walked back into the boot room. "Anything seem odd?"

Charles locked the back door and took the umbrella from her. "Not that I can tell."

Ruth removed the other umbrellas from the stand and used the torch on her phone to peer inside the empty receptacle. At the bottom was a cup-shaped receptacle where the posh umbrella had rested. "Here's something." She took Henry's umbrella back from Charles. The ferrule had several grooves. Ruth lined it up with the ridges inside the cup and slotted it into place. She shifted the umbrella to one side, and there came a soft click, but nothing else happened.

Ruth slid out the umbrella again and examined it. "When I worked for the police, we got calls about an old guy in the park, threatening some teenagers with a sword." She checked the handle closely. "When we arrived, we found him seated on a bench. Not a sword in sight, only a walking stick."

"How could people mistake a walking stick for a sword?" Charles asked.

"They couldn't." Ruth gripped the gold ring on the

umbrella, slid it down and twisted it one half of a turn. "The sword was hidden within the walking stick, similar to this." Ruth pulled the handle, and it came free.

However, instead of a sword hidden inside, an ornate key with a crosshatch pattern in the bow was revealed, and as she removed it, the cap on the other end of the umbrella retracted into the shaft.

Ruth held the key up to the light. "Anyone know what this is for?"

Charles gaped at it. "I do."

22

Amgine Hall's master bedroom, situated in one of the original castle sections of the house, was an oval room with stone walls, a four-poster bed, wooden chandelier, various rugs, and an open fireplace.

Charles faced an antique wardrobe—oak, with fine carvings of peacocks and various flowers, all intricately detailed.

"This is a French armoire." Greg looked impressed. "Mid-1800s."

"My father's prized possession," Charles said. "Gifted to him by Grandmama after his marriage to my mother."

"Heck of a wedding present," Ruth said. "All I got from John's mother was a scowl."

"Is it any wonder?" Margaret said. "You killed her bonsai tree."

"I did not." Ruth cleared her throat. "Just forgot to water it when she went on holiday. Anyone could make that mistake."

"She left you a note," Margaret said.

"It was vague."

"Giving specific instructions on when and how to water her beloved bonsai."

Ruth mumbled, "Couldn't read her handwriting."

Margaret waved a hand at the wardrobe. "You do realise if you'd listened to me in the first place and broken this open, we could've cut the need for most of this running about."

Charles brushed two fingers over his moustache as he considered the item of antique furniture. "I'm not breaking it." He held up the key. "Thanks to Ruth, now we don't need to."

"You haven't looked inside this since Uncle Henry died?" Greg asked.

"No." Charles glanced at Margaret, and then unlocked it.

If Carter already followed these clues, Ruth thought, *why did he return the key to the umbrella?*

Charles took a deep breath and opened the wardrobe.

Various suits hung from hooks, with an old leather suitcase in the bottom.

Charles knelt and opened it. "Empty." His shoulders slumped. "No will."

Margaret sighed and looked at the ceiling. "Would have been too easy. Right, Henry?"

"We're not finished with the riddle." Ruth motioned to Greg.

He removed it from his pocket and scanned the list of words. Then a smile swept across his face. "Lawsuit."

They all frowned at him.

"Don't you get it? Lawsuit. Law. Suit." Greg pointed at the suits hanging inside.

Ruth groaned. *A play on words.* Something else she was terrible at.

"But which suit is it referring to?" Margaret asked. "There's ten of them."

Charles indicated a black suit on the far right. He pulled back the lapel to reveal a shimmering gold lining.

Ruth whistled. "Fancy. How do you know it's that one?"

Charles let out a slow breath. "A friend of my father's, Ernest, was accused of embezzlement. He had no way to defend himself. My father not only hired a top lawyer, but also appeared in court to defend Ernest as a character witness."

"Did Ernest get off?" Greg asked.

"He did." Charles released the lapel and stepped back.

"That's not the end of the story," Margaret said. "Ernest saved your mother's life."

Greg's eyes widened.

"Not far from here, in fact," Charles said. "Killean. She was on her way home, rounded a bend in the road, swerved an oncoming motorcycle, and crashed. Knocked her unconscious, and the car caught fire. Ernest happened to be passing when he saw what had happened."

"Pulled Jean free of the wreckage," Margaret said.

"You see, if Ernest had wound up in jail," Charles said, "he—"

"Wouldn't have been there to save her life," Greg finished with a look of amazement.

Charles stared at the suit. "My father never wore this again but kept it as a reminder of his friendship."

"No kind action ever stops with itself," Ruth said in a sage tone.

"A quote of yours?" Charles asked.

"Amelia Earhart."

Also, as a police officer working in a close-knit community, Ruth had witnessed several acts of kindness that had thrown out roots in all directions, and then those roots had grown new trees. All it took was that first act to encourage others.

She nodded at Henry's suit. "May I?"

"Be my guest." Charles stepped aside.

Ruth lifted it from the hook, and a click and a whirring came from behind the wardrobe. She froze. "I'm sensing a theme."

However, as with the removal of the umbrella in the boot room, nothing else happened—no apparent secret doors or hatches sprang open this time either.

Ruth ran her fingers over the sides and back of the wardrobe, but found nothing out of the ordinary. She laid the suit on the bed and set about examining it. Ruth felt the lining, the stitching, and then she checked the pockets in turn. "There's something in this inside pocket." Ruth ran her fingers over the top edge. "Someone has sewn it shut." She looked at the others. "We need a knife."

"I've got one." Greg fished in his pocket and pulled out the Swiss Army knife he'd pilfered from the attic. He went to hand it over to Ruth but hesitated. "Sorry, Aunty Margaret. I forgot." He offered her an apologetic look. "May I have this, please?"

She stared at the red object in his hand. "What is it?"

"A birthday present from me to you," Ruth said through tight lips.

Margaret shrugged. "Of course you may have it, Gregory."

He smiled and handed it to Ruth.

She muttered under her breath as she pulled out a small blade and set to cutting the stitches across the inside pocket. Once done, Ruth handed the pocketknife back to Greg, and peered into the opening. "Well, that's not what I expected."

Ruth reached into Henry's jacket pocket and pulled out a first-place rosette, with red and gold ribbons.

"What on earth is that doing in there?" Margaret said.

Ruth flipped it over, but the back was blank. "One of your mother's?" she asked Charles.

"Another proud day in my parents' lives," he said. "When her horse won the Hatton Derby. A hundred-to-one shot."

"All she got was a ribbon?" Greg said, incredulous.

A flicker of a frown crossed Charles' face too. "Now you come to mention it, no. She received a splendid trophy."

"May we see it?" Ruth asked.

"Of course." Charles strode from the bedroom.

Ruth returned the suit to the wardrobe, prompting a loud clunk and a whirring. Then she followed the others down the corridor, into Charles's mother's horse room.

He pointed to a two-foot-high silver trophy on a stand. "This is the exact replica my father had made for her. The original had to return to the derby for the following season."

Ruth examined it. The trophy had all the past winners' names engraved, all the way up to Jean Andrews. She lifted the lid and peered inside. *Empty*. Then Ruth hoisted the trophy from the plinth by its handles and looked over at Greg. "Anything underneath?"

Greg examined the underside for a second, then shook his head.

With Greg's help, Ruth set the trophy back down, and then she pursed her lips as she thought about the riddle. Her gaze moved around the room, taking in all the other trophies, rosettes, and ornate salvers. "Something in here has to be related to our search." But nothing leapt out at her.

Ruth examined the picture of the riddle on her phone. All that remained was the sentence they had yet to decipher, and the letter *U*. Ruth stared, and a few seconds later she groaned.

"What is it?" Margaret asked.

Ruth couldn't help but shake her head. "The letter *U* in the riddle part we solved. It's not a letter."

"Then what is—" Charles groaned too.

Margaret's expression turned blank. "What am I missing?"

"It's a horseshoe." Ruth swept an arm around the room.

Greg's brow furrowed. "There's like a million things in here related to horses. How are we supposed to know what to look for?"

Ruth turned on the spot, and then she stared at the plinth with the porcelain horse statue. Suddenly, she understood. Ruth waved a finger at it and addressed Charles. "It was supposed to be here."

Realisation swept across his face. "Of course. I moved it after my father died."

"Moved what?" Greg asked.

Charles motioned to the trophy and the rosette in Ruth's hand. "Diamond Joy. The winner of those. Now I understand. My father wanted us to look at the horse statue. The one I moved."

"And it explains why Carter took it from its new spot." Ruth examined the plinth. "We need to return it."

Charles tapped Greg's arm. "Help me." They first removed the porcelain statue and set it in the corner of the room, then left to fetch the bronze version.

Ruth continued to examine the plinth in closer detail.

A craftsperson had made it from oak and steel, and the plinth appeared to be fixed to the floor by hidden bolts.

"Ruth?"

She looked up at her sister.

Margaret glanced back at the door and kept her voice low. "I wanted to thank you for everything you've done so far. Charles and I were at our wits' end. We wouldn't have even started without you."

Ruth ran her fingers around the bottom edge of the plinth. "You're welcome."

"I mean it," Margaret said. "You've saved the island."

Ruth stood. "We haven't found the will yet. The task isn't complete until we do." Although, she was flattered by her sister's faith.

Margaret lifted her chin. "I know you'll succeed. You always do when you put your mind to it." She rested a hand on Ruth's shoulder in a rare sign of affection. "Thank you. And as far as the re—" She pulled back as Greg and Charles carried the horse statue into the room and set it on the plinth.

Now it was in position, Ruth walked slowly round it, and examined all the details. "Carter went to the effort of bringing this back in here for a reason. He must have figured out something we haven't."

"It would appear Carter knew many things he neglected to share." Charles' jaw clenched.

"I can't see why he brought it back in here, though." Ruth rested a hand on the horse's saddle. "Is this the exact orientation it was in before you moved it?" she asked Charles. The base of the statue was octagonal, so there were seven other positions to set.

"It faced the door, as it does now," Charles said.

Ruth brushed her fingers over the horse's mane and head. "What are we missing here?" She motioned to Greg. "Read out the line for this horseshoe clue again."

He removed the sheet from his pocket. "You'll find me in a puzzle, not in a riddle, and in you, never him."

"We have only one more part after this?" Ruth asked.

"Right," Greg said. "The death bit."

Ruth stepped back, clasped her hands behind her back, and glared at the statue as exasperation clawed at her chest. "From what we can gather from his last movements, Carter did something with this statue, and then some time after that he wound up in the dining hall. There, Maddie overheard him telling someone about the family motto on the plaque."

"After, he went to the study," Charles said.

"Which is where we found him," Margaret added with a shudder.

"But if there's only one clue remaining, why is there a further two steps?" Greg asked. "Why did Carter look at that plaque and then go to the study?"

Ruth crossed her arms and considered the riddle. "You'll find me in a puzzle."

"You think that's why Carter had that puzzle box?" Greg asked.

Ruth's eyes narrowed in concentration. She walked around the statue again, hoping for some other clue to miraculously leap out at her. "Somehow, this led Carter to the family crest, and then on to the puzzle boxes, but I can't see the connection." She ground her teeth. "We're still missing something, but what?"

Greg read from the sheet. "Remember you're alive, even though they're dead." He looked at Ruth. "Could the answer be something to do with the mausoleum? Is it a full circle?"

Charles leaned against the doorframe. "Carter went to the dining room, not outside."

Ruth gripped the horse statue. "Everything else has had some sort of mechanism built into it. Some way to lead us to the next location." She ran her fingers down the sides. "This is solid. Nothing moves. Which leaves us with . . ." Her hands slid down to the plinth. However, Ruth had already examined it in detail, and found nothing. "Why would Carter bring the statue in here? It's as if they have to be together to—" Ruth froze. "It's a key."

"What's a key?" Margaret asked.

"Diamond Joy." Ruth waved a finger at it. "The statue needs to be on this plinth. Which means it's the key, and the plinth is the lock. That's why Carter had to bring it in here." She gripped either side of the horse and attempted to turn it clockwise, but it wouldn't budge. Ruth took a breath and tried in the opposite direction.

The statue rotated the top lip of the plinth anticlockwise by one face and clicked into position. Then there came a mechanical whirring of cogs, and a panel slid aside in the base to reveal a bronze knight, twelve inches tall.

"Well done, Ruth," Charles said. "Bravo." He squinted. "I've never seen it before."

Ruth reached into the hidden compartment and lifted out the statue of the knight. She examined it for a moment, and then, given the knight's posture and spacing of their legs, and the fact they were bent at the knees, Ruth knew what had to be done. "Help."

Greg hurried over and took the weight on one side. Together they hoisted the rider and slotted it onto the horse.

When they released the equestrian, leaving her in the saddle, the whole statue dropped by an inch. Ruth cried out and reached for it, but stopped herself as a new mechanical thunk came from within both the statue and the plinth.

Something vibrated beneath the floorboards, then the helmeted head turned to face the right.

All three of them watched in amazement.

"What's it supposed to mean?" Margaret whispered.

"I know exactly what it means." Ruth faced the other three. "Now it's time to kill two birds with one stone." She balled her fists. "We're going to trap the killer, and then uncover the will." She squeezed Margaret's arm. "It's almost over." She hurried from the room.

23

In the downstairs corridor, once sure they were in a spot it would be hard to overhear their conversation, Ruth beckoned for Margaret, Charles, and Greg to huddle close. She whispered, "When we go into the study, sit at the table by the window that's open, and follow my lead. Don't say anything other than brief responses to what I'm talking about. Understood?" Her plan was spur of the moment and risky, but it was all she could come up with under such pressure and time constraints.

"You think the killer can hear us when we're in there?" Margaret murmured.

"I'm banking on it." Ruth recalled the blueprint of the house and addressed Charles. "Open the exterior door to the laundry room, but make sure all other external doors remain locked. Bolt them too, so there's no way for someone to open them from the outside. Double-check." Ruth glanced about. "Then I want you to call Captain Barney, tell him the laundry room door is open, and ask him to meet us in the study."

Charles' face dropped. "You think the captain is involved?"

Ruth's balled her fists. She didn't have time to explain. "Take Greg with you. Come straight back here when you're done. No deviation."

Charles hesitated, then nodded, and marched off with Greg.

Margaret's expression turned grave. "You're really going to try to trap this phantom person?"

"We have no choice," Ruth said. "We can't complete the riddles until we do. Otherwise they could pounce at the last second and take it from us." Ruth opened the door to the study, and the two of them went inside and sat at the table by the window. She then took a breath and said in a loud, clear voice, "We've checked the dining hall. There's nothing in there that can help us."

Margaret stared at her, and then realisation dawned on her face. "Shouldn't we check again?"

"Later." Ruth stretched. "I need to think." She turned in her chair and looked over at the blackboard. "Clearly the knight turning their head like that is a clue. I know I've seen something similar but can't remember where." She faced Margaret again. "Can you think of any object that has that knight on it? I was sure it would be among the armour in the dining hall." She gave her sister a hard look, reminding her to be vague in her answers.

Margaret blinked. "I— I don't think so."

Ruth interlaced her fingers and rested her elbows on the table. "Then we're missing something. We can't finish the riddle until we figure it out."

"But we're so close," Margaret said.

The study door opened. Charles and Greg marched into the room and sat at the table.

"What did we miss?" Charles gave Ruth a small nod.

She sat back. "We'll have to check out the dining hall again in a while. There must be something that helps us finish this riddle."

Margaret studied her watch. "Noah and the police will arrive in a little over an hour."

Ruth's stomach did a backflip.

To burn off some nervous energy, she stood and paced the study, with her hands clasped behind her back. Ruth was about to go over what clues she'd so far gathered, and see if there was anything she had overlooked, when there came a knock at the door.

"That must be Captain Barney." Charles strode over and opened it.

However, it wasn't Captain Barney, but Ray.

Ruth stared in confusion.

"What are you doing here?" Margaret said, as if reading her mind. "What's happened? And why are you prowling about the house on your own?"

Ray looked at Ruth. "I've got something to tell you."

Charles stepped aside. "Come in."

Ray shook his head and kept his focus on Ruth. "Alone."

"Not a chance," Greg snarled.

Ruth raised a hand. "It's okay."

"You can't be serious." Margaret frowned.

"I'll be right here." Ruth stepped into the hall and closed the door behind her. "What's this about?"

Ray clenched and unclenched his fists, and shuffled from foot to foot. "I had to tell you. It's been bothering me."

Ruth inclined her head.

Ray took a deep breath. "Yesterday morning, Betty caught Carter in the boot room. He was hunting for something."

Ruth kept her expression neutral. "Go on."

"He didn't say what it was, only that he couldn't find it. Carter was irate. Bordering on manic." Ray looked at the door behind Ruth and lowered his voice. "He asked Betty to help him with something. She says he didn't tell her what, only that it would mean Noah could claim his rightful inheritance."

Despite herself, Ruth's eyebrows shot up. "Carter *was* in cahoots with Noah."

"He told Betty all about him," Ray said. "Carter explained Noah's plans to turn the island into a high-class hotel resort, and said if Betty helped him, he'd make sure she had a job for life. Double pay too."

Ruth stared as she tried to comprehend. "Betty told you all this?"

"Last night."

"Why didn't she say something to me?"

Ray shrugged. "You'll have to ask her. But I'm telling you. I don't want them to turn this place into a hotel. I like working here. Good pay and free accommodation. Why would I give that up for some rich Australian guy's crazy plan?"

"Who else has Betty told?"

"Everyone," Ray said.

Ruth nodded as the new information sank in.

Carter had conspired with Noah. Which meant he could've burned down the solicitors, thinking they had another copy of the will, and then hunted for the one here. In desperation, he'd then told other people.

Did someone team up with Carter and then betray him?

That same person had gone on to murder Maddie.

Of course, Ruth had no evidence of any of this.

She blew out a puff of air. "Thank you."

Ray hesitated. "I'm sorry I didn't tell you sooner." Then he hurried off.

"Stay in your room for the rest of the day," Ruth called.

Ray waved a hand in acknowledgement and rounded the corner.

Ruth stared after him for a few seconds as the full weight of what he'd told her sank in, and then she hung her head and traipsed back toward the study.

Outside the door, Ruth remained frozen, gripping the handle, as she thought about what she would tell Margaret and Charles.

Carter had conspired with Noah, and the chances were he'd then partnered up with another member of staff to help him with the riddle.

Ruth's money was on Josh.

Their plan had been to locate the will and not to hold it to ransom, but to destroy it. Of course, the island estate would then split between Charles and Noah. As Margaret had feared, without the finances to defend themselves, Noah would force a sale and take it for himself.

Ruth's chest tightened as another thought struck her— the motorhome accident. Josh had faked a mishap not to claim insurance, not to scam her, but to delay Ruth's arrival, leaving Carter able to finish the riddle and find the will in peace. His surprise and unease at seeing Ruth and Greg in Alec's cottage had clearly been an act.

However, Josh's plan hadn't worked, so he'd raced back to the island with Fisherman Fred's help, and snuck into the study with Carter while Ruth and Greg had lunch in the dining hall.

During that time, Carter and Josh must have had their altercation, and Carter fell to his death. Whether manslaughter or murder, the crime was a heinous one, and Ruth was determined to bring Josh to justice.

She composed herself, turned the handle on the study door, and stepped inside.

"What on earth was that about?" Margaret asked.

Ruth sat at the table next to Greg, opposite her sister and brother-in-law. Ruth considered lying, concealing the truth for now, knowing the reaction she was about to face, but she couldn't keep it a secret.

However, Ruth also could not risk this new theory being overheard. She glanced at the open window. "Nothing much. He wanted to know when they could go about their business. I told him to wait for the police."

She opted to not say anything about Josh for the time being, not until she had solid proof and could be certain. Right now, it was nothing but a theory.

Besides, given Ruth's insistence on an interview with Josh earlier, the way she'd chased after him, there was a good chance he'd be wary of her now.

She needed to be smart about this.

The door to the study opened, and Captain Barney stuck his head in. "Everything a'richt?"

"Thank you for coming." Ruth stood, glad to avoid her sister's inevitable reaction. She indicated for Margaret and Greg to stay put, but for Charles to follow her out.

"This way, please, Captain." Ruth led him through the house and into the kitchen. No one else was there. The house staff must have been in their rooms. She pointed to a seat at the table.

Captain Barney sat with a puzzled expression. "Am I in trouble?"

Once Charles had slipped into the kitchen, Ruth shut

the door and whispered to the captain, "We're close to finding out who sank your boat."

His bushy eyebrows lifted. "Is that so?"

"You left the laundry room door unlocked?" Ruth asked.

Captain Barney looked between Charles and her. "Was I nae supposed to?"

"You did the right thing." Ruth took a deep breath and hoped her plan worked. "Would you mind staying here in the house until we call for you?" Having an extra pair of rugged hands about the place could come in handy if there was any confrontation with the killer imminent.

It was clear Barney could more than handle himself, and Ruth doubted someone would attempt to murder him.

Captain Barney nodded. "Sure."

"We could be some time," Ruth added.

"Nae problem," he said. "I'll make a cuppa."

Ruth smiled and ushered Charles from the room.

In the hallway, he leaned in to her. "Are you going to explain what you're doing?"

"It's time to catch a murderer."

Charles stared at her. "How?"

"I made it very clear in the study that we can't continue without the plaque."

"The one you left in the underground room," Charles said. "Why not get it?" Realisation swept across his face. "Ah, you want the killer to put it back?"

"I do," Ruth said.

"You think the murderer is the phantom?"

"I believe they're the same person, yes." Ruth's stomach tensed. "But we'll need to trap them to prove my theory."

"In the dining hall?"

Ruth shook her head. "We must see that plaque again. I forgot to take photos, and it could have a hidden compartment. So I have a better idea." She edged her way down the hallway, to the corner. Ruth pointed to the inner laundry room door and placed a finger to her lips.

Charles nodded.

However, they didn't have long to wait. A few minutes later, the door to the laundry room opened, and a figure rushed past the end of the corridor.

Charles went to go after them, but Ruth grabbed his arm.

"Wait here." Ruth darted from the corridor into the laundry room. Once there, she locked the door to the outside, and with a lot of effort, snapped the key in the lock, making sure there was no way to open it again.

Ruth raced back to Charles.

He whispered, "Now what?"

She raised a hand, and her ears strained.

A few minutes more and the footfalls returned.

She held her breath as the figure rushed past the end of the corridor in the opposite direction, and as soon as they had closed the inner door to the laundry room, Ruth ran over and locked it, sealing them inside.

Charles joined Ruth, and they peered through the circular window.

In the laundry room, Josh whirled around. His eyes met theirs. "What are you doing?"

Charles' face twisted with anger. "You." He stabbed a finger at the window. "You did this."

Ruth took his arm and pulled him away.

Josh banged his clenched fists on the laundry room door. "Let me out of here. You're making a mistake."

Ruth spun on her heel, marched through the house with Charles and stopped outside the dining hall. She opened the door and peeked inside. Sure enough, Josh had placed the Andrews family crest back on the wall.

"I'll fetch Margaret and Greg." Charles hurried off.

However, after a glance at Maddie's body, Ruth closed the door again and pressed her back against the woodwork.

They were close to the end.

She could feel it.

Charles returned with Margaret and Greg in tow.

"What happened?" Greg looked toward the dining room door behind her.

"Your grandmother just captured the culprit," Charles said. "Quite clever. A simple and effective solution. He'll hold there until the police arrive."

Margaret spoke through clenched teeth. "They're in there?"

Ruth shook her head. "Somewhere safe."

"Who is it?" Greg asked.

Ruth hesitated, and then she let out a long breath. "You were right all along. It's Josh." She eyed her grandson and braced herself.

Margaret's expression hardened. "Where is he?"

Charles rested a hand on her shoulder. "Best you don't know the answer to that, my love. Let the police deal with him. He's going nowhere. We can finish the riddle in peace."

Greg's face dropped. "Wait. Who's the phantom, then?"

"Must be long gone," Charles said. "Josh found the hidden room and has been using it. Not a big surprise, given the fact he works in the garden."

Ruth wasn't so sure about that theory.

"That's how he overheard us?" Margaret asked. "Through the open window? He was hiding in the garden and eavesdropping on our conversations?"

"Started by listening in on Henry." Ruth tapped her

pocket with the notebook. "He copied down conversations. That's how he knew about the will." It was damning evidence, and she'd hand it over to the detective. Ruth faced the dining room door. "Give me a minute."

"I'll come with you." Greg stepped beside her.

"But Maddie—"

Greg took a deep breath. "I won't look."

Ruth checked the time on her phone. They only had thirty-five minutes until Noah, his lawyers, and the police arrived.

"But even if we can solve these final parts of the riddle, Carter smashed the puzzle box," Margaret said. "Whatever was inside, Josh must have taken. We should demand he hand it over."

"He can't have taken anything," Charles said. "If that were the case, then why return the plaque?" He nodded at Ruth. "It was a shrewd way to confirm your suspicions."

"Give us a few minutes." Ruth opened the door and slipped into the dining hall with Greg.

24

As Ruth and Greg marched across the grand dining hall, Ruth wondered if there was an afterlife, and whether Henry watched them right now.

Is he smiling down at us, pleased with his crazy riddle and the fact we're all running about like lunatics, trying to solve it?

"Should we cover her?" Greg said. "You know, Maddie. It's respectful, right?" He eyed a stack of table linen.

"I'd love to, but we can't disturb the scene." Ruth lifted the plaque from the wall and examined the hook. No hidden mechanisms like the other items they'd discovered.

She muttered the remaining words of the riddle under her breath, "Remember you're alive, even though they're dead. Remember you're alive, even though they're dead." Ruth frowned. "I can't see what it has to do with this crest. There are no other inscriptions." She widened her eyes. "Ancestors?"

"Remember you're alive, even though they're dead." Greg beamed at her. "That has to be it."

Ruth examined the list of Andrews family members on

the back. "Hmm." She returned the plaque to the wall and stared at it. "I'm not so sure. This must be wrong."

"How can it be?" Greg said. "The horse statue and rider. The turned head." He waved a finger at the plaque. "They match. Same as this. Andrews family crest."

Ruth pursed her lips.

This is where Carter wound up before the study. Maddie confirmed that, but . . . "What if Carter made the same mistake we're making right now?" After all, some riddles had been open to interpretation. "We've missed something." Ruth huffed in frustration. "It doesn't match Henry's other answers. There's no mechanism. No link or clue to the will's hiding place."

They were so close to solving the entire riddle, but this final part was infuriating. She clenched her teeth. For a moment, Ruth considered Henry might have died before he'd finished setting up all the clues, but she dismissed the idea.

After all, the elaborate nature of the setup, using the entire house as the game, would have taken him many months to plan and then construct in secret. In fact, now Ruth came to think of it, the blueprint dated back decades. Henry had played the ultimate long game.

"Maybe we're not missing anything." Greg stepped close to the plaque. "Look at these." He pointed to sections of the family crest on each side of the knight.

Ruth leaned in for a closer look.

What she'd assumed was a simple tartan pattern, or crosshatch design, was in fact a series of interlocking rectangles and squares.

"What do they remind you of?" Greg asked.

"A puzzle box." She stared at the family crest design.

Something still seemed off. This plaque didn't fit in with the rest of the riddle. The rectangles were like the puzzle boxes, sure, and she could understand the connection Carter had made, but they weren't an exact match. In her view, it had to be a coincidence. Carter had made a mistake.

But what are we missing? What wrong turn did we take?

There was nothing else for it—Ruth needed to go back a step. Alone. With a clear mind and free to look again without undue pressure.

"Come on." She marched across the room with Greg, and they stepped back into the hallway, meeting up with Margaret and Charles. "Wait here, please," Ruth said to the three of them, and she raced up the stairs, across the landing, and into the horse room.

To her surprise, the rider on the statue had now reset, facing the door again.

Ruth grabbed the base, turned it, and there came the familiar whirring of gears, and the vibration beneath the floorboards.

As before, the rider's head turned to the side.

Ruth glared at her. "So? What am I missing?" She circled the statue, hunting for more clues, but nothing stood out.

Frustration gnawed at her insides.

They were almost out of time.

She returned to the front. "The only thing that moves is her head," Ruth murmured. "Her head? Why? It's almost as if she's looking at something over . . ." Ruth followed the equestrian rider's gaze to the photograph on the wall—the image of the Andrews family and Diamond Joy.

A younger Henry, in his fifties, and Charles, in his early thirties, stood on either side of a sleek dark horse with ribbon around its neck. Jean, decked in her rider gear, held a silver cup, and all three Andrews family members smiled at the camera.

Ruth hurried over to the photo.

Behind them were a set of stands filled with spectators, and to the left of those was a funfair, complete with carousel, a haunted house, and a Ferris wheel painted in bright reds and yellows.

Ruth inhaled. "Okay." With her heart pounding in her chest, she ran from the horse room and back downstairs. She raced past Margaret, Charles, and Greg. "Quickly. This way. Hurry up." Ruth threw open the door to the study and went in.

Ruth found the hidden switch in the bookshelf and swung it open to reveal Henry's secret office.

Inside, she faced one shelf full of his mechanical devices. "This is what we're supposed to find." Ruth pointed at the model of the Ferris wheel. "It's what the bronze rider was looking at upstairs. In the picture on the wall. That's why her head turned to the side."

Charles' eyes widened. "Of course. In the photograph. I remember."

Ruth examined the Ferris wheel and then tried to turn it around to look at the back, but Henry had bolted it to the shelf.

"He didn't want us to move it." Greg leaned in. "Which means . . ."

"It's part of Henry's riddle."

Ruth found a lever on the side. She looked over at Margaret and Charles.

They both nodded.

Ruth held her breath and turned the handle.

Nothing happened.

"Oh, come on." Exasperated, she tried again, but got an identical result.

"Is there some way to wind it up?" Greg asked.

"It's winding me up," Ruth muttered.

"The Ferris wheel is not clockwork," Charles said.

Ruth stared at him. "What do you mean?"

Charles pulled a tray from the base. "You put water in here, and then light this part." He hinged a door open to reveal a glass reservoir filled with paraffin, and a wick. "It's steam powered."

The front doorbell rang.

All four of them stiffened.

"Who's that?" Greg whispered.

"They're early." Margaret looked at her watch. "Why are they early?"

"Fred must have ended his fishing trip," Charles said.

Margaret's expression hardened. "Remind me to cross him off our Christmas card list."

"Is anyone left on there?" Ruth got a grip of herself. "Keep them busy."

Margaret blinked. "For how long?"

"I don't know." Ruth glanced at the Ferris wheel. "Make them drinks. Put on a coffeepot. Tell them it takes time for it to percolate. Settle them into the sitting room. Make them biscuits. I don't care, just do whatever it takes. Buy me some time."

The front doorbell rang again.

"The police will want to start their investigation straight away," Margaret said with a look of incredulity.

"Let them," Ruth said. "But keep them out of here."

"And what about our friend in the laundry room?" Charles asked.

"Don't tell the police about him yet," Ruth said as she thought it through. "Hold off for now. I'm concerned they'll want to interview us all if they know about Josh. They'll demand explanations. I want to find the will first. As soon as it's safe, then tell them about Josh." When the doorbell rang for a third time, Ruth waved Margaret and Charles off. "Go. Hurry."

They hesitated for a second and then raced away.

Ruth squeezed Greg's shoulder. "Let's finish this." She faced the Ferris wheel again. "How did Charles say we get it working?"

Greg removed the tray. "We fill this with water."

Ruth motioned to the study. "There's a jug in there from lunch."

Greg marched off and returned a minute later with the tray. "I only put a little bit of water in here. Otherwise we'll be waiting ages for it to boil." He slid the tray back into the base of the Ferris wheel. "That should do it."

"Now what?" Ruth asked.

Greg opened the hatch below. "Now we need some way to light the wick."

Ruth looked about but couldn't see a handy lighter anywhere. She circled the desk and opened each drawer in turn. In the lowermost right-hand drawer she found a packet of matches.

Ruth gave them to Greg.

He lit the wick, set the flame to maximum intensity, and then closed the hatch.

"And now what?" Ruth's impatience grew exponentially with every passing second.

Greg stepped back. "It will take a few minutes."

Ruth's eyes widened. "A few minutes?" She paced the room, and her stomach twisted into knots as three minutes turned into four, and then into five. "Come on. Come on."

Finally, steam rose from a vent.

Ruth raced back to Greg. "That's it?"

"Almost." Greg turned a dial on the side, held his breath, and pulled a lever. Nothing happened. "Hmm." He checked the dial again, turned it all the way up, and then pulled the lever for a second time.

Still nothing.

"You have got to be kidding me."

Greg examined the wheel and mechanism. "Doesn't look jammed."

"We're missing something," Ruth murmured.

"Like what?"

"Remember you're alive, even though they're dead."

Greg screwed up his face. "Right. Ancestors?"

Ruth shook her head, and her gaze moved to the three painted solar systems at the Ferris wheel's hub. Each one had a sun with planets orbiting. "Remember you're alive, even though they're dead."

Although, what if they're not planets? Not suns? And definitely not solar systems?

Then it suddenly clicked into place.

Ruth chuckled.

Greg looked between her and the Ferris wheel. "Grandma?"

"Remember you're alive, even though they're dead." She pointed at the image. "Not solar systems. They're atoms."

Greg stared for a few seconds, and then realisation dawned on his face. "Remember you're alive, even though they're dead. You're alive, but the atoms that make you aren't." He blew out a puff of air. "How did you figure that out?"

"I have no idea." Ruth pressed the middle, and the hub

cover hinged aside to reveal a second lever. She swung it down. "Try now."

Greg flipped the other lever, and the Ferris wheel began turning. "Yes."

Something moved beneath the floorboards, as though a mechanical beast stirred.

Ruth followed the sound to the door, but then the Ferris wheel stopped with a clunk. She spun back. "What happened?"

Greg adjusted the dial as steam rose, and he pulled both levers again, but the Ferris wheel didn't move this time. "It's jammed."

Something beneath the floorboards then slid back toward the contraption, as though resetting itself.

Ruth threw her hands up.

"I don't get it." Greg scratched his chin. "It should work."

Ruth's gaze drifted from the Ferris wheel to the floor, and then over to the study door. "It's a mechanism," she murmured. "Like the others."

Greg looked back at her. "Huh?"

"Could they all have something that connects—" Ruth smacked her forehead. "Of course. Now it makes sense." She beckoned for Greg to follow her. In the study, Ruth marched over to the table with the blueprint. "Look at this." She indicated all the blacked-out sections. "We wondered why Henry redacted these areas. Now we know."

Greg nodded slowly, and then he shrugged. "I don't get it."

"All these different areas have a mechanism attached. That's what Henry was hiding. Machinery running through the entire building. In the floor and the walls." Ruth ran her finger over the blueprint. "All these blacked-out areas are next to where we found puzzle pieces." She pointed at the attic, then the master bedroom, the horse room, and pantry, plus boot room. Ruth thrust a finger at the door to the study. "There too." She indicated the corresponding location on the blueprint. "He wasn't hiding the secret office, but the mechanism."

"Are you saying they're all linked?"

Ruth took a breath. "It's like those mechanical toys and contraptions Henry made, only scaled up a thousand times. A giant Rube Goldberg machine."

Greg gave her a dubious look. "Nothing connected to the device in the well. It's electronic, not mechanical."

"We don't know what it activates," Ruth said. "A motor somewhere? A switch? Could be anything."

Greg still didn't look convinced. "What about the mausoleum?"

"That was the start, with the braille. I don't believe it's part of the house mechanism." Ruth looked to the door and lowered her voice. "Remember the onion in the pantry? When I moved it, something clunked in the floor."

"And revealed that hatch in the wall," Greg said.

"But that's not all it does." Ruth tried to contain her excitement, but butterflies ravaged her stomach. "Same thing happened in the attic. And with the wardrobe, but didn't activate anything obvious. Same with that switch in the stair's newel cap." Ruth took a juddering breath. "When I went back to check the rider on the horse, it had reset. My guess is it must have taken five or ten minutes to do that. I bet they've all reset since, but it still gives us enough time. Exactly how Henry designed it."

Greg inclined his head. "Enough time?"

"We need to hurry." Ruth pointed at the corresponding locations on the blueprint as she spoke. "Go to the attic and activate the mushroom, then the wardrobe hook in the master bedroom, and finally, the rider in the horse room. Meanwhile, I'll activate all the ones downstairs. We'll meet back here. Got it?"

"I think so." He blew out the wick on the Ferris wheel.

"And don't get caught," Ruth warned him. "We've only got one shot at this, and not enough time to explain ourselves."

25

R uth opened the study door and peered into the hallway.

Voices came from further down.

She pressed a finger to her lips and slipped through, with her grandson close behind.

Together, they tiptoed along the corridor, staying close to the wall. At the door to the dining hall, Ruth held her breath and peeked around the doorframe.

Sure enough, Doctor Cleaves examined Maddie's body at the far end, while Margaret, seated opposite Detective Murray at the table, answered his questions in a slow, sombre voice.

Ruth pressed a finger to her lips and motioned for Greg to step around her when no one was looking.

He darted past the door, and she followed a second later.

The next door down also stood open by a few inches, and more voices came from inside.

Clearest of all was Charles. "I'm not signing a damn thing until I've read it all. Stop pressuring me."

Greg raced up the stairs, while Ruth hurried down

another corridor. At the end she headed into the conservatory.

Once there, Ruth peered into the well, cupped her hands around her mouth, and called, "Yoo-hoo." A few seconds later, the device repeated her call, but as before, there came no click or whirring. However, the light on the device turned from red to green.

Ruth pulled back, and hoped that did the trick.

She raced from the conservatory, down the hallway, and darted into the kitchen.

Captain Barney sat at the table, mug of coffee in front of him. "Everything a'right?"

"It's fine. Thank you for waiting." Ruth hurried into the pantry. She twisted the onion, and this time a loud clunk came from the wall and floor. Ruth winced and murmured, "Hope that's a good sign." She returned to the kitchen, smiled at Captain Barney as she passed him, and then raced into the boot room.

She returned the key to the umbrella, which pushed the tip out. "That's why Carter returned the key. He was trying to figure out what the mechanism does." Ruth replaced the umbrella in the stand, aligned the grooved ferrule inside the cup, turned it, and received a reassuring clunking.

She stepped back into the corridor and froze.

The door to the laundry room stood open.

Ruth's heart jumped into her chest. She crept over and peered into the room.

Josh had gone.

With blood pounding in her ears, Ruth stared into the empty laundry room, hardly believing her own eyes.

"What's happened?"

Ruth leapt out of her skin and spun around, fists raised.

Captain Barney stood in the corridor. "Something wrong?"

"Oh, it's you." Ruth let out a breath. "There's no time to explain, but Josh has escaped." She waved a finger at the laundry room. "We locked him in there."

"Why would—" Captain Barney's bushy eyebrows rose. "Ye think he murdered Carter? Maddie?"

Ruth tried to clear her head. "I need to get back to Greg."

"Leave Josh to me." Captain Barney cracked his knuckles.

"He's dangerous," Ruth said. "If you find him, let Detective Murray know. Please be careful."

"I've dealt with worse."

Ruth hesitated. It wasn't a good idea to let the captain loose on a murderer, especially considering Josh had sunk his prized possession, but she was out of time. "Don't do anything that can get you into trouble." She squeezed his hand, and then hurried away.

Fearing for her grandson's life, and cursing herself for suggesting they split up to perform the tasks, Ruth ran from the corridor, and across the hall.

She twisted the newel cap on the stairs and received the electrical spark in confirmation of a solid switch.

Ruth pulled back. "Hopefully, that's it."

She snuck past the sitting room door, then stopped at the dining hall, heart pounding, trying to get her breathing under control and failing.

Chest heaving, Ruth peered around the doorframe.

Margaret was still giving her statement to the detective in a low drone, while the doctor now sat nearby, making notes and filling out forms.

Detective Murray rested his chin in his hand and looked like he was about to fall asleep.

Ruth darted past, ran into the study, and closed the door behind her. She then locked and bolted it for good measure, before facing the room. "Greg? Please tell me you're back." Ruth ran to the hidden office door and slid to a halt. She let out an enormous sigh of relief.

Greg stood by the desk. "You were quick." He grinned. "But I was quicker." Sweat glistened on his forehead.

Ruth bent double, panting. "Thank goodness you're okay."

Greg's brow furrowed. "Why wouldn't I be?"

Ruth winced and straightened. "Josh escaped."

Greg stared at her, motionless and unblinking. "He's what?"

"Must have picked the lock. He's gone." Ruth then inclined her head. "No. That can't be right." Her heart sank. She removed the laundry room door key from her pocket and held it up. "The loop."

"What loop?"

"On Carter's belt." Ruth closed her eyes. "He had a leather loop, but with nothing on it." She groaned and looked at Greg. "I bet it was for a set of keys." Ruth smacked her forehead. "What butler doesn't have a full set of keys for every door in the house? Josh took them from him." It seemed so obvious now.

Sure, if Josh was the phantom, he must have had keys to external doors, especially if he still stole food from the kitchen. That was why Ruth had made sure Charles bolted the doors from the inside, forcing Josh to enter via the laundry room. She'd broken off the key, but then neglected the internal door.

Ruth shook herself and motioned to the Ferris wheel. "Hurry." She peered into the study. The door to the hallway was still closed and locked, with the bolt across. Even if Josh had Carter's keys, he couldn't open it.

Greg lit the wick beneath the Ferris wheel again and then adjusted the dial. As soon as steam issued from the vent, he pulled on the levers, and the Ferris wheel rotated.

The familiar whirring and grinding reverberated beneath their feet, and the pair of them followed it from the office into the study, where it intensified.

Ruth turned on the spot and prayed no one overheard.

Greg gasped and pointed.

They backed toward the fireplace as the middle of the parquet floor shifted. Its wooden tiles slid under and past one another as though it was a giant puzzle box. And then the circular section with the labyrinth pattern rose into the room.

Beneath the wooden slab was a glass cabinet, four feet high, with six shelves crammed full of diamond-encrusted jewellery: necklaces, earrings, tiaras . . . On the bottom shelf sat handfuls of gold coins, and among them was an A4 card file.

Greg dropped to his knees. "A glass safe, hidden beneath our feet all this time?" His eyes sparkled. "Amazing. I've seen nothing like it before."

"It explains where Jean's jewellery vanished to," Ruth said. "Henry didn't sell it after all." There was enough there to finance the island for many years to come. "Clever Henry." She smiled. "That's why he left the riddle for Charles." She waved a finger at the jewellery. "That's what he had in mind, not the will. He kept it in there for safekeeping, but Henry assumed the jewellery would be the real prize." Ruth nodded at the file and took a step toward the safe, but her attention flittered to an open window.

She stiffened, and her breath caught.

Someone had undone the bolt and propped the window open with a spade handle.

For a second, Ruth thought of Josh. However, he hadn't had time to escape the laundry room, run round the back of the house, unbolt the window, and then climb through. Which only left—

Ruth spun round at a gasp.

Alec had hauled Greg to his feet and now held a knife to his throat.

Ruth raised her hands and glanced at the armchairs. Alec must have been seated in one of them this whole time, obscured by the high back. In her haste to solve the riddle and find the will before Josh, Ruth had made a basic error.

Greg winced as the head groundskeeper pressed the knife into his neck.

"Make a sound," Alec growled. "Either of you, so much as a peep, and the boy gets it."

Greg offered his grandmother an apologetic look, as if he blamed himself, and his legs trembled.

Doing everything she could to remain calm and clear headed, Ruth kept her hands raised, her voice level. "No one needs to get hurt."

Alec kicked a duffle bag across the floor to her, and then motioned at the safe. "Fill it."

Ruth's whole body quivered as she scooped up the duffle bag and headed to the glass cabinet. She opened the door, grabbed handfuls of jewellery, and shoved them into the bag. "You knew this would be here, didn't you?"

Alec hadn't been after the will at all.

"All of it," he snarled. "And be quick."

Ruth rested the open duffle bag against each shelf and swept her arm from front to back, sliding the contents into it. Then she scooped out the gold coins from the bottom shelf and loaded them into the bag too.

Once done, she faced Alec.

He nodded at the remaining file.

"You don't want that," Ruth said. "Take this and go." She strained to hoist the bag, took a couple of faltering steps forward, and fearing she may dislocate her arms, she placed the duffle bag on the floor between them. Then Ruth retreated, hands raised.

Alec increased his grip on Greg's neck while glaring at Ruth. "I told you to put it in the bag."

"Why?" Greg croaked. "It has no value to you."

"I know what it is," Alec said. "And it ensures you don't follow me. If you do, I'll destroy it."

"And how do we expect to get it back?" Ruth asked. "Are you going to post it to us?"

Alec adjusted his grip on the knife.

Greg winced.

"Okay, okay." With extreme reluctance, Ruth removed the file from the safe, slipped it into the duffle bag, and retreated again.

"Get back." Alec said. "Further." Then, still with a tight grip on Greg, Alec walked them both over to the duffle bag. He growled in Greg's ear, "Pick it up."

Greg bent at the knees and hoisted the duffle bag with a grunt.

Then, Alec holding the knife to Greg's throat, his gaze locked on Ruth, they circled her and backed to the open window. Once there, Alec said, "Set the bag down. Slowly."

Greg did as he asked. Alec then shoved him away, the teenager stumbled, and Ruth caught him.

A second later, Alec hoisted the bag, leapt through the window, and ran.

Ruth grabbed Greg's shoulders and scanned him from the tip of his head to his toes. "Are you hurt?"

Greg swallowed and looked as though he was about to faint. "I'm fine."

"Are you sure?" Ruth examined his neck.

"We're on an island," Greg said. "Where will he go?"

Ruth released him. "There's only one way off." Fists balled, Ruth marched across the study, determined to end this once and for all.

To steal was one thing, but to murder two people and then threaten the life of an innocent teenager were other matters entirely.

Anger boiled within Ruth as she rushed into the dining hall, and over to Margaret and Detective Murray. "The will," she panted. "We found it."

Greg remained by the door with an anxious expression, rocking back and forth.

"You found it?" Margaret's eyebrows lifted. "Really?" She jumped to her feet. "Well done, Ruth."

"A safe." Ruth thrust a thumb over her shoulder. "In the study all along. Right under our feet."

"Oh, thank goodness. You've saved us." Margaret cracked a rare smile. "Quickly. Hand it over to Charles before he signs our lives away."

Ruth cringed.

Margaret's face dropped. "What now?"

Ruth turned her attention to the detective. "The killer you're after is the head gardener."

"Alec?" Margaret's voice rose.

"There's no time to explain in full," Ruth said. "But Alec murdered Carter and Maddie, and now has the contents of the safe. That's what it's been about."

Margaret sat back down.

"You have proof?" Detective Murray asked, as if enquiring about the weather.

"For the safe robbery, yes," Ruth said. "In the form of a duffle bag filled with stolen jewellery. Alec has it." Ruth ignored Margaret's spluttering. "I expect you'll find forensic evidence for the murders. Alec is getting away, but I know where he's heading."

Detective Murray got to his feet, his expression dubious. "Show me."

Margaret went to follow.

Ruth shook her head. "Stay. Tell Charles. Stall them a bit longer." Ruth then ran from the dining hall with Greg and the detective in tow.

They jogged across the hallway, unbolted the front door, and hurried out. The three of them hurried down the front path, past the lawn, and the hedge maze, and on through the brick archway.

Ruth stopped short of the cliff elevator.

Detective Murray opened the door and ushered Greg inside. "What's wrong?"

"Grandma has cleithrophobia."

"I'll meet you there." Ruth took a deep breath and descended the steps as fast as she could, while holding the handrail, praying she didn't trip.

Images flashed through her mind: Alec when they'd arrived, tipping his cap at them; Alec in his armchair inside his cottage; and Alec and Josh standing in the dining hall, peering at Maddie's body.

Did *Alec murder her, slip back to the garden, and feign innocence?* Then, at Helen's scream, both he and Josh had come running. *Are they working together?*

At the bottom of the steps, having reached the base of the cliff before the boys, Ruth stumbled along the pontoon, trying to catch her breath, and clutched at a stitch in her side.

Halfway along, she stopped dead in her tracks.

At the far end of the pontoon, next to the boat, were Captain Barney and Josh. On the boat was a bald-headed man in his late seventies, who had to be the boat's owner: Fisherman Fred.

Greg and the detective caught up to Ruth.

"They're in on it," Greg breathed.

Ruth hesitated. "I don't think so." She hurried over to them. "Have you seen Alec?"

Captain Barney gripped Josh's shoulder. "Hauld yer horses until ye hear this one's story."

Detective Murray stepped forward, but Ruth threw out an arm.

"Josh explained it all to me," Captain Barney said. "Caught him sneaking round the side of the house. I'm here to help put it right."

"I was trying to stop Alec," Josh said. "We then thought he'd come here next."

Ruth shook her head. It all now clicked into place. She thought back to the motorhome accident, and if she was right, Josh had been used. But that would have to wait. "Who let you out of the boot room?"

"I don't know," Josh said. "I thought I heard the lock click. By the time I tried the handle and opened it, they were gone."

Ruth faced Greg and the detective. "I bet Alec let him out."

"Right," Greg said. "Because they're working together."

"Alec let him out so we'd wind up chasing him instead." She thrust a finger at Josh. "Which we've done. He's a distraction." Ruth's gaze moved to the cliff. "Alec's not coming here, which means he's planned another way off this island."

"How?" Detective Murray said. "Fred has the only boat available. We had to wait all day for him."

Ruth took a deep breath and closed her eyes, picturing the beach, the cave, the lighthouse and—

Her eyes flew open. "I know how Alec's going to escape." She looked over at Captain Barney. "Have you stored anything of yours in the lighthouse recently?"

He frowned. "I dunnae go in there. Why?"

"Stay here in case Alec changes his mind and doubles back," Ruth said. "Guard the boat. Don't let him anywhere near you." She motioned to Detective Murray and Greg. "You two, this way."

They hurried back along the pontoon and to the path on the left, heading up the hill toward the lighthouse.

"Can you explain what's going on?" Detective Murray asked. "Or are you going to have us run about like headless chickens?"

Ruth looked back at him. "Alec pressed a knife to my grandson's throat until I emptied the safe of jewels into a bag."

"So, a robbery," Detective Murray said.

"And murder. Possibly two."

They crested the brow of the hill and continued their march toward the lighthouse.

"He killed Carter," Greg said.

Detective Murray's eyebrows knitted. "That was an accident."

"Manslaughter at the very least," Ruth said. "And you saw Maddie's body. That was definitely a murder."

Greg screwed up his face. "The axe was a giveaway."

"We'll have a crime scene examiner out here by the end of the day," Detective Murray said.

Ruth paused at the door of the lighthouse. "Then you'll get the forensic proof you need." She peered inside. As expected, the crate nearest to her now stood empty, and the motor had gone. She stepped back and motioned to the path. "This way." As they hurried toward the clifftop, Ruth said to Detective Murray, "I know we're all suspects, but please at least take my word for it—someone is trying to escape the island. Not the actions of an innocent party."

The three of them stopped at the top of the cliff and stared down to the beach below.

A compressor sat at the shoreline, running, filling an inflatable raft with air.

"Where is he?" Greg looked about.

Ruth's eyes narrowed. "He'll be nearby."

Greg raced down the stairs.

"Wait," Ruth called after him. "Be careful."

Detective Murray hurried after Greg, and Ruth brought up the rear.

By the time she'd gotten halfway down, Greg was already sprinting across the beach.

Ruth's stomach twisted into knots, and she looked about for Alec, but still couldn't see him.

Greg stopped at the boat, pulled out the pocketknife, selected the biggest blade, and jammed it into the rubber hull. A loud *pop* knocked him back several steps, followed by a rush of air.

Someone shouted, "Hey."

Ruth spun round.

At the top of the steps, duffle bag in hand, was Alec.

He looked from the boat to Ruth, snarled at her, and turned to leave, when someone appeared, as if from nowhere, and slammed into Alec like a rugby player, tackling him to the ground.

Lungs burning, Ruth raced back up the steps as fast as she could. By the time she reached the top, Captain Barney had Alec pinned to the ground, face in the dirt.

"Keep still, if ye know what's gud fer ye." Captain Barney bent Alec's arm up behind his back.

Alec groaned.

Ruth leaned against a wooden railing, bent double, about to pass out. "Well. Done. Captain."

26

Detective Murray escorted Alec onto the fishing boat, where Fred used some old rope to tie him up.

With some obvious effort and strain, Greg held the duffle bag out to Ruth. "Should we give this to him? It's evidence."

"Hold on." Ruth slipped out the folder. "Now you can."

Once they'd finished securing Alec and had him seated, Greg handed over the duffle bag.

Detective Murray checked inside, and his eyes bulged from their sockets. He passed it back. "Hold on to it. Touch nothing. We'll need to check for fingerprints."

"You won't find Alec's in there, but speaking of finger-prints . . ." Ruth pulled her phone from her pocket. "I have pictures you can use as evidence. There's a fingerprint in the attic you'll need to look at. It's more proof of what they were up to. Him and Carter. The places they visited, hunting for answers to the riddle."

"Riddle?" Detective Murray let out a slow breath. "I'll look at everything when I come back." He glared at Alec. "After I've processed him, I will return with the crime scene examiner." Detective Murray looked at Ruth. "Please lock the doors to the dining hall and study. Keep everyone's movements to a minimum. I'll want to interview everyone."

Ruth addressed Alec. "Why did you kill Maddie?" When he scowled and looked away, she said, "Maddie caught you taking the plaque from the dining hall, didn't she? The family crest?" Her stomach tightened. "What happened? At that moment she realised your involvement? Did Maddie spot the family motto and put two and two together?" Ruth clenched her fists and fought back anger. "She threatened to go to Charles and Margaret?" Ruth pictured Maddie turning to leave, only for Alec to snatch the axe from the wall and strike.

Alec still didn't meet her gaze.

"Answer me," Ruth shouted.

"Don't worry," Detective Murray glowered at Alec. "We'll get it out of him. The whole sordid story."

Captain Barney untied the ropes fore and aft, and Fred started the engine.

"Oh, and another thing," Detective Murray said to Ruth. "Please pass on my apologies to the doctor and tell her what happened. I'll be back soon."

Ruth let out a slow breath, calming herself. "We'll take care of her until your return."

Detective Murray waved, and the boat chugged away.

"That was quick thinking," Ruth said to Greg as they headed back along the pontoon toward Josh. "Puncturing Alec's inflatable boat?" She waggled a finger at him. "Reckless, though. So don't do it again. Your mother would never forgive me if something bad happened to you."

"Got it." Greg winked.

Ruth chuckled and looked over her shoulder at Captain Barney. "And you saved the day. Thank you."

He waved off her compliment. "Dinnae mention it."

When they reached the end of the pontoon, Margaret and Charles stepped from the cliff elevator.

"What on earth's happened?" Margaret, pale-faced, stared at the boat as it left.

Ruth handed the folder to Charles.

He opened it and read the paperwork inside.

"The will?" Margaret wrung her hands. "Is it okay?"

Charles looked up. "Everything's going to be fine."

Margaret's shoulders relaxed. "Oh, thank goodness for that. It's over."

"Not quite." Ruth beckoned Josh. "Charles. I think it's time to meet your—" Ruth inclined her head. "Half-brother?"

"Ruth." Margaret tutted. "Don't be absurd."

"It's not the only explanation that fits the facts," Ruth admitted. "But the most probable." She winked at Josh.

He looked away with a sheepish expression.

Margaret shook her head. "You've lost your mind."

"He's the phantom," Ruth added for good measure.

Charles frowned. "But the phantom has been on this island—"

"Over forty years," Ruth said with a fervent nod. "John and I saw you in the cave, Josh. Did you spot us too? That day Henry banished us from the island?" It now made sense why he'd reacted in such an extreme way. John and Ruth had come close to discovering his dirty little secret.

Charles stared at Josh. "You— You were the one living in that room?"

"Not recently," he muttered. "A long time ago. I still go down there sometimes. The room has been there for centuries, part of the old castle basement levels, but Henry modified it for my needs. He did it in secret."

Margaret's mouth opened, but no words came out.

"My guess would be Josh joined the island as assistant groundskeeper soon after we spotted him," Ruth said.

"I was sixteen."

"It was Henry's plan?" Ruth asked. "A good idea to hide the truth by keeping you in plain sight. And how long were you on the island before that?"

"Two years."

"You were the redheaded boy," Charles said with an incredulous look. "But you drowned."

Josh shook his head. "I was only swimming. I went back to my room. They couldn't find me. And when they asked at the house—"

"No one had heard of you," Greg finished.

"Henry was really angry with me," Josh murmured.

Up until that moment, Ruth wasn't sure how she now felt about Henry. On the one hand, he was a genius for turning his entire house into a giant puzzle. But, on the other, now all this came out about his dirty secrets, especially forcing a child to live alone underground for two years to keep an affair under wraps, was both abusive and cruel.

In his wake, Henry's actions had resulted in murders, trauma, and unnecessary stress, some of which could have been avoided if he, and others, had been honest from the start.

"Why didn't my father tell me about you?" Charles asked Josh.

"I'm partly to blame," Josh said. "Needed a quiet life. No hassle. Wasn't interested in Henry's money. All I wanted was to follow my gardening passion." He lowered his head. "Henry came up with the idea to employ me when I was old enough. I just had to wait it out until then."

Margaret unstuck her tongue. "This is insane. You're claiming to be Henry's love child? Who was your mother?"

Josh looked away and mumbled, "Marie Atkins."

"My father's accountant," Charles said. "But she—"

"Died," Josh said. "That's why Henry suggested I could stay here, on condition I remained quiet and told no one. Then when I turned sixteen, he gave me a job as assistant groundskeeper. I've worked here ever since." He lifted his head. "And I kept my promise until now."

"If you're the phantom," Greg said, "why are you stealing food? Bit risky, isn't it? You don't need to do that anymore."

"When I first lived in that underground room, Henry couldn't bring food to me every day, for fear of being discovered. He unlocked the door to the boot room, and I'd sneak in at night and take what I needed." Josh glanced toward the clifftop. "I was only supposed to go to the kitchen, but sometimes I'd look about the house, while everyone was asleep. Since Henry made me assistant groundskeeper, and now I live in the house, I sometimes sneak out to my old hidden room, and take food with me." His eyes glazed over. "I like being alone sometimes."

"Where's your proof of all these wild claims?" Margaret asked. Although, her voice had lost its harshness.

"Could get DNA tests," Greg suggested. "Charles and Josh—it would show whether they're related. Easy to do. Spit in a vile and post it."

Margaret cringed.

Ruth didn't think they needed proof, but that would be for Charles to decide. She pulled the journal from her pocket. "Is this yours?" she asked Josh.

"Alec's," he said. "I stole it to show what he'd done. I was gathering evidence. Alec sat outside the study window, listening to conversations. It's all in there." Josh's expression intensified. "That's how I know what Henry and Carter had discussed. The rest Alec told me when he demanded I help."

"Alec murdered Carter?" Margaret asked.

"They were working together."

Ruth cleared her throat as more pieces of the puzzle slotted into place. "That's also how they knew about the safe's existence?"

"Henry told Carter about the jewels." Josh refocussed on her. "He said Charles thought he sold them when his mother died, so it would be a nice surprise. They'd fetch enough money to keep the island running for decades."

"And then some," Ruth said. So far, what Josh had told them made sense. Well, to a point. All of it would need corroborating. "And according to the journal, Carter knew about Noah too?"

"Henry complained Noah kept harassing him," Josh said. "Noah said he was his son too, but Henry refused to leave him anything in his will. Henry complained to Carter and showed him the emails, but Carter made a mental note of Noah's email address. Carter then contacted Noah directly and offered to destroy both copies of the will in exchange for payment."

"I still can't believe what he did." Charles shook his head. "Carter? He was so loyal."

"He hated the island and wanted to move to France," Josh said. "Carter needed more money, but he wasn't interested in the jewellery because he had no way to sell it. Noah agreed to pay him off."

"Did they think there were copies of the will at the solicitors?" Ruth asked.

"Yes, and the security was too much for Carter to bypass, and with all the documents locked away, there was no way to get to the copies of the will easily." Josh took a breath. "So, the day Henry died, Carter paid some kids to burn it down, and then he started his hunt for the one here."

"But there were no copies with the solicitor," Ruth murmured.

Josh looked between them. "Toward the end, with only a couple of clues left to solve, Carter emailed Noah and said he was close. Noah told him to destroy the riddle."

Margaret glowered. "But he didn't. Why?"

"Probably because he wanted Noah to frame it and hang it in the new hotel," Greg said through gritted teeth. "Rub it in Charles' face."

"I don't know what his reason was," Josh said. "Anyway, Carter got stuck on the last parts of the riddle, so he asked Alec for help."

"Carter flew the riddle up to the lighthouse so Alec couldn't get hold of it," Ruth said. "He memorised the final lines, which then made him valuable. Gave him protection. Alec thought the puzzle box was the last step, so they fought, and Carter fell, taking the riddle with him."

"However, you found it and reignited the hope." Charles considered Josh. "How did you get involved in all this?"

"I thought something was going on, so I eavesdropped on one of their conversations. Alec caught me. I tried to warn him it was a bad idea, told him to stay clear, but he wouldn't listen. I found his journal later."

Ruth took a breath as the gravity of the situation sank in. "Going back a step, what happened the morning Carter died?"

"Alec helped him with the riddle as planned," Josh said. "They were close to the end, but heard you were on your way."

Ruth considered him for a few seconds. Josh had faked

the accident to slow her down. Alec clearly wanted to buy some time to find the safe and get off the island.

Josh's expression turned downcast when he noticed Ruth staring at him. He muttered, "Alec threatened me. I had no choice. I'm sorry."

"Can I just say fer the record," Captain Barney chimed in. "I had no idea what this guy was up to." He glared at him. "Wud ne'er have given him a lift to the mainland 'n' back if I had."

"You're in the clear, Barney," Charles said. "Don't worry."

Captain Barney nodded and stepped back.

"How did Alec threaten you?" Margaret asked Josh.

"He started off by saying he'd tell you about me." Josh looked between Charles and Margaret. "But then he got nasty and threatened to hurt you both if I didn't do what he asked."

"Even so." Charles brushed his moustache with a sweep of his fingers. "You should have come to us. Explained what was happening."

Ruth inclined her head. "Would you have believed him?"

Charles hesitated and then looked away.

"I refused to help Alec anymore." Josh's eyes welled with tears. "I wanted nothing to do with it, but then he killed Maddie. That's when I tried to stop him again."

"What happened?" Ruth asked.

Josh stared at the ground. "I was round the corner, unloading bags of compost from the trolley. That's when Alec must have snuck into the dining room to take the plaque."

"But Maddie caught him," Ruth said.

Josh swallowed. "When I came back, I saw Alec slip the plaque into the wheelbarrow, hiding it among the leaves."

He looked up at Ruth. "Then we heard the scream and came running."

"How did you wind up with the plaque?" she asked.

"I took it from the wheelbarrow when he wasn't looking, and stashed it in my room. Alec went nuts, but I feigned innocence." Josh let out a breath. "When he then overheard you talking about it, Alec realised what I'd done and demanded I put it back."

"Who flooded our house?" Margaret asked.

"Alec?" Ruth studied Josh.

"I didn't know about that until after he'd done it," Josh said. "I'm not sure what he was trying to do."

"Slow us down again," Ruth said. "Those were Alec's boots in the shed." She knew she hadn't spotted them outside his front door on the way into his cottage. "And then when that failed, when I recovered the riddle from Henry's office, Alec had no choice but to let us continue, and then he waited to ambush us."

Josh focussed on Charles. "I'm not interested in the will or your money. I only wanted to keep my job. It's all I've ever wanted. You must believe me."

Charles stared at Josh for a long while, and then said, "It appears you and I have a lot to discuss."

"Not until we evict that obnoxious Noah and his spiteful lawyers from our property," Margaret said. "As far as I'm concerned, it's his fault this happened."

Charles put an arm around Captain Barney's shoulders. "Thank you for helping."

"Yer welcome."

"How about you come back up to the house with us?" Charles said. "We'll start by sorting you out a new boat. I'm sure we'll find one suitable on the internet."

"Happy with the auld one," Barney said as the six of

them headed toward the cliff elevator. "Help me get her repaired 'n' dried aff, that'll be fine fer me."

Margaret turned around and gave her sister a rare smile.

"Have I earned your forgiveness?" Ruth asked.

She'd done the right thing telling their mum about their dad's affair all those years ago, but Ruth had to admit that for her entire life she had gotten so caught up in the forensics, the cold facts, the determination to solve mysteries, that she could lose sight of the human tragedy.

"I'm sorry," Ruth said. "I'll do better."

Margaret placed her hands on Ruth's shoulders. "We also have a lot to discuss. A lot of damage to repair. But yes, Ruth, I forgive you. Of course I do." Her face softened. "Can you forgive me?"

Ruth stepped back. "Almost."

Margaret frowned. "What?"

"I almost forgive you," Ruth repeated. "But you can push our relationship over the finish line by giving me your steak and ale pie recipe." Her eyes sparkled, and she flashed her teeth.

Margaret let out a breath. "Yeah . . . Not a chance."

Ruth's face dropped. "I just saved your island."

"I know, Ruth, and I'm grateful. I really am. But that's too high a price to pay." Margaret walked away and linked arms with Greg.

Ruth ground her teeth and trotted after them. "I've tried a million combinations. What am I missing with the recipe? but I can't figure it out." Frustration boiled within her. "You must tell me what the magical ingredient is."

As they walked, Margaret leaned in to Greg and whispered something in his ear.

His eyebrows lifted. "Really? Wow." He looked back at

his grandmother. "I never would have guessed that in a million years."

Ruth glared at him.

Margaret, Charles, Captain Barney, and Josh stepped into the elevator.

"I'll go this way with Grandma." Greg waved a hand at the stairs.

"Don't you dare tell her what it is." Margaret closed the door, and the elevator started its ascent.

Ruth gripped Greg's shoulders. "What's the magic ingredient?"

Greg made a zipping motion across his lips.

"Now listen here—" Ruth's phone vibrated in her pocket. She gave Greg a hard look and muttered a few choice words under her breath as she checked the display. "An email." Her spirits lifted as she read.

"What now?" Greg asked. "I'm knackered. I want to sleep for a month."

"It's a job," Ruth said. "Next week. A food consultancy gig like no other." She shook her head as she scanned the details. "I'm impressed."

Greg's eyes narrowed. "What is it?"

"Oh, Gregory." Ruth pocketed the phone and headed on up the steps. "You're going to love it. Absolutely *love* it."

He groaned, "I bet I won't," and traipsed after her.

Continue reading for a sample of . . .
MURDER ON THE FINSBURY FLYER
OUT NOW

Thank you for reading! We would be incredibly grateful if you could leave a star rating or review. Your invaluable support is

**vital to the Ruth Morgan Mystery Series' success and can make
all the difference.**

**To be notified of FUTURE RELEASES in the Ruth Morgan
series, click on the author name "Peter Jay Black" at Amazon (on
any of Peter's book pages), and then "Follow" in the top left. OR
visit peterjayblack.com and join the free VIP list.**

Also grab a FREE copy of
DEATH IN BROOKLYN
*A Short Story set in the Fast-Paced
Emma & Nightshade Crime Thriller Series.*

IMPORTANT
*Please remember to check your spam folder for any emails. You
must confirm your sign-up before being added to the email list.*

~

MURDER ON THE FINSBURY FLYER
CHAPTER ONE

Ruth Morgan, her teenage grandson Greg, and a perplexed
Scottish car park attendant found themselves in a peculiar
standoff. They stared up at a steel bar swathed in yellow and
black tape, several feet above their heads.

Ruth cleared her throat and tried not to allow desperation to edge her voice. "You're absolutely positively sure
there's no way to raise it?" She waved a hand at the bar in a
dramatic fashion. "This height-restriction thing. You can't
make an exception for us?" Ruth had a sneaking suspicion
batting her eyelids wouldn't help.

Indeed, the car park attendant gawped at her as though

she'd informed him aliens had landed in Scotland nine hundred years ago and built Edinburgh Castle using nothing but space rays and stardust.

Ruth sighed and looked from the unyielding bar to the rooftop of her motorhome. The former was two inches lower, so zero chance her beloved tin palace would slide underneath. Plus, it was already evening, so they didn't have time for this nonsense.

Her narrowed eyes swept the car park on the other side of the barrier. It sat there all flat and concrete-y, taunting her with its smug, featureless expanse. To add insult to injury, her client had reserved ten spaces in the far corner. Ample room, but no way to reach it.

Ruth growled. "Just blinkin' typical."

They were on their way to her first paying food-consultancy gig in almost a month. A vital job she hoped would get things back on track since the disaster on board the *Ocean Odyssey*. It promised to be a high-profile affair too, with plenty of future clients to impress, so Ruth did not want to be late.

"So near, and yet so far," she said through clenched teeth.

For a fleeting moment, Ruth considered abandoning Greg with the motorhome and forging ahead on foot. But deserting her grandson was unthinkable. Well, almost. Besides, Greg was far nimbler than Ruth, and even with the element of surprise in her favour, he would catch up to her in a few paces.

The three of them flinched at the blast of a car horn.

Greg peered round the side of the motorhome. "There's like fifteen cars waiting behind us now."

"What do they expect me to do?" Ruth pulled her long

black coat tight, and adjusted her bright pink beanie and scarf. "It's not as if I can reverse out of here now, is it?"

They'd followed a narrow lane between buildings to reach the current predicament, and Edinburgh's mazelike roads weren't renowned for their motorhome-accommodating girth.

Another car horn blared, this one more incessant and higher pitched.

Greg's cheeks flushed scarlet. "So embarrassing."

"Nonsense. It's not our fault." Ruth eyed the car park attendant.

He blinked at her. "I didnae set the height restriction. It's nae my fault either." His gaze shifted to the motorhome.

Ruth let out another long breath. "Nothing else for it, then." She motioned to Greg. "Go on, before I change my mind."

His brow furrowed. "Huh?"

Ruth pointed at the bar high above their heads. "Climb up there."

Greg gaped at her. "And do what, exactly?"

"See if you can unbolt it."

"The bar? How?" Greg flinched at another blasting car horn.

"We must have tools in the motorhome. I'm pretty sure there's a screwdriver in the bottom of the utility cupboard. Try that."

Greg shook his head with a look of pained exasperation. "It's got a broken handle."

Ruth faced the car park attendant. "Do you have an adjustable spanner?"

"No."

"Pliers?"

"No."

"Anything at all that may help?"

He glanced up at the bar. "It's welded in place."

"A saw, then?"

"Yer nae removin' it," the car park attendant snapped. "Boss would kill me."

Ruth threw her hands in the air. "Well, that leaves us with only one alternative." She couldn't believe how thoroughly unhelpful the men were being.

"What are you going to do?" Greg asked in a hushed voice, as though fearing her actions would set off a chain reaction of bad karma.

Ruth inclined her head. "I thought I'd play upbeat calypso songs and ask my giant motorhome to kindly limbo under the nasty bar."

Greg snorted. "That's your plan?"

"Would be if I could find a big enough grass skirt at such short notice." Ruth smirked. "It still is my plan, in a manner of speaking. Sans the music and the Caribbean attire." She tapped her chin. "Although now you mention it, I do fancy a trip to Trinidad and Tobago." Ruth looked up at Scotland's overcast sky and shivered.

Yet another car horn blared.

Ruth poked her tongue out at her grandson, marched around the motorhome, waved at the not-so-patient drivers, and knelt by a rear tyre. She removed the dust cap and pressed a key into the valve.

Air hissed.

Greg rushed over to her. "What are you doing?"

"Solving a problem with a bad idea." Ruth then muttered, "Story of my life." She nodded to the other side. "Do that one."

Together, Ruth and Greg released pressure from the motorhome's tyres at the back and then moved to the front.

As the wheeled metal mansion dipped, Ruth peered up at the bar.

The car park attendant looked at her as though she were mad. Or a genius. It was hard to tell.

Once they were done, Ruth straightened. "Come on, Gregory." She stepped on board the motorhome with a supreme level of confidence this would do the trick and slid into the driver's seat.

MURDER ON THE FINSBURY FLYER
OUT NOW

To be notified of FUTURE RELEASES in the Ruth Morgan series, click on the author name "Peter Jay Black" at Amazon (on any of Peter's book pages), and then "Follow" in the top left. OR visit peterjayblack.com and join the free VIP list.

Also grab a FREE copy of
DEATH IN BROOKLYN
*A Short Story set in the Fast-Paced
Emma & Nightshade Crime Thriller Series.*

IMPORTANT
Please remember to check your spam folder for any emails. You must confirm your sign-up before being added to the email list.

PETER JAY BLACK
BIBLIOGRAPHY

DEATH IN LONDON
Book One in a Fast-Paced Crime Thriller Series
https://mybook.to/DeathinLondonKindle

Emma leads a quiet life, away from her divorced parents'
business interests, but when her father's fiancée turns up
dead in her mother's warehouse, she can't ignore the threat
of a civil war.

Unable to call the police, Emma's parents ask her to assist
an eccentric private detective with the investigation. She
reluctantly agrees, on the condition that when she's done
they allow her to have her own life in America, away from
the turmoil.

The amateur sleuths investigate the murder, and piece
together a series of cryptic clues left by the killer, who seems
to know the families intimately, but a mistake leads to the
slaying of another close relative.

Now dragged into a world she's fought hard to avoid, Emma
must do everything she can to help catch the culprit and
restore peace. However, with time running out, could her
parents be the next victims?

"Pick up Death in London today and start book one in a
gripping Crime Thriller Mystery series."

***

DEATH IN MANHATTAN
Book One in a Fast-Paced Crime Thriller Series
https://mybook.to/DeathinManhattanKindle

When someone murders New York's leading crime boss, despite him being surrounded by advanced security, the event throws the underworld into chaos. Before anyone can figure out how the killer did it, he dies under mysterious circumstances and takes his secret to the grave.

Emma's uncle asks her to check out the crime scene, but she's reluctant to get involved, especially after the traumatic events back in London. However, with Nightshade's unique brand of encouragement, they figure out how the killer reached one of the most protected men in the world. Their lives are then complicated further when another member of the Syndicate is murdered, seemingly by the hands of the same deceased perpetrator.

Emma and Nightshade now find themselves in way over their heads, caught up in a race against time, trying to solve clues and expose a web of deception, but will they be quick enough to stop a war?